LONGARM REMOVED THE CUFFS . . .

Francy promptly slapped him hard across the face. He reached round and pulled her to him . . .

"I hate you," she snarled, her face muffled against his chest. "Damn you, let go of me!"

"Not till you say you'll stop beating at me," Longarm said. He tightened his pressure on her body.

"I will like hell!" Francy continued to struggle. She thrust her hip against his groin, trying to break his grip around her back. The aroma of her body, musky and heated, filled his nostrils . . .

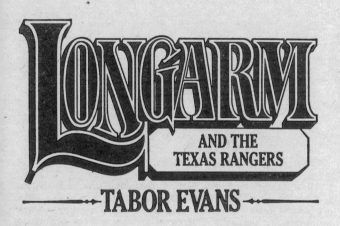

LONGARM

AND THE TEXAS RANGERS

——→ TABOR EVANS ←——

j

A JOVE BOOK

Printed in the United States of America

Library of Congress Catalog Card Number: 79-84079

First Jove edition published August 1979

10 9 8 7 6 5 4 3 2 1

Jove books are published by Jove Publications Inc., 200 Madison Avenue, New York, N.Y. 10016

Chapter 1

For the tenth time that night, Longarm swore at the mist shrouding the rock-studded hillside. The heavy white fog had settled down at dusk, growing thicker as darkness deepened. It spread a thin film of moisture over the already wet soil, left a slick coating on the rocks that surfaced from the brown earth, and hid the snagging mesquite shrubs that tore at his clothing and the prickly pear clumps that left spiny souvenirs in his stovepipe calvary boots as he zigzagged across the slope.

"Damned lousy country, old son," he muttered to himself as he blinked up at the sky, trying to guess where the moon was by now.

When he'd stopped for a breather and to light a fresh cheroot a while back, he'd looked at his pocket watch. It had been just two o'clock then, and he guessed he'd been moving for at least two hours since then, as steadily as the rugged country would allow. He'd learned, though, that there were times when an unpleasant hour would seem to double itself, so he stopped again and checked the time. It was a few minutes before four.

"I've got to be close to the place by now," he said under his breath. "But I'd sure give a pretty to know how the hell I'm going to see a big dead cottonwood in this kind of mess."

He was still trying to locate the moon, but all he could see overhead was a halo of scattered brightness. The moon itself could be centered anywhere in the wide nimbus the fog created, and it was still more than an hour before the sun was due to rise. His booted foot slipped on another of the small, slick chalkstone boulders that lay hidden under a thin layer of moist soil. To keep from falling, Longarm steadied himself with a heavy yank on the reins of the horse he was leading. The claybank gelding tossed its head and almost pulled Longarm off his feet.

This time he swore at the horse instead of the weather. It made him feel better to think that at least the animal could hear him, and the fog couldn't. That feeling lasted only long enough for him to realize that neither horse nor fog could understand or reply.

Well, hell, he thought as his anger faded, *I guess this ain't the first wild-goose chase I've been sent on. I know Billy Vail wouldn't have sent me if that letter had smelled bad to him. So if Billy was right, I better keep on chasing.*

Longarm's chase hadn't begun suddenly or unexpectedly. Nearly three months ago he'd walked into his chief's office, a bit late as usual, to find Vail turned away from his desk and its overflow of the paperwork the chief marshal for the Denver district so detested. Vail was looking out the office window, and didn't turn around to greet Longarm when he heard the door close.

It wasn't Vail's way not to have some remark ready about his deputy's habitual tardiness, and Longarm didn't quite know what to say. Finally, after a moment of puzzled silence, he asked, "You got something special on your mind today, Billy?"

"That telegram on top of my reports file." Vail's tone was distant, thoughtful. "You better read it."

Longarm picked up the scrap of yellow flimsy and read:

DEPUTY J C MCCLINTOCK DENVER OFC DEAD TODAY GUNSHOT WOUNDS RE-CEIVED ATTEMPTED HOLDUP SHIPMENT COINS VIA U S MAIL STOP INFORM DISPOSITION BODY STOP
                 G MOORE INSPECTOR USPS

The wire had come from Fort Worth, Texas. He looked up from the flimsy to find that Vail had swung his chair around to face him.

"You know how I felt about Mac," the chief marshal said quietly. Behind the controlled words, Longarm could sense the anger Vail was holding back.

"You set a right big store by him, I know, Billy. And from what little I've seen of Mac, he was pretty much of a man."

"There's damn few who'll ever know how much of a man he was." Vail's eyes were fixed on the wall beyond Longarm. "He was just about as close as I ever got to having a big brother. If it hadn't been for him, chances are I wouldn't be sitting in this office right now."

"The hell you say." Longarm frowned. He'd never had any idea that Vail and the murdered McClintock were so close, though he'd known their friendship went back through the years.

"Sit down," Vail said. It was less an order than a friendly invitation. "I guess you'd better know a little bit about Mac before you take out after whoever killed him."

Longarm sat down in the red morocco chair that stood beside Vail's desk, stretched his feet out, and lighted a cheroot. He waited patiently for his chief to pull himself out of the past and back into the present.

"Mac was my company commander during the War," Vail went on after a while. "Promoted me to top sergeant and wanted me to put in for a commission. Which I guess I'd've done, if the fighting had lasted much longer. Then I went back to the Texas Rangers and Mac wound up in the marshal's service. He was chief deputy in Austin then, so we always kept in pretty close touch. Then, when the Texas State Police were organized to replace the rangers, I saw how the new outfit was going to be run, and I didn't want any part of it, so Mac put me on as a deputy marshal. We worked a lot of cases together. Texas was still pretty wild then."

"It ain't changed much yet," Longarm put in when Vail paused, carried back into his memories. "Still too damn much land and not enough people to tame it. Maybe it never will be tamed, from what I've seen of it."

"Sooner or later it will be," Vail said absently, then

7

went on, "When this job here in Denver fell vacant, Mac was the first one it was offered to by the bigwigs in Washington. He didn't want it; said he was getting too far along to carry such a big load. How he did it, what sort of strings he pulled, is something I can just guess at, but I've seen enough by now to know it must've taken a lot of doing to get me the job. He did though. Took a while, but he pulled it off."

"Man like him," Longarm said, "How'd it happen that he was riding shotgun on a mint shipment?"

"Because he wanted to stay about halfway active instead of retiring. Didn't want to sit in a rocking chair for the rest of his life. It was his idea for me to carry him on the extra roster, and call him in on things like the mint assignment. Damn it, Long, how in hell could he have got killed on a piddling little job like that?"

Longarm shook his head. "Beats me. Hell, Billy, when you come right down to it, why would any out-law in his right mind think about taking on a U.S. Mail coach? He'd have to know the outside doors are always locked, all the registered mail and insured shipments are kept in a double-locked cage inside the car, all the clerks carry iron, and there's a shotgun guard on duty for the run."

"That's what you're going to find out. I want you on the next train out of here for Fort Worth. Talk to this postal inspector, Moore. Backtrack that job. I want to pull the trap myself when it comes time to hang who-ever shot Mac."

Longarm tried his best, but he couldn't seem to get a handle on the case. He'd spent two weeks backtracking on the mail-coach robbery, which he found had taken place northeast of Fort Worth, on the I-GN mainline while the train was rolling south from Texarkana. As far as he could learn, it had been a one-man job, not the work of any of the outlaw gangs that hid out in the Ozark foothills. Whoever the lone gunman was, he'd vanished without a trace. Longarm had wired the chief marshal for instructions, and had been ordered back to Denver.

Billy Vail's tight-lipped attitude had just about faded when the letter came. It was in a dog-eared envelope

8

with a streak of grime obscuring the blurred ink of the cancellation stamp. The paper the letter was written on was a sheet torn from a coarse school tablet, and the scrawl of blunted pencil straggled across the crumpled page. Vail passed the letter over to Longarm without comment. Squinting at the smeared postmark, Longarm struggled through the few lines of almost indecipherable script that the missive contained.

Mister U S Marshal,
    You want to know who killed your man on the train? It was Sim Blount. If I get a reward, I'll turn him over. Be waiting by the big dead cottonwood on Hutto Creek outside of Round Rock two weeks from now at daybreak.

Longarm finished puzzling out the handwriting and returned the letter to Vail without comment.

"It came from Round Rock, all right," Vail told him. "At least that's what Pinky says."

Pinky was the nickname the chief marshal's staff had given to Marty Collier, who claimed to follow Alan Pinkerton's scientific detection methods and was recognized as the Denver office's expert with magnifying glass and chemical investigative methods.

"Now, I never said it didn't, Billy," Longarm answered. "Only where in hell or Texas is Round Rock at?"

"It's a little jerkwater town north of Austin about twenty miles. You'll be leaving right away. I've already got my clerk fixing up your travel vouchers, and he'll have your expense money ready too, when you stop by his desk on your way out."

"Suppose nobody shows up? It strikes me that's a hell of an uncertain appointment to be keeping."

"Then you go back the next morning and the next, for a week. After you're sure you've found the right cottonwood tree, of course."

"Sure." Longarm frowned thoughtfully. "This Sim Blount fellow—you ever hear of him?"

Vail nodded. "I had him looked up. Simaeus Blount. He's in the files. The clerk's made a copy of his jacket for you to take along. You can study it on the train. He's been running with Greb Walker's gang."

"Hell, I thought they'd all been rounded up and were waiting to stand trial. How come Blount was missed?"

"I haven't figured that out myself yet. Now, damn it, quit wasting my time and yours and get moving." Longarm, remembering, thought he'd never heard Billy Vail sound as deep-down angry as when he added, "I want Blount. I want him in court to answer for killing Mac. And this is one time when I wouldn't mind pulling the trapdoor that'll drop a man at the end of a noose!"

Fishing a cheroot from his pocket, Longarm sat down on a cold, mist-slicked boulder that loomed suddenly at his side. He knocked his heels against the rock to kick off some of the clods of loam that clung to his boot-soles and made his footing on the loose hillside soil even more treacherous. The flare of the match that he flicked across his thumbnail was momentary company, and the red dot of the cigar's glowing tip at least gave him something to focus his eyes on, making the ghost-liness of the fog seem less oppressive.

While he puffed, he wished he'd had time to scout the area before he'd had to set out to meet the writer of the anonymous letter. There hadn't been time, though. He'd had the choice of getting off in Austin and taking potluck on a horse from one of the local livery stables, or riding the train on to San Antonio where he'd be sure of getting a good cavalry-trained remount from the big quartermaster depot stables at the new permanent fort the Army was building there. He'd decided against risking an uncertain horse, and the extra time he'd spent in backtrailing from San Antonio had kept him from arriving in Round Rock with a day to spare before keeping the appointment arranged by the letter.

Nobody he'd asked in Round Rock the night before had been able to pinpoint the big dead cottonwood on the bank of Hutto Creek. Most of the men he'd talked to, at supper in the boardinghouse and in the saloon later, had thought his question was a joke of some kind. About all he'd learned was the general direction in which the creek ran before it emptied into the San

10

Gabriel River north of the town. As for dead cotton-woods, everybody knew there were a few of them on the slope that ran down to the creekbed, but nobody could put a finger on the tree Longarm was hoping to find.

Upslope, a rock began rolling almost silently over the soft earth that slanted down to the creek. Longarm dropped his cheroot and stepped on it to douse its red glow in the same movement that brought him off the boulder with his Colt drawn.

Straining his eyes and ears to pierce the mist, he crouched behind the stone on which he'd been sitting. Beside him, the claybank gelding stomped, its big hoof thudding on the damp soil. Longarm slapped the animal's leg and the horse quieted.

Another small noise reached his ears—the clicking of pebbles disturbed by a footstep. Longarm froze. His only motion was the darting of his eyes as he tried unsuccessfully to see through the swathing gray-white haze that wrapped him in protective invisibility, but also hid from him any enemy from whom he might need protection. The small noise he'd heard was re-peated, but still there was nothing visible.

Longarm waited, his Colt ready. In front of him the mist swirled. Longarm had the muzzle of his .44 cen-tered on the disturbed spot and was ready to trigger the weapon when, through the swirl, he saw the white muzzle and tall antlers of a deer. He let out the breath he'd been holding. The almost inaudible exhalation was enough to spook the buck. It reared, stomped, snorted, and dashed off, disappearing at once in the fog. Long-arm chuckled.

"Damn deer was spooked worse than I was," he said under his breath.

Then, suddenly, he sobered. From the way the buck had reacted, Longarm realized that the animal had been spooked a few minutes earlier, by who or what-ever had started it moving down the slope. Instead of holstering his Colt, Longarm kept it in his hand.

I'll bet I ain't the only one looking for a big dead cottonwood in this pea soup, he told himself. As though to underscore his thought, the claybank whinnied.

Longarm strained his eyes again, as uselessly as before. From somewhere in the mist, a light voice called, "You there, mister? Because if you are, I hear you, only I can't see you."

"Who in hell are you?" Longarm called back.

"Well, if you're waiting for somebody who wrote a letter to Denver two weeks ago, you're in the right place," the hidden speaker replied. "If you ain't, say so, and I'll go about my business."

"I'm the one you're looking for," Longarm said. He could tell that whoever was speaking was following his voice, getting closer. He kept the Colt in his hand.

"You the U.S. marshal?" the speaker asked.

"Yep." Longarm didn't see much point in explaining his exact status as a deputy marshal. He knew by now that he'd connected with the author of the letter. "Just keep on coming ahead till I can get a look at you."

"You better keep on talking." The voice was even closer now. "I didn't count on there being such a fog this morning. Just say something now and again, and I'll find you."

"I'd say you just about have." Longarm kept looking around, but his eyes still couldn't penetrate the mist. "You can't be more'n a few steps away."

Again the mist swirled, the disturbance that precedes a moving body. Longarm didn't bother to raise his Colt this time. Whoever was behind the fog didn't even know his identity, and he didn't imagine that the letter had been designed to bring somebody from Denver to Texas just to get bushwhacked.

A shapeless form could be seen now where the fog was roiling. Longarm holstered his Colt; he didn't want to give an unfriendly first impression. The form took shape as it drew closer, and he could make out the pale blob of a face under a hat with a pulled-down brim. The stranger took substance almost instantly, and Longarm could see that he wore a nondescript coat reaching almost to his ankles, and that the face was that of a youth still too young to shave. The face matched the light treble of the voice to which he'd been replying—that of a youth not yet deepened into manhood.

"I'm Custis Long," Longarm said, "deputy U.S.

12

marshal out of the Denver office. Are you the one who wrote us that letter about Sim Blount?"

"Yes. I didn't know whether it'd get to the right place, but since the newspaper story said the man who got killed was from the Denver marshal's force, I thought I'd try."

"You did just right," Longarm assured him. "You know where Blount is?"

"I'll tell you that when you tell me what it's worth to you to get your hands on him. Outlaw like he is, killed a federal lawman, I guessed there was a reward out on him."

"There is. But it's payable after I take him, not right here and now. I reckon you can see why."

"I reckon." The youth looked around nervously. "Listen, Marshal Long, this isn't a real good place for us to talk. Will you follow along to where I'm staying? I've got coffee on, and it's warmer and a lot more comfortable than out here on this hill."

Longarm couldn't see any more reason now for the youth to lead him into an ambush than he'd seen earlier for a letter to have been sent to bring him down from Denver to be bushwhacked. He said unhesitatingly, "Sure, I could do with some coffee; it's been a while since I ate. And anything beats this damn fog. Let's go."

For the first time, the young man seemed to notice the claybank gelding. A frown rippled over his face and he said, "I—oh, I guess I forgot about your horse."

"There ain't any reason I'd have to leave him here, is there? Like a cliff to climb up, or a deep, wide gully to get over, something like that?"

"No. I just forgot him, that's all."

"If it's a far piece, we can ride double," Longarm offered.

"No need, Marshal, it's not all that far. Come along."

As he followed the youth along the slippery, sloping ground, Longarm found himself looking forward to getting inside, out of the damp air, and drinking a cup of coffee. His breakfast had been a few bites of the jerky he carried in his saddlebag; the boardinghouse where he'd managed to find a room in Round Rock didn't start serving breakfast until six o'clock, and he'd set out an hour after midnight. Aside from his usual wake-up sip or two of Maryland rye and the jerky, his stomach hadn't been given anything to keep it busy, and it was beginning to inform him of the fact.

Commanding his rebellious innards to keep quiet, Longarm followed his guide, who appeared unworried by the fog as he led them in a series of long zigzags that allowed them to climb the upslope with the barest possible effort. They moved in silence. The stillness of the fog-shrouded air was broken only by the occasional clacking of a stone dislodged by their feet on the uncertain ground, and by the muffled clopping of the claybank's hooves in the yielding soil.

Their walk seemed longer than it really was because of the slow pace the young man set. Actually, Longarm reckoned they'd been moving for only twenty minutes or so when the white haze off to their right began to grow perceptibly brighter, then took on a pinkish tinge. Longarm watched it, welcoming the sunrise that the glow indicated. He'd begun to lose his taste for traveling blind.

A dark bulk grew out of the fog ahead of them. The youth stopped and turned to Longarm. "Tie your horse to that mesquite bush over there. I don't want him inside with us."

Trying to figure out what the young stranger meant brought a new frown to Longarm's face; the remark didn't seem to make any kind of sense. He looped the rein over the bush, though, and slid his Winchester out of its saddle scabbard.

"You think you're going to need that?" the youth asked.

"No. But seeing as how I don't know who might be passing by this way, I sure don't aim to make somebody a present of it by leaving it here while we're wherever we're going."

His reply appeared to satisfy the other, who nodded and started in the direction of the shadowy mass that loomed in front of them. As they came closer to it, Longarm could see that the shadow was a cliff that rose abruptly, cutting at an angle across the slope they'd been traversing. The youth walked onward unhesitatingly, and Longarm got ready for a climb. Then he saw

14

the mouth of a cave, a black splotch against the dark gray face of the bluff. He followed his guide inside.

In the cave, the air was clear of mist, and he could see a gleam of light ahead, the slow flickering of a dying fire somewhere around a bend in the passageway, deeper inside the cavern. The youth's form, shapeless in his ankle-length coat, showed in silhouette as he led the way.

Underfoot, moist loam gave way to solid rock that grated underfoot, dry and hard, as they walked. They rounded the bend in the passage and entered a chamber so high that its ceiling was invisible. Only deep blackness met Longarm's eyes as he tilted them upward. The cavern wasn't especially broad where they were standing, but beyond the range of the dying firelight it widened out into a black void that matched the darkness overhead. All at once, the youth's odd remark about not wanting the horse inside with them made sense. A horse in a cave could really stink up the air, if it was kept there very long.

"Make yourself at home," the young man said. He'd gone at once to the dying fire, added a few fresh sticks of wood to the fading embers, and was now hunkered down, nursing the newly placed sticks into flame.

"Thanks. I'll just go take a squint at what's back in the dark there first, if it's all the same to you." Without waiting for a reply, Longarm picked up one of the smaller pieces of firewood that was bursting into flame, and with his rifle still cradled in the bend of his elbow walked back toward the dark end of the cavern.

Though the blackness that his torch only partly dispelled made the big space away from the fire seem boundless, Longarm explored it thoroughly. Only after he'd satisfied himself that there was no one lurking back there, and more importantly, that there were no side passages leading off the high-domed chamber, did he feel at ease. He walked back to where the youth was still nursing the fire with fresh wood.

"Satisfied?" the young man asked. Then he added quickly, "Not that I blame you for wanting to be sure, Marshal. I did the same thing when I first got here. For all I knew, Sim could've beat me here and been waiting for me."

15

"Sure. None of us likes to take chances." Longarm tossed the branch that had served him as a torch onto the fire, which was now burning briskly.

In the better light, he looked around the bright circle cast by the dancing flames. A bedroll was spread on the floor of the cave, between the fire and one wall. Several wooden boxes had been stacked one atop the other against the almost vertical rise of white stone, to make a cabinet of sorts. In one of the boxes, tin plates caught the flickering firelight and threw back a glimmer of silver. A skillet and an iron pot stood in another box, and some crumpled paper sacks and a few airtights had been crammed into a third. A water bucket stood beside a washbasin on still another box that had been upended near the improvised storage shelves, and a shotgun leaned against the wall behind it.

Pegs driven into the wall—Longarm had already judged that the stone of which the cavern was formed must be soft because of its chalky appearance—supported a few shapeless garments that might have been anything; their identity was unguessable. A yard or so away from the pegs on which the garments hung, a stub of a tree branch had been pegged into a crack in the stone. It supported a side of venison. At least Longarm thought it was venison; it might have been a calf. He couldn't tell from this distance just what the animal had been, because chunks of meat had been cut from the carcass.

"You live here?" he asked the youth. He went to the wall and laid his Winchester across two of the clothes pegs.

"I do right now." The stranger looked up from the fire, which turned his beardless face a rosy pink. He was adjusting two of the sticks of fresh wood to lie parallel, just far enough apart to support the coffeepot that he held in one hand. "It's safer for me to stay here than it would be in town, where Sim might happen to see me."

"You're saying Sim Blount's in Round Rock?"

"I didn't say that, Marshal Long. For all I know, he might be. Or he might not be. I don't think he's there right now, but Round Rock's a place he goes to visit

16

often enough, so I don't want to take any chances that we might both be there at the same time."

"Sounds to me like you're carrying a grudge against Blount, or he's toting one against you. Is that why you wrote that letter, saying you'll show me where to find him?" Longarm asked.

"I'd just as soon not talk about what's between Sim and me until we've settled some things about that reward money." _

Longarm nodded slowly, not surprised. Informers usually insisted on getting their pay before they gave out any information. He said, "The reward's in two parts. There's five hundred dollars that'll go to whoever hands Blount over to me, or tells me where to find him. Then there's a thousand more if he stands trial and gets convicted of killing McClintock."

Longarm couldn't see the youth's face, but he read the disappointment in his voice when he said, "That's not as much as I thought it'd be."

"It wouldn't even be *that* much if the man he killed hadn't been a U.S. Marshal. In case you didn't know it, son, rewards ain't generally paid except when the man they're offered on gets convicted."

"I know that. What bothers me is, how am I going to be sure I'll get my money?"

"If you're afraid I'll try to claim it if I arrest Blount, you don't need to worry. There's a rule against us deputy marshals getting any part of a reward for bringing in a man." This wasn't the first prospective informer who'd brought up the question of how he could be sure he'd get paid.

"I wasn't meaning to say you wouldn't be honest, Marshal. I just want to hear you tell me you'll see that I get every penny that's coming to me."

"I'll give you my word on that, all right, as long as you'll guarantee to tell me where you'll be when you're due to get paid. I've got to know that, because I can't come looking for you to deliver it, and if a reward ain't claimed by whoever it's supposed to go to, the money goes back to the U.S. Treasury." Longarm looked at the youth with a bit more respect than he'd felt so far. The young man was proving brighter than he'd expected from his first impression. He went on,

"That coffee ought to be hot enough to drink by now. Why don't you pour us a cup, and we'll get down to business?"

Wordlessly, the youth poured the coffee and stood up, holding out a cup to Longarm, who was getting ready to light up a cigar to go with the steaming brew. Longarm took the cup and sipped appreciatively.

"Now that's right good," he said. "All right, son, let's talk. You might start out by telling me your name."

"You might start out by not calling me 'son' anymore," the youth retorted, pulling off the battered felt hat that had kept Longarm from getting a really good look at his face.

A shower of hair, honey-gold with streaks of darker gold, cascaded from beneath the hat and fell to the youth's waist. The face now framed by the hair suddenly lost all the qualities of maleness that Longarm had thought he'd seen in it during the brief glimpses he'd gotten through the mist-shrouded darkness on the way to the cave.

"Great God a'mighty!" Longarm's mouth fell open. The cheroot he'd been ready to light dropped to the ground. You ain't a boy at all! You're a woman!"

"I've been wondering how long it was going to take you to find that out," she said. She smiled, her full red lips framing glistening white teeth.

Looking at her in the firelight, Longarm wondered why he hadn't realized sooner that it was no boy who'd met him and led him to the cavern. Though the woman's voice was low and husky, and though she still had on the long, shapeless coat that effectively disguised her figure, there was now no mistaking her femininity.

He said, "Guess I just took for granted that a woman wouldn't be likely to meet me out in the middle of noplace to hand over an outlaw killer."

"I didn't set out to fool you, Marshal. You made the mistake, remember. I just didn't set you straight until it suited me. You're not going to hold any hard feelings about it, are you?"

"Not for a minute." Longarm hoped he didn't sound as sheepish as he felt. "Like you say, it was my fault to start with." He shook his head, and a grin crept slowly over his face, replacing the anger that, for a moment, had set his lips in a straight, hard line. He went on, "Well, you've sure set me right. Now get your coffee, and we'll talk about how you aim to turn over Blount. I still want to know your name, too."

"I'm Netta Maze." She picked up the cup of coffee that she'd left sitting beside the pot when she stood up. With more than a trace of defiance in her voice, she asked, "I suppose you've already guessed why I wrote that letter about Sim?"

Longarm nodded. "It don't take much guessing. I'd say he's played you some kind of mean trick, and you're out to get even."

"That's about the way it is." Netta glanced around the cave. Its floor was bare except for the pile of tumbled bedding between the fire and the wall. "There's nothing we can sit down on while we talk, except for my bedroll. But it'll be warmer than sitting on this cold stone floor, even if it won't be much softer."

"It'll do fine." Longarm stepped over to help Netta as she bent to straighten up the blankets and fold them into a pad.

Over her shoulder, she said, "You don't have to worry about Sim. If I know him, and I don't think anybody knows him better than I do, you won't have to go far to take him. He ought to be on his way here right now."

Chapter 2

Longarm had already started for his rifle when Netta's next words stopped him.

"There's not that much of a hurry, Marshal." She finished folding the bedding and stood up. "Sim's not going to walk in here anytime soon. He won't move by daylight. I don't know which one of his holes he's ducked into, but whether he gets here today or tomorrow or the next day, he won't come around the cave here until it's dark."

"You're sure about that?"

"I'm sure."

"Sounds like you know him real good."

"I do; I told you that. Sim's been on the run before, and he knows how bad he's wanted. You're not the only one after him, you know."

"Oh, I figured that. I imagine the rangers and a bunch of local sheriffs and policemen would like to get their hands on him."

Longarm was studying Netta Maze, trying to decide just how much of what she said was safe to believe. He watched while she shed the long coat that had hidden her shape until now. Looking at her slim figure, clad in blue denim shirt and jeans, Longarm thought he might have taken her for a boy even without the coat.

Netta saw him looking at her. "I hope you're not shocked because I'm wearing pants. I know fast women are the only ones who're supposed to wear them in public." Then, with a wry smile, "Hell, Marshal, I don't have to stage an act for you, do I? You know I'm a fast woman, and so do I."

"Now, that don't bother me one bit," Longarm replied. "I never have worried about how fast a woman is, if I like her."

She smiled. "You're one of the few men I've found who'll admit that."

From her face, Longarm reckoned Netta's age at somewhere past the mid-twenties, maybe pretty close to thirty. It had a few lines of maturity on it that he hadn't been able to see outside and hadn't noticed until now, in the soft glow of the firelight.

Her figure was boyish, though; it certainly wasn't that of the overstuffed dowagers Longarm saw on Broadway or Colfax Street in Denver, or the lard-fleshed saloon girls he encountered when out on his assignments. Netta's hips were just a shade shy of being narrow. The loose denim shirt she had on bulged only slightly over her breasts, which he took to mean they weren't the baggy, floppy kind. The trimness of her tucked-in waist and the clean lines of her buttocks indicated that her ribs and back would be straight rather than softly rounded. The loose jeans hung in a straight line from her taut stomach to her ankles, with no sign of bulging thighs.

Netta's face contradicted the spareness of her body. It was broad and a bit fleshy, with a firm, rounded jaw-line and full lips and cheeks. Her cheekbones were low and square; her gray eyes, so light a gray that at times they seemed almost colorless, were set deep, shaded by thin lashes and heavy brows. Her nose had been broken at some time, Longarm guessed. It veered to one side between brow and tip, and its bridge bulged slightly. Her nostrils were thin and arched, and flared out when she smiled.

In spite of their lack of color, Netta's eyes weren't expressionless. They met Longarm's own blued-steel eyes without flinching or dropping. She let him finish looking at her, aware of his inspection, but allowing it to pass without comment. Then she folded her legs in a single lithe, economical movement, sat down on the folded blankets, and sipped her coffee.

Longarm said, "Just to settle my mind, maybe you better tell me how come you're so sure Blount's heading this way, and why you figure you know just when he'll get here."

"That's easy." Netta studied her cup for a moment, her full brows pulled together, before she said more. "I left Sim right after he killed your friend—the deputy marshal guarding the money shipment, I mean—in the mess he made out of robbing the mail coach. Sim had to go on the run, of course, and that didn't bother me. I'd hid out with him before, so I knew what it was going to be like. But I didn't know he was going to be so mean and ugly to live with."

Longarm broke in, "I guess you have to tell me the best way you know how to, Netta, but what I want to know is what I just asked you about. What makes you think Blount'll come here, and why do you figure you know when he'll show up?"

"Sorry, Marshal. I guess I was rambling all over the place. I know Sim's going to come here because I let him know this is where I'm going to be. And I know his habits. He won't show himself anyplace during daylight when he's hiding out."

"Now you're cutting down to the bone." Longarm nodded, then continued, "All right. If you left him, how did you let Blount know you aimed to head for this cave here?"

"I know who passes tips on to him, men he talks to all the time, even when he's hiding. I went to the one Sim's always trusted the most and told him I was coming here. You understand, I just let that part of it slip out like it was an accident. If I'd told him and asked him to get word to Sim to meet me here, Sim would never show up. He'd smell a trap."

"That makes sense," Longarm said. "Now, who's this fellow you told all that to? I want to look him up. My chief wants to know where Blount got the tip that that mint shipment was on its way out of Denver. Nobody was supposed to know about it."

Netta shook her head. "I won't tell you who tips Sim off; they never did me any harm. And I don't know who gave him the tip about the money shipment, but it wasn't the man I went to."

"If you feel like telling me later, there might be another reward for it," Longarm suggested.

"No." She shook her head again. "I'll help you take Sim, but nobody else."

22

Longarm didn't push her. He said, "All right. Go on with what you was telling me."

"I left Sim in Fort Worth," Netta continued. "It took me a while to make up my mind where to go, so I just laid low there until I could decide. Then, after I wrote that letter and said I'd turn Sim in to you folks, I waited until I was pretty sure things would time out right, and then I told Sim's tip-off man. That was four days ago. I let him know I wasn't leaving right away, but I let on to him that I had to hide out too. I knew this man wouldn't know how it was between me and Sim, so I was pretty sure he wouldn't waste any time getting word to Sim where I'd be."

"You've used this cave to hide in before?" Longarm asked.

"More than once. Not me by myself, but when I'd be hiding out with Sim after he'd pulled a robbery. It's really his hideout, not mine."

"Well." Longarm chewed thoughtfully at the edge of his mustache. "It sounds pretty thin, but I guess I got to take your word that you knew how to set things up so Blount'd be here."

"Don't worry, Marshal," Netta reassured him, "Sim's going to be here. Oh, I'll grant you, I gambled. I guess you can say I gambled twice: once, when I took the chance that Sim wouldn't be here himself when I picked out the cave as the place to bring him to for you to arrest him; and I guess I gambled a little bit when I let Sim's tip-off man know I wasn't going to come to the cave right away."

"Looks to me like you're pretty much of a gambling lady," Longarm observed with a half-smile. He'd relaxed a little after hearing Netta's explanation.

"I am. I always have been." Netta smiled back at him. "And you've got to admit, it looks like I'm going to win both my bets, this time."

"It does right now, but you won't be certain till the payoff's made, will you?"

"I'm willing to take my chances. As long as you're willing to wait with me."

"That's what I came here for," Longarm reminded her. Then he added, "Only one thing bothers me."

"What's that?"

"How come you're so sure Sim Blount's going to look for you here, especially, like you say, after you quit him, walked out on him?"

"I've quit Sim, but he's not going to let me get away that easy. I know too much about him," Netta replied calmly. "Sim won't be coming here to try to talk me into coming back to him. He'll be coming here to kill me."

Longarm stared at the girl. "You're joshing me."

"You think so, Marshal Long? Just take a look at this."

Netta's free hand darted to the neck of her denim shirt, and her fingers nimbly undid the top buttons. She pulled the shirt open, revealing the shallow valley between her small breasts. Longarm saw a long, thin scar that started in the hollow at the base of her throat and ran down the middle of her chest to disappear above her waist, where the shirt remained buttoned. As an expert on scars, Longarm could see that this one was new, so recently healed that it was still pink; it had not yet faded to match the ivory hue of the satin-smooth skin across which it ran.

"Did Blount give you that?" he asked.

She nodded. Her lips were pressed together grimly, her face hard. "He put his mark on me in Fort Worth, when I told him I wasn't going to stay with him any longer."

"Easy to see why you figure he owes you something. Can't say I blame you for wanting to collect." Longarm pondered for a moment before adding, "If you look at it one way, though, you got off light. He could've killed you right then and there."

"He intended to," she said bitterly. "He was after my throat, said he was going to slash it from ear to ear. I grabbed his wrist and hung on as hard as I could. That's when the knife dragged down my chest. When I thought Sim was going to break my hold on his wrist, I kicked him in the balls. He doubled up, and I broke the water pitcher over his head. If I hadn't been afraid I was bleeding to death, I think I'd have stayed around long enough to finish him off while he was still knocked out."

Longarm got a vivid picture of the struggle in spite

24

of Netta's calm, dispassionate description. She might have been relating something that had happened to another woman. His mind felt easier, too, after hearing her story. It proved, better than any protests she might make, that she was turning Blount over as a calculated act—not as the result of an emotional, spur-of-the-moment decision. Longarm had seen too many of the latter misfire when, at the critical moment, anger faded. He had no doubt that the trap Netta had set would snare Simaeus Blount. And he no longer had any hesitation about trusting Netta Maze.

"You think Blount's likely to show up tonight, then?" he asked.

Netta shrugged. "Tonight or tomorrow night. It's not like I could name the day or the hour, Marshal. One thing you can depend on, though. Sim's going to try to get rid of me as soon as he can. As long as I'm alive and walking around and able to talk, I'm a threat to him. He's not going to wait any longer than he has to."

"If there's a chance he'll get here tonight, we better be figuring out how I'm going to take him alive. I sure as hell don't aim to drygulch him. My chief wants to see him stand trial."

"That's something for you to work out, Marshal. I'm bringing Sim here; it's up to you to take him. Alive or dead, I don't care which."

"You better care, Netta. The difference is pretty big. If he forces me to kill him, Blount's only worth five hundred in reward money to you. If I get him back to stand trial, he's worth fifteen hundred."

"I didn't realize that until you told me just now," Netta said thoughtfully. "I don't know what you expect me to do to help you, but—"

"For openers, you can tell me someplace where I can hide my horse, seeing as how you don't want it in the cave. If I leave that claybank hitched outside, where Blount can see him—"

"Oh, hell, I overlooked that. Bring the horse inside here, then. You can tie him up at the back, where he won't stink up the rest of the cave too much. And we ought not to have to stay here long enough for that to matter, anyhow."

"That takes care of one thing, then. Now, what if

Blount doesn't show up for two or three days? We'll need food and water."

"If you don't object to having venison every meal, that side I've got hanging up won't be too high for us to eat off of for the next three or four days. I had to shoot the deer with a shotgun, and I ruined most of the rest of the meat. There's plenty of wood for cooking, so we don't have to worry about that. But the only water's what's left in the bucket."

"Where do you fill it?"

"At a spring about fifty yards from the mouth of the cave. With two of us, though . . ."

"I've got a two-quart canteen hanging on my saddle-strings. With what the bucket'll hold, that'll see us through."

"What else do we need then?" she asked.

"Well—" Longarm grinned. "A bottle of good Maryland rye sure would make the time pass faster and help me think better."

"I haven't got rye, but there's a half-bottle of pretty good brandy in one of those boxes against the wall. Will that pass?"

"It sure as hell will have to, seeing as it's a three-hour ride to the nearest saloon and back." Longarm stood up and stretched his massive frame. "If you're right about Blount not being liable to get here till after dark, I've got plenty of time to come up with a scheme to take him without having to kill him." He picked up the water bucket and started toward the mouth of the cavern. "Suppose I fill this up and lead the gelding inside. Then we won't have to go out again, in case he comes early to scout things out."

Before Longarm reached the bend in the cave, Netta called to him, her voice provocatively husky, "Marshal, I hope that brandy really does make you think fast, because I've got a scheme of my own to make the time pass while we're waiting. If you're the man I think you are, that is. I warned you a while ago, I'm a fast woman."

Longarm had ignored the challenge implied in Netta's earlier confession that she was a fast woman, but he decided he couldn't let this one pass by. He said, "I don't let my pleasure get in the way of duty, Netta.

But since I'm sure now that we'll have plenty of time before I go on duty, it looks like you'll have a chance to find out if I'm a fast enough man to catch up with you. We'll see about it when I get back."

In spite of Netta's certainty that Sim Blount wouldn't risk traveling during daylight, Longarm stopped just inside the mouth of the cavern and scanned the area well before he stepped outside. It was daylight now. The foggy mist that had obscured everything in the hours before dawn had given way to a fine, drizzling rain, tiny droplets of moisture that didn't really fall, but rather seeped down from a slate-gray sky. Visibility was much better, but it was still limited to perhaps two or three hundred yards around the base of the towering bluff that the cave pierced.

Standing in the mouth of the cave, concealed by the shadows of the arched portal, Longarm looked for signs of movement, but saw none. The claybank gelding was the only living thing in sight. The horse stood with its head down and its shoulders hunched, as though to protest the tiny droplets that gathered on its rusty coat and slowly ran off its belly to puddle on the ground below. Longarm hadn't taken the bit out of the gelding's mouth before he'd entered the cave; for all he'd known then, he might have needed the horse in a hurry. Now he snapped the bit free of the headstall to let the animal graze on the clumps of grass that grew among the mesquite.

A hundred yards away, he saw the pewter-gray water of Hutto Creek at the bottom of the gentle slope that ran to its banks. Cottonwoods grew along the creek, and their massive boles were shelter enough for a sniper. Longarm walked slowly down to the little stream, stepping carefully from one rock outcrop to the next, his eyes flicking from tree to tree. Still, nothing moved. The soft earth around the cottonwoods at the water's edge showed no footprints except the scratches of raccoon claws and the deep crescents left by deer hooves. Satisfied, he went back to the gelding, picked up the water bucket, and led the horse to the spring. He filled the bucket before letting the horse drink its fill. Then he led the gelding back to the cave.

Netta had built up the fire and was holding the

coffeepot, with the ground coffee already in it, waiting for him to return with fresh water. She looked questioningly at Longarm, and he shook his head.

"Nobody's been moving outside. I scouted around a little bit, as much as I could without leaving my bootprints all over the place. Looks like you're right about Blount waiting till it's dark," he told her.

"I wasn't worried. I knew we'd have a while. Do you want some brandy now, or will you wait until the coffee's ready?"

"Nothing wrong with having one now and one with the coffee too, is there?" He went to the box-cupboard and rummaged out the brandy. He tilted the bottle for an experimental sip, and found the liquor too sweet for his taste. It lacked the sharp, authoritative bite of his accustomed Maryland rye, but it was better than nothing. He offered the bottle to Netta, but she shook her head.

"I'll wait until the coffee's brewed."

They might, Longarm thought, have been in a room in Denver, talking about having a drink before eating, instead of in a cave somewhere about half-past Texas, waiting for a murdering outlaw to show up. He led the gelding back to the dimly lit recesses of the cavern. He didn't unsaddle it, but untied his bedroll from behind the saddle and took off the animal's headstall. He snapped the bit back on the headstall rings, looped the ends of the leathers together, and passed them over the horse's neck. The claybank, like any good cavalry-trained mount, was used to standing with no more tether than the weight of the bit and headstall dropped to the ground beside its forefeet. With the bedroll under his arm, Longarm went back to the fire and sat down crosslegged beside Netta, who was sitting on the pad of folded blankets, watching the steam as it began to gush from the coffeepot's spout. She said, "If it'll help you do your scheming, I've been trying to think how Sim's going to act when he gets here."

"You mean what he'll do first, things like that?"

"Yes. Sim's a suspicious man, which means he's careful. And he's a nasty man, which makes him sneaky. I think he'll try to creepy-crawl into the cave and take me by surprise, after he figures I've gone to sleep. Then he'll want to hurt me somehow, beat on me, maybe cut me a little bit with that knife he likes to use. Then he'll want to fuck me. And then he'll be ready to kill me."

Netta delivered the catalog of her ex-lover's expected actions in a matter-of-fact, unemotional voice.

Longarm asked, "And what the hell am I supposed to be doing while all that's going on?"

"You're going to be waiting back there by the horse, in the dark, until Sim's so taken up with what he's doing to me, and what he aims to do to me, that he won't see you when you come after him."

Longarm said nothing for a moment while he considered Netta's plan with a thoughtful frown. He decided he didn't like it very much. It was a woman's scheme, too fancy, too chancy. He'd been thinking about waiting just inside the cave entrance for Blount, and taking him before the outlaw had a chance to get more than a few steps past the mouth.

"You'd be risking too much, being bait like that," he told Netta with a dubious frown. "I don't think much of your scheme."

"It's my idea. You didn't ask me to be the bait, even if we both know I'm the only bait you've got. If you want Sim alive, I think that's the only way to handle it."

Longarm grimaced a bit, and rubbed the back of his neck with a large, calloused hand. "Maybe. I ain't so sure." He still didn't credit Netta with hating Blount enough to take the chance of being killed with a quick stab before he could move from the back of the cave to where her imagined scene was taking place. He went on, "What if he don't behave the way you figure he will? Your scheme's no good unless he does."

"He will," she said definitely.

"What makes you so sure, Netta?"

"Knowing Sim the way I do."

"That still don't guarantee a thing."

"I think it does. Sim's a little crazy, you know, where his women are concerned."

"Crazy, how?"

"He likes to hurt them. Look."

Netta stood up, turned her back on Longarm, and

ripping open the fly of her jeans, she pulled them down to her knees. She was wearing nothing under the jeans. The firm flesh of her tapered thighs gleamed in the reflected firelight. So did the curve of her taut buttocks, in spite of the dozen or more thin, white, triangular scars that marred their smoothness. Longarm blinked and his eyebrows drew together. A muscle in his jaw twitched.

She spoke over her shoulder: "That's Sim's work. When he'd be in one of his crazy moods, he'd take his knife to bed with us. Then, just when I was ready to go off, he'd jab the point into my butt, so I'd scream and squirm a lot while I was coming. That got him off with a bang that he couldn't get any other way."

"Christ!" Longarm gasped. He stepped closer to Netta and ran his hand over the scars. They were knife wounds; no mistaking the lumpy flesh that lies under a stab scar. "Why'd any man want to do a thing like this?"

"I don't know," Netta replied. "Maybe Sim figured he'd scar me up so other men wouldn't have anything to do with me. Maybe he really hated me deep down inside, and just wanted to hurt me. I never did understand why."

Longarm had begun to grow excited the minute his hand had touched Netta's skin. She'd made it plain that she was expecting him to slide into her sooner or later, and that if she had her way, it'd be sooner. He wasn't sure he should take the invitation, in spite of the growing pressure of his erection against his clothes as he ran his hand over Netta's soft, bare flesh. She sensed his hesitation, and the reason for it.

"I'm not playing bait just to give Sim a chance to get at you, Marshal," she said. "I'm just a woman who needs a lot of loving, and I've gone without a man too damn long."

When Longarm didn't reply, she straightened up and turned to face him. Her hand went to the bulge that was showing at his crotch. "This feels like you want to put it in me as bad as I want you to." For a moment her hand wandered, measuring, exploring, then she said, "God! Is what I'm feeling real?"

"It's real enough." Longarm's hands crept around

Netta's hips. His fingers traced the crease of her buttocks, then crept between her thighs and found her warm and wet. "I reckon it's about time you got what you've been after ever since we come in here."

Netta hadn't waited for his invitation. While he was talking, she'd worked his fly open and stepped out of her jeans. She clasped her hands around his neck and levered herself up by pressing her elbows against Longarm's chest. She straddled him, but couldn't swing her hips far enough back to get him inside her.

"Well, damn it!" Her breath gusted in frantic eagerness as she strained to arch her body and take him in. "Aren't you going to help me even a little bit?"

Longarm helped her by sliding his elbows under her knees and lifting her weight from her arms. She dropped a hand to guide him into her, shuddering ecstatically as she felt his penetration.

"Oh God, if you only knew how good that feels! I haven't been filled up for so damn long!" Her head went back, her hair streaming in a golden flood, as she rocked her hips to pull herself tightly against Longarm's groin. She sighed, a soft tremolo that began deep in her throat, but after a moment sharpened and turned into a whimper. "Oh, damn it! I can't be this quick, but I am! It's too soon to come! Too soon! Too—ohh, my God!"

Longarm supported Netta while her body arched and writhed and quivered. He held her until he felt her muscles grow limp and then tried to slip his arms from beneath her knees. She locked her ankles behind his back and kept him from moving.

"No I can't stop now!" she protested. "Please! You're still good and hard! I came too fast, I need more! A lot more!"

"You'll get more," he promised. "Only let's get our clothes off first. I guarantee I'll give you all you can take, but damn it, I've still got my gunbelt on, and I like to be comfortable when I'm pleasuring a lady."

Chapter 3

Longarm didn't hurry. There was still a lingering doubt in his mind about Netta. She was too accommodating, too eager to combine her revenge on Simaeus Blount with her own personal satisfactions. Longarm had seen woman-baited traps before, and he couldn't shake off the uneasy feeling that he might just be stepping into one now. He took his time about walking over to the cavern wall where he'd hung his coat and vest, stopping to take another sip of brandy.

Netta was spreading out the bedroll she'd folded into a sitting pad earlier. She worked with a quick economy of movement, her hands sure in their job of unfolding and rearranging the bedding, her legs and thighs gleaming ivory in the firelight under the flapping tail of the denim shirt she still had on. She looked up to see Longarm watching her and making no move to take off his gunbelt and clothing.

"What's wrong, Marshal?" she asked. "Don't tell me you're still afraid I'm playing pigeon for Sim, and leading you into some kind of trap."

"I ain't just sure what I think," he told her. "I grant you, there's not any reason for me to question this setup you've got here, or what you told me about Blount. Especially after that letter you sent the office in Denver."

"Then what's eating at your mind?"

"I can't rightly say."

"Maybe you didn't enjoy that sample we just had as much as I did," she suggested, "even if you seemed to. Well, I'm sorry if you didn't get anything out of it, but I couldn't help letting go so fast. I told you, it's been too long a time for me."

"Now that wasn't it at all," he protested. "The way

32

you was riding a minute ago, I could tell what you said about needing a man was the truth. And I guess that makes the rest of what you told me true, too."

"It is. I don't know anything else I can say, if you've still got doubts. I'd say I've proved my case pretty well. By now, either you believe me or you don't."

"Oh, I reckon I believe you, Netta. I got no cause not to, when you come right down to it. In my business, though, a man learns to be suspicious."

Longarm was removing his gunbelt as he spoke. He hung the belt on one of the pegs that supported his Winchester while he shed his flannel shirt, then wrestled off his cordovan cavalry boots. He skinned out of his brown twill pants and balbriggans at the same time, and let them fall to the stone floor. Before turning to go back to the bedroll Netta had arranged, he slid his Colt from its holster.

Netta was sitting down on the bedding. She'd taken off her shirt, and now her small, high breasts winked their pink nipples in the soft glow of the fire. She studied Longarm as he walked toward her, and a smile grew on her face. He moved easily, walking heel-and-toe on the cold stone. He saw Netta's eyes travel up and down his tall frame, taking in the play of the smooth muscles in his thighs as he walked, the sinews corded on his flat belly, the width of his shoulders, the lithe movement of his hips. He stopped a short distance from the edge of the bedding.

"Damned if you're not a hell of a fine piece of man," she said. "But I knew that already, didn't I? Even if you've lost that beautiful hard-on you had, you still look fine to me, Marshal—" She stopped short and shook her head, frowning. "It's silly, I guess, but I don't remember what you said your first name was. I can't keep calling you Marshal Long now, can I?"

"I reckon not. First name's Custis. Only my friends use a nickname I answer to a lot faster than the real name my folks gave me. It's Longarm."

"Longarm it is, then." He was near enough now for the dim light from the fire to let her see the puckered scars he'd picked up in the course of his career as a lawman. "My God! Here I've been feeling sorry for myself because of the scars Sim marked me with, and look at you!"

"Scars don't bother me none, Netta. There's not any of mine I'm ashamed of, even if I got some of them by not paying attention when I ought to've been, and they make me feel like a fool sometimes." Longarm laid the Colt beside the bedding, where he could reach it quickly. "Just in case," he told her. "Seeing as we don't know precisely when Blount might show up."

"It's still the middle of the morning," she reminded him. "You don't have to worry about Sim risking his neck by parading around in daylight, even off in the woods."

"All the same, I aim to keep on being careful."

"Not so careful that you can't put your mind on me for a while, I hope." Netta reached up to fondle him. "I've got the feeling you were just getting started good when I spoiled things by coming too fast, a minute ago."

"You didn't spoil a thing for me, Netta. And if you keep on working at me that way, I'll be ready to prove it to you. There's something about a woman's soft, warm fingers that makes me perk up real fast."

"So I'm feeling."

Longarm scissored his legs to lower himself beside her on the blankets. Netta leaned across him, and began rubbing her breasts across the matted curls of his chest hair. She exhaled gustily as he put an arm around her and pressed her to him. Her face turned up to Longarm's as she sought his lips for a deep kiss.

When they were both breathless from the prolonged intertwining of their tongues, and had pulled apart by unspoken mutual consent, Longarm said, "I guess you're ready for me to keep my promise, Netta."

"I sure am. And you are too; I've got the proof in my hand."

She pulled herself to her knees without releasing her grip on him and, still kneeling, spread her thighs wide enough to guide him into her. Longarm leaned back on his hands, keeping his arms straight, and straightened his legs so that Netta could lift one knee over them. She sank down on him slowly, her eyes closed, until she was sitting on his thighs. Longarm could feel her

34

inner pulsing as she leaned slowly forward, prolonging her impalement, her breath catching in her throat as she took him into her moist, waiting warmth.

"Just don't move for a minute or two," she begged. "I like the feel of you going into me a little bit at a time."

"You call the turn this time, Netta. I told you I'd do whatever you wanted, and I try to keep my promises."

There were minutes of timelessness as Netta lowered herself with infinite slowness, and then Longarm felt her tightening around him in a drawn-out series of contractions and releases, like the gentle squeezing and relaxing of a hot, wet hand. Then Netta began to rock her hips, slowly at first, but gradually going faster and faster while her mouth opened, her red lips stretched taut over her white teeth, and her eyes squeezed shut as her breathing grew gusty.

"I'm getting there too fast again," she panted. "But I don't want to stop. I want to go on and on and on!"

"Go ahead," he invited. "Don't worry about me right yet. I got a lot of wind left. You take your pleasure the way you want to. There's lots of time yet."

"You're sure?" the words came from her throat on a trembling column of air. "Because I—I—oh, Longarm! Hold on! Hold on to me! Squeeze me tight! Break me in two!"

Longarm wrapped his arms around Netta and squeezed as tightly as he dared. Her body seemed fragile to him, her breasts crushed flat against the muscles of his chest, her ribs flexing under the pressure of his forearms. She groaned, a trembling seized her, and she began jerking spasmodically, whimpering deep in her throat. Longarm held her until the quivering stopped and she sagged limply against his chest.

"You all right?" he asked gently.

"I'm fine. Wonderful," she gasped. "But I did it again, didn't I? Came before you were ready. What're you doing to me, Longarm? I'm not usually so hot that I can't hold on a while. And damn it, I want to hold on! I want to keep going forever!"

"Nobody can do that, Netta. But maybe you're trying too hard. Maybe it's like you said, you've done without a man too long. Let's see what happens now."

35

Without leaving her, Longarm lay back, still holding his arms around her. He waited for her to straighten out her legs, then rolled her gently over on the blankets. Her muscles were still lax. She let him move her without protesting, and kept her eyes closed, her arms hanging loosely.

For several minutes, Longarm did not move, but lay on her lightly until her breathing returned to normal and the limpness left her muscles. Then he began to stroke gently, smoothly, and, after a few moments, felt Netta's breathing match the rhythm of his stroking. Her eyes opened and she stared up at him.

"I'm all right now," she smiled. "I guess I was just mad at myself for a minute. Don't stop, Longarm. It feels good again. Better than before, if that's possible."

Longarm nodded. He speeded his strokes gradually, withdrawing a bit farther each time. Netta's legs opened and came up to wrap around his hips. She smiled again, but her expression was still languid. Longarm maintained his steady pace, a slow, unhurried rhythm, until he felt her begin to tense again. Even then he did not change, but maintained the even tempo he'd established until he felt her thigh muscles start to quiver. Then he began to thrust, to pound into the girl's pulsing depths. He was building to his own climax now, still in control, still pacing himself deliberately.

Longarm felt himself tightening, and started now to pound hard, with longer, deeper thrusts that set Netta to whimpering once more. He knew her signs by now, and held back until the cries from her throat pulsed almost in a steady stream before he felt his own frenzy coming on. As fast as he'd been thrusting, he moved faster, probed deeper.

"Now, Longarm, now!" Netta cried. "Oh, hurry up! I can't hold back any longer! Give it to me now! Now!"

Panting, Longarm jabbed and pounded until his own body shook, and then, with a final, tremendous lunge he plunged forward, flowing and shaking, and lay quietly on the trembling form of the girl beneath him.

Neither of them moved or spoke for several minutes. Then Netta said with a sigh, "That was the best ever. God knows, I never had any man give me what

36

you have. Why couldn't I have met you six years ago, instead of Sim?"

"I guess it just wasn't time for us to get together," he replied. A yawn followed his words and caught him by surprise.

"You want to sleep awhile?" Netta asked. "I'll stand lookout, if you're tired."

"Oh, I'm all right. What I need right now's some more coffee and another tot of that brandy and maybe a bite to eat."

"You stay where you are. I'll fix us something, after I get your coffee and brandy."

Netta brought Longarm a cup of coffee and the brandy bottle, then busied herself at the fire. She added fresh wood, bringing welcome heat and light into the cavern. Neither of them had made a move to dress; it was as though they'd reached an unspoken agreement that any clothes they put on would only have to be taken off later.

Soon the aroma of frying venison steaks filled the big cave. Longarm suddenly discovered that he'd forgotten how hungry he was; those few bites of jerky he'd nibbled at and called his breakfast had been eaten a long time ago. He looked at Netta again; she'd taken the venison steaks out of the skillet and was slicing potatoes into the pan.

"If it's all the same to you, I'll take that steak by itself. I'll be starved to death before them spuds get done," he told her.

"All they have to do is heat," she said. "I boiled them the other day. I never was much of a cook, and my biscuits aren't anything to brag about. I'll have you eating in two minutes."

"All right. I guess I can wait that long."

True to her promise, Netta brought their plates to the bedroll before the two minutes had passed. Longarm held out the brandy bottle, but she shook her head.

"I don't need it. Brandy wouldn't give me any better feeling than I've got right now."

Longarm nodded, tilted the bottle himself, and turned his attention to the food. He made two haunch steaks disappear and finished his potatoes while Netta was eating the single steak she'd cooked for herself.

37

"Now that was a real tasty breakfast. Or whatever meal you'd call it," Longarm said, putting his plate down. "I thought you said you couldn't cook, Netta."

"I said I couldn't cook biscuits. And I can't, or much of anything else. My talents are in the bedroom, not in the kitchen; I found that out a long time ago."

"Stop talking like you're an old woman. I'd guess you can't be more than, well, twenty-four, twenty-five."

"Add about five years and you'd come closer." The corners of Netta's mouth drooped. "Sometimes I think it ought to be fifty years, instead of five. Maybe a hundred, if you count the time I spent with Sim."

Longarm recognized the symptoms. People not used to facing danger usually began to get nervous as the time for a showdown drew closer. He said, "Blount bothers you a good bit, don't he?"

"You're damned right he does, Longarm. I know he won't be satisfied until he kills me. And I don't suppose it makes much difference how old I feel, I'm sure not ready to die yet."

"Quit fretting, Netta. You're not about to die. Just get rid of those bad ideas that keep pushing into your head. We're going to scheme up a way to grab Blount before he can do any harm to you or anybody else."

"I wish I was as sure of that as you are."

"It's my business to do jobs like that, you know."

"I know. That's what I keep telling myself, but my stomach still drops down to my ankles when I think about it."

"Here." Longarm handed Netta the brandy bottle. "Take a good swallow or two of this. It'll make you brighten up."

Obediently, Netta took a big swallow from the bottle. She blinked away the tears the liquor brought to her eyes and grinned. "You think I'm scared, don't you? Well—" she tossed her head back defiantly— "I guess I am."

Longarm pulled her close and put his arms around her. "It don't do a bit of harm to get scared once in a while."

Netta nestled her cheek against his chest. "I guess you're going to try to make me feel good, and tell me you've been scared a lot of times."

38

"Being scared makes you move more carefully. Saves your life sometimes."

"When was the last time you were scared, *really* scared, Longarm?"

He couldn't find an answer at once. Finally he said, "I disremember the exact time, but there've been some."

"Well, if you set out to make me feel better, I'd say you have. Even if it took a little white lie to do it." Her hand was stroking Longarm's chest, her fingers combing through the thatch of dark brown hair that covered it. Bit by bit, she dropped the hand to his groin and began to fondle him. "You can make me feel even better than I do now, you know."

"I'm always ready to make a pretty girl feel better."

"So I can see. And feel." Netta shifted around, and stretched out on the bedroll. "And I'll help you feel better too."

She bent her head down and Longarm felt the moist tip of her tongue tracing the length of his swelling shaft. Her lips caressed him, kissing and nibbling gently, before she took him into her mouth. Now Longarm lay back and let himself enjoy her caresses. He stretched a hand out to find her buttocks, and parted the firm mounds to slip his fingers between her thighs, then began to rub and finger her moist inner lips. Netta spread her legs to give his hand freer play, and engulfed him deeper with her busy mouth. He swelled and grew harder as her tongue continued rasping gently over him.

Suddenly she stopped and raised herself on her hands, still bending over him. "Do you like to come this way, Longarm?" she asked.

"If it pleasures you for me to, I'll like it."

"I'd get more pleasure if you'd just as soon be old-fashioned again."

Longarm rolled over. Netta moved to slip under him and opened herself to him. She was wet and slick as he entered her, and he didn't hesitate or go in gently this time, but thrust full-length with all his strength. She brought her groin up to meet his, and their bodies ground together. For a few moments, until he found his rhythm, Longarm jammed into her almost brutally. Netta dug her fingers into the taut muscles of his back and clung to him as his hips rose and fell. Then the

39

first exhilaration faded, and he slowed his tempo. His lunges became slower, more deliberate, his pressure at the depth of his penetration more prolonged.

"I can stay with you this time," Netta whispered. "And it's even better than it was before. Take all the time you want to, Longarm. The longer you make it last, the better it'll be for both of us."

He prolonged their embrace until both of their bodies were filmed with perspiration, though the fire had by this time died to a red glow of coals, and the coolness of the cavern began to bring a chill into the air around them. When at last Netta began to whimper and gurgle joyously, he pounded hard, letting himself go in the final few deep thrusts that drained him and left her sprawled under his relaxed body.

They lay quietly until the chill of the air began to reach their cooling skins. "I'd better tend the fire," she said. "Not that I want to. I can still feel you in me."

"You lay quiet," Longarm told her. "I'll stoke up the fire."

He stood up and padded on bare feet to the woodpile, then put fresh branches on the dying coals, hunkered down, and blew on them until the dry wood burst into flickering flames. He went back to the bedroll. Netta was asleep, her lips curled in a contented smile. Longarm grinned.

She's a right good woman, old son, he told himself. *I guess she was telling the truth earlier, when she said she needed a man right bad.*

Picking up his Colt, Longarm went to the cavern wall and holstered it in his dangling gunbelt before starting to get into his clothes. He made short work of dressing, pulling on his underwear and pants in the same manner in which he'd shed them, as though they were a single garment. He tucked in his shirttail, stomped his feet into his boots, and slipped his arms into his vest. Taking from the vest pocket his watch, which had his double-barreled .44 derringer clipped to the other end of its chain, Longarm looked at the time. The afternoon was well along; the hands indicated two o'clock. If Netta was right in her prediction that Simaeus Blount wouldn't reach the cave until after dark, there was plenty of time in which to make a plan to take him.

Thoughtfully, Longarm fished a cheroot from his vest pocket, flicked a match into flame across his thumbnail, and lighted up. The gray smoke from the cigar eddied through the air and mingled with the sparse thread of smoke rising from the mesquite branches he'd added to the fire. From the darkness at the back of the cavern, the claybank gelding whinnied. Longarm filled the graniteware washbowl with water from the bucket, carried it back to the dimness where the horse stood, and put the basin down to let it drink.

Back by the fire, he picked up the brandy bottle and tilted it to his mouth, his eyes catching the play of flames through the sides of the bottle while he took one swallow and followed it with another. He looked at Netta; he'd been careful to move quietly, and she was still sleeping deeply. The smile she'd worn when he'd looked at her earlier hadn't left her face.

Setting the brandy bottle back in the cabinet, Longarm strapped on his gunbelt, spending several minutes in making sure the holster was at the height and angle that suited him best. Lifting his Winchester off the clothing pegs, he then walked softly toward the cave's entrance.

Even before he reached the opening, the sound of raindrops splashing on wet earth told Longarm what to expect. He stopped just inside the shelter of the entrance, and watched the raindrops pouring down from a somber sky. Down the slope that fell away from the cave's mouth, the ground was puddled with patches of standing water; the shining surface of the puddles was pocked by the steady fall of raindrops.

Here and there, little rivulets flowed from the puddles to cut grooves in the wet, soft soil as they ran down to join the creek. The brown limbs of the mesquite brushes had been turned a shiny black by the rainwater that clung to them; in the dim, soft light they stood out starkly against the softer hue of the soaked earth. The tan boles of the few cottonwoods visible from the mouth of the cave were streaked with dark runnels from thin, zigzagging streams of water flowing down their striated bark. The skins of the clumped prickly pear plants glowed like freshly polished green leather, and the patches of their needles cut sharp yellow lines across their rounded faces. The rounded rocks that studded the black loam between the sparse vegetation gleamed bone-white, their domed tops giving the earth the appearance of a graveyard from which the skulls of people long-buried were arising.

It had been Longarm's idea to walk a short distance along the base of the bluff, to some point where he could look down at the creek and watch for signs of movement while he relieved himself, but the rain cancelled that plan. Standing under the overhang, he cradled the Winchester in his elbow while he opened his fly and arced a yellow stream out onto the wet ground.

His eyes kept busy, moving, scanning the terrain. All he saw was the dull gray of the draining clouds, the trees, the brush, the cacti, and the rocks. In all that bleak, rain-soaked landscape, nothing moved. Satisfied, Longarm turned and went back into the cavern.

Chapter 4

Netta was still asleep. She'd curled up, her legs drawn up to her chest, her head almost touching her knees, her long blonde hair streaming over the rough blanket and down her back. Longarm didn't disturb her. He stood beside the bedroll for a moment, looking at the firelight gleaming on the scarred skin of her buttocks, and wondering what led women to outlaws like Sim Blount. He shrugged the thought aside when he found no answer. Then he went over to the wall, replaced the Winchester on the pegs, took the bottle of brandy, and sat down at the base of the wall, leaning back against the pale, cold stone while he lighted a fresh cheroot before taking a warming sip from the bottle.

He went over in his mind the details of the terrain outside. There was no cover anywhere close to the entrance. On all sides, the slope bore only scattered vegetation, no thick bushes, no closely spaced groves of trees where he could wait in hiding and watch and listen for Blount's approach. The cottonwoods were wide-spaced, and the thin-leaved mesquite bushes would not conceal a man's form. The cactus offered no cover, either.

You got a problem here, old son, Longarm told himself. *But let's just eat the apple one bite at a time.*

Twenty minutes later, he was still chewing on the first bite, a long way from the core. There was no way to take Blount outside the cave. The only thing he could see to do was to let the outlaw come in, using Netta as a decoy. Then Longarm could step from the shadows back in the area where the claybank gelding was, and face the man down. It wasn't the solution Longarm would have preferred, but it was the only one the situation seemed to offer. He'd lighted a fresh cheroot and was taking a swallow of brandy when Netta spoke.

"My God! How long have I been asleep?"

"Maybe an hour, give or take a few minutes."

"I looked for you to come back and lie down with me. I sleep better with a man's shoulder for a pillow, you know."

"I didn't know, but I'll remember next time. You didn't seem to be having any trouble though."

Netta grinned happily. "I was ready for a rest, after that last good one we had, Longarm. I'd've thought you'd be, too."

"I just wasn't sleepy, and you were snoozing so peaceful I didn't want to bother you."

"Being bothered by you is a pleasure. You can come bother me again right now, if you feel like it."

"Oh, I always feel like it. Thing is, though, Netta, we better not take any more time pleasuring right now. It's getting late, and there's a heavy rain falling. Dark's going to come early tonight."

"What time is it?"

Longarm looked at his watch. "Right on three o'clock. It'll be full dark by five, unless this weather breaks, and there didn't look to be much chance that it will, when I was outside."

Netta jumped up and stretched. She looked around for her clothes, saw her jeans on one side of the bedroll and her shirt on the other, and grimaced. She said, "I was really in a hurry, wasn't I? But I told you how long it'd been."

"Sure you did. And it'd tickle me if we could go right back and start all over again, but we just ain't got the time."

"Why didn't you wake me? I didn't intend to sleep at all."

"There wasn't any reason to wake you up. Besides, I wanted to just set quiet and do some thinking."

"About how we're going to handle Sim?" Netta had gathered up her scattered garments and was putting on her shirt.

He shrugged. "Mostly that. Can't say I made much headway, though."

"Well, you didn't like my original idea. The only

44

other one that I can think of would be for me to stand just inside the mouth of the cave, like I was waiting for Sim. He'd see me right away, and see I was by my-self. But you could be hiding in the dark, just inside the opening, and when he got close enough, all you'd need to do would be to step up and take him." She was buttoning her shirt while she spoke.

"Don't forget, I want Blount alive," Longarm reminded her.

Netta had wiggled a foot into one leg of her jeans. She stopped and stood with the other leg poised in midair, and looked questioningly at Longarm. "I'm not forgetting. What's that got to do with it?"

"You stop and think a minute, and you'll see why trying to take Blount outside the cave won't work."

Frowning, she shook her head. She pulled her jeans up over her slim hips and started to button them before replying. "I suppose I'm dense, but I don't see what you're getting at. Why wouldn't it work for me to stand in the cave-mouth?"

"On a bright day, I guess you could. Blount'd be in the sunshine. He couldn't see back into the shadows where I'd be. All he'd see would be that black opening. I could take a quick, long step, and I'd have him before he'd be able to draw."

"Well, then?"

"I thought it out, Netta. With the weather outside like it is today, there ain't much difference between the light out in the open, on the slope coming up, and the light inside the cave. Instead of being right inside the opening, I'd have to go back ten or fifteen feet. That'd be far enough to give Blount all the time he needed to see me coming and pull his gun before I could grab him. I'd have to kill him, and that ain't what my chief wants me to do."

Netta thought for a moment, then said with a frown, "I guess you're right. Well, if you can't come up with anything better, we'll have to go back to my original idea, won't we?"

"I ain't got the right to ask you to do that, Netta. It's just plumb too risky."

"It was my idea to start with, remember? And I've

45

told you, I'm willing to take any kind of risk to be sure Sim's put away where he can't ever get at me again."

"I know what you said. The thing is, there's a difference between what you're ready to do and what I'm ready to let you do."

"To hell with that, Longarm!" Netta's eyes flashed angrily. "You're not going to tell me what I can or can't do! You wouldn't tell a *man* what he could do, how much of a chance he could take, if he was in a situation like this. Would you, now?"

"No." Longarm shook his head. "No, I reckon not."

"All right then. We'll do it the way I worked out before you got here." She tied her shoelaces and stood up.

"If that's how you want it," Longarm agreed. "Only you got to keep him from noticing me while I'm pussyfooting up here from the back. I've got to get near enough to get my hands on him before he can go for his gun." He paused for a second or so before adding, "You seemed pretty sure Blount would want to play around with you for a while—"

"I said he'd want to fuck me before he kills me," Netta broke in. "Maybe he'll wait until I start to come, and stab me then. I know Sim. That's the way his ugly, twisted mind works. Damn it, I showed you proof of that."

"I know you did. But if you don't feel up to doing it—" Longarm began.

She cut him off. "I didn't say that. I guess I can stand having him touch me again without letting him see how disgusted I am at the idea."

Longarm gazed fixedly into her eyes for a moment, then said, "I don't like the scheme, but it's the only way I can see that'll give me time to move in on him."

"Yes. It's the only way." Netta was silent for a few seconds, then said, "Don't worry about it. I'll bait the trap all right. It's worth it to me, and not just for the reward. I'd do it for nothing. I don't think there's much I wouldn't do if it'd get me free from worrying about Sim catching me."

"It's settled, then," he said.

"As far as I'm concerned, it is. How long do you think we ought to wait before we set things up in here?"

"Well, you've said all along that Blount won't show out in the daylight, but what kind of odds would you give that he might figure a dark, rainy day's as good as night?"

"About fifty-fifty. I didn't stop to think about the weather. You're right, though. He'd know that if he bundled up and pulled his hat down over his face like anybody'd do out in the rain, there wouldn't be much chance he'd be noticed. Damn it, Longarm! He might be on his way here right now!"

"I sort of figured that, too."

"We'd better set the trap, then," Netta suggested.

"Any time you're ready."

"I'm as ready as I'll ever be, I guess. No, there's one thing I've got to do first, go outside and squat a minute."

"You can go back there where my horse is, if you don't want to get wet," he suggested.

"No. I'll go outside. I need to breathe fresh air for a minute or so, before Sim gets here to stink things up. And if he doesn't show up tonight, we'll be waiting a long time until it's safe for us to stir around." She said over her shoulder as she started for the entrance, "I'll be right back."

Longarm looked around the cavern, making a mental note of the items belonging to him that he'd have to carry back to his hiding place. He couldn't leave anything lying around that might give Blount any hint of his presence. All he saw that would be obvious giveaways were his bedroll, his canteen, his coat, and his Winchester.

"Hell's bells," he muttered. "That's only one good load. Might as well take it back there now and save time later, in case I need to duck out of sight in a hurry."

Putting on his coat, Longarm lifted his rifle off the pegs and tucked it under one arm. He put the bedroll under the other arm, picked up the canteen by its webbed strap, then carried the light load back into the darkness, not bothering to take a torch. There was plenty of time for him to go back later with a lighted branch, tend to the claybank, spread his bedroll so he'd have a comfortable place to wait, and carry the

47

brandy back so he'd have something to sip on now and again.

He moved slowly into the darkness of the cavern's back recesses, giving his eyes time to adjust to the darkness. The gelding heard him coming and nickered hopefully. Longarm reminded himself that he'd have to give the horse food before settling down. With any luck, they'd be out of the cave and on their way back to Denver the next day, with Blount in custody. He dropped his bedroll on the stone floor and laid the Winchester carefully beside it. The gelding nickered again.

"You ain't been forgot, fellow," Longarm said. He knew the claybank couldn't understand his words, but would be reassured simply by the sound of a calming voice. "I'll get back and tend to you pretty quick."

Back in the main chamber, he hunkered down by the fire. It was burning low again. He added a few of the scrawny mesquite limbs, little bigger than twigs, and when one of them blazed up, he lifted it to light the cheroot he'd taken from his pocket. He'd had a few puffs and was thinking about getting the brandy bottle when it struck him that Netta had been gone a long time, much longer than she should have been. He frowned, levered himself to his feet, and started toward the mouth of the cave. He didn't really expect Simaeus Blount to show up so early, but just in case the outlaw had been the cause of Netta's delay, Longarm slid his Colt out of its holster as he walked.

There was little difference between the firelit interior of the big cavern and the gray dusk that showed the cave's arched mouth in dim outline as Longarm approached it. He reached the opening and hesitated for an instant before stepping outside. While he stood looking out, trying to pierce the veil cast over the area by the early, rain-filled dusk, he heard footsteps splashing toward the entrance. He started to step outside just as Netta rounded the corner of the arch.

"Longarm!" she gasped. "Thank God! Sim's right behind me!"

Blount was following her more closely than Netta realized. While Longarm's attention was still on her, listening to her warning, a man's stocky form loomed

48

behind Netta. Her body in his line of fire prevented Longarm from shooting. The other man had no such compunctions.

"You dirty bitch!" he snarled. He lifted the pistol he'd been carrying in his hand and let off two quick shots.

Both slugs struck Netta in the back. The impact of the bullets sent her lurching forward. She fell against Longarm, her arms flailing. One of her arms fell over Longarm's gun hand, pulling it down before he could shoot. He tried to lift his arm, but the weight of Netta's inert body was too much; his hand was held too low for him to hope to hit the outlaw.

Blount fired again as he was turning to run, but missed. The fugitive started down the muddy slope. After a dozen long leaps he lost his footing and fell, tried to get up and failed, then settled for rolling over and over down the incline leading to the creek, raising big splashes from each puddle he encountered.

Longarm was finally able to raise his gun hand. Supporting Netta with his left hand, he snapshotted at Blount's rolling form. By now, the outlaw was thirty or more yards away, almost invisible against the dun-colored earth, his body obscured by the water he sent splashing up around him each time he thrashed around in a roll. In the growing darkness, Longarm could not aim. He tried one more long-range shot, then lowered Netta to the ground inside the cave's mouth and started chasing Blount.

After seeing the outlaw's fall, Longarm did not try to run. He picked his way carefully to keep from falling himself, but before he'd covered a half-dozen steps, he realized there was little point in trying to pursue. He was just turning back when, somewhere ahead of him, the orange-red muzzle-flash of a shot cut the night, followed by the sharp crack of a rifle shot. The slug buzzed over Longarm's head and he dodged into the questionable shelter of the nearest mesquite bush.

"Stand where you are!" a voice called through the dimness. "Texas Rangers! You're under arrest! If you move, I'll shoot to kill the next time!"

Longarm hesitated only a moment before sending a high shot in the general direction of the muzzle-blast and dropping down for better shelter in the scanty heart of the bush.

Another flash of orange split the darkness and another slug whistled above Longarm's head. He returned the shot, knowing as he fired that he was shooting blindly.

Longarm called, "I'm a U.S. marshal! If you're a ranger, hold your fire and take after that son of a bitch that's getting away!"

Hoofbeats splashed at a distance, then a second set of hoofbeats plopped on the wet ground in the general direction from which the rifle shots had come. Longarm did not move until the noise of the horses had faded and died. He got up then, and slipped and skidded upslope to the mouth of the cavern. Netta was lying where he'd left her. Her pulse was faint, and even in the near-darkness he could see the bloodstain on the back of her shirt. He picked her up and carried her inside.

Carefully, he laid her on the bedroll and went to the water bucket, where he soaked his handkerchief in the cold water. Back at the bedroll, he mopped Netta's face until she stirred and her eyes opened.

"Sim did what he came to do, didn't he?" she asked. Her voice sounded as though it were coming from a far place. "He's killed me, I think."

"Now don't go getting bad ideas," Longarm replied. "I'll take care of you. You'll be all right, as soon as you get over the shock."

"You don't have to lie to make me feel good, Longarm," she whispered. "I've seen people die. I know how I feel."

"You always feel worse than you're really hurt."

"I couldn't feel the way I do unless I'm going to die."

Longarm searched for words, but none would come. He kept on mopping Netta's face with the wet handkerchief. Her skin was a dull white now, beginning to bead with cold sweat.

"Well, it's the truth, isn't it?" she demanded.

"I don't know, Netta. I've seen people shot a lot worse than you are, and get over it."

"I'm not going to, though. All I am right now is a

head floating around somewhere, Longarm. I can't feel my body at all."

"Like I said, that's just shock. I've been where you are, with a bullet or two in me, and I'm still walking around."

"If I was going to live, you'd be putting a bandage on me."

"I'm just getting ready to do that. Before the shock wears off. It won't hurt as much that way."

"There's an old shirt of mine stuffed in the cabinet. It's about all I've got that you can use."

Longarm went to the stacked boxes, found the shirt, and tore it into strips. He took off the blood-soaked shirt Netta was wearing and raised her gently from the blankets. She tried to help, but feeling was returning to her now, and any move she made brought a grimace of pain to her face.

When he saw the location of the bullet wounds in Netta's back, Longarm knew the bandage was a waste of time, but he finished wrapping it around her and tying off the ends. Then he pulled the blanket over her shoulders, which were already beginning to feel chilly to his touch. She lay back, and her eyes closed. Belatedly remembering the brandy, Longarm went to the cabinet and got it.

"Here," he said. "Take a swallow of this. It'll make you feel better."

He held the bottle to her lips. Netta swallowed obediently, then a cough tore through her body. Pain twisted her face.

"Oh, damn!" she gasped. "I can sure feel my body now. And it hurts. Did you hurt when you got shot, Longarm?"

"I sure as hell did. Every time. But I got over it, just like you will."

"Maybe you're a lot tougher than I am."

"Maybe. But you're a pretty tough lady, Netta."

"Thanks. That's one of the nicest things anybody ever said to me." Netta tried to raise a hand to reach Longarm, but her strength wasn't equal to it. She said, "Sit down by me a little while, will you, Longarm? All at once, I feel lonesome."

"No need for you to. I ain't going to leave you."

Longarm folded his legs under him and sat down on the cold stone floor beside Netta. He went on, "Now you're going to rest a little while. Then I'm going to bundle you up and carry you into Round Rock to a doctor."

"You really think a doctor can do me any good?"

"It's worth trying. Never say—" Longarm caught himself in time to bite off the last word.

"Die?" Netta finished for him. She smiled weakly. "I always thought I'd be afraid to die. But you know something? It doesn't scare me a bit, right now."

"It'll be better if you don't talk," he cautioned her. "Try to save your strength for that ride into town."

"You're lying again, aren't you?" Netta managed another wan smile. "Hell, Longarm, I've known enough men to tell when one of you lies to me. You do it better than most, though." She lay silently for a moment before adding, "But you do a lot of things better than most men."

"You'll get well, Netta."

"Promise me?"

"Of course I promise you."

"Will you promise me something else too?"

"Just about anything. What?"

"Don't let Sim get away. Keep after him until you catch him. Or kill him, I don't care which."

"You know I aim to do that."

"You'd do it whether I asked you or not, wouldn't you?"

"I'd have to, Netta. It's my job."

"Was I part of your job too, Longarm? Earlier, I mean, when you had that big, beautiful tool of yours inside me and you made me feel like I was floating on a cloud? Was that just part of your job?"

"No, Netta. That wasn't part of the job. And you know I'm not lying to you this time."

"Good. I'd hate to think I was just part of a job somebody did because he had to, not because he wanted to. You know—" She stopped short and gasped, her mouth contorting.

"Don't try to talk anymore now," Longarm commanded.

Netta sighed, a deep exhalation that seemed to ex-

52

haust her. Suddenly, Longarm could see that her eyes were staring sightlessly at him from her bloodless face.

Longarm felt for a pulse in her throat, but found none. He covered Netta's face with the blanket and picked up the brandy bottle. He took a long swallow, then followed it with another. Absently he reached into his pocket and took out a cigar, dragged the head of a match across his thumbnail, and lighted up. He looked at the blanket-covered form while the match burned until the flame reached the skin of his fingers, then he let the burned shriveled stub fall to the stone floor.

Damn Blount, Longarm thought. *It was just a waste to kill that woman. All she wanted from him was to be left alone.*

Puffing a cloud of smoke into the still, cool air, Longarm reached again for the brandy bottle. There was just one good drink left in it. He raised the bottle to his lips and was swallowing the last drop of brandy when somebody spoke from behind him.

It was a man's voice, harsh and commanding. "Freeze, mister! You better prove to me you're a U.S. marshal, or you're likely to be a damn dead outlaw!"

Chapter 5

Longarm didn't twitch a muscle. He was still holding the brandy bottle at eye-level in his right hand, and did not lower it. His left held his cheroot, which he'd been about to put back in his mouth, and he kept that hand motionless too.

In a quiet, conversational tone he said, "I guess you're the Texas Ranger that let off a couple of blind shots over my head a while ago, outside?"

"You guessed right, mister. Name's Will Travers. C Company out of Waco. You want to hang a name on yourself?"

"Glad to, ranger. Custis Long, deputy U.S. marshal from the Denver office."

"Denver? What the hell are you doing way down here in the middle of Texas?"

"Trying to run down a skunk named Blount. He just killed this woman laying here, but that's beside the point. I'm after him for gunning down one of our men when he was trying to rob a U.S. Mail coach of a gold shipment from the Denver Mint a few months back. That was up around Texarkana."

"I remember," Travers said. "Your name's Long, is it? You the one they call Longarm?"

"I've answered to the name."

"You worked that Laredo Loop case, then. So did one of our boys. Remember who he was?"

Unhesitatingly, Longarm replied, "Nate Webster. Took out a rurale who was fixing to backshoot me down in a hellhole called Los Perros."

Travers's tone was a bit grudging, as though he was disappointed. "All right. You can let your hands down and turn around. I guess you're who you claim to be, all right."

Longarm lowered his hands. He dropped the brandy bottle and clamped his cheroot in his mouth. Then he turned to face the ranger. He said, "You knew right along I wasn't lying, ain't that right, Travers?" When the ranger made no reply, he went on, "If I hadn't been who I said I was, you know damned well you weren't going to find me still hanging around here, after you yelled out who you were."

"I figured it that way, sure. But don't blame me for making certain I was figuring right," Travers said.

"Oh, I don't. No hard feelings. I'd most likely have done just what you did."

Longarm was pretty sure he'd have tagged Travers as a ranger even in a chance encounter on the street or in a saloon. The Texan was clean-shaven, ignoring the conventional male adornment of a beard or mustache. His face was long, running to a lot of jaw under thin lips. *Mean lips,* Longarm thought. His eyes were pale, almost colorless, set deep in his head, surrounded by a network of squint-wrinkles that showed up even in the dimly lit cave.

Travers had on a light tan Stetson, with a mid-Texas crease. His light gray flannel shirt was very much like the one Longarm was wearing, but it was several shades paler, almost white. A shirt like that marked a lawman wearing it as being either very brave or very reckless; light-colored articles of clothing offered prime targets in a nighttime shootout. A bright cerise silk neckerchief was knotted around the outside of his shirt collar. There was no badge on his shirt pocket, but Longarm hadn't expected to see one. Like U.S. marshals, the rangers carried their badges in their wallets. Below covert-cloth trousers with narrow legs, Travers was wearing Texas-style boots, with long, narrow toes and high heels. Texans made a point of boots like that, boots that identified their wearer as a horseman, a man who'd swing into the saddle just to go across the street. The spurs on the boots were another Texas trademark. They were ornate, of shiny steel, with gold-chased rowels the size of silver dollars.

Longarm recognized and approved of the ranger's business equipment. Travers's gunbelt was worn high, with the holster in a cross-draw position on his left side. The butt of the revolver that protruded from the holster identified the weapon as a Colt .45 single-action. Instead of cartridge loops, he carried his spare shells loose in a pair of pouches. Seconds wasted in thumbing reloads from loops, especially with fingers that were cold or wet, had gotten more than one man killed needlessly.

Travers said, "I couldn't run Blount down. Not in the dark, in this kind of weather, and me getting a late start after him."

"You still after him for that mail coach job?" Longarm asked.

"That and a lot of other things. Mostly, though, because he gunned one of our boys down about three weeks ago."

"Matter of pride now, I'd say." Longarm's remark wasn't a question, just an affirmative comment. "Well, there's another count of murder against him now." He indicated Netta's blanket-shrouded body.

"His girl, wasn't she?"

"Used to be. Before he cut her ass and tried to slit her throat. That scared her so much that she turned him in to us."

"I was just getting around to asking how you happened to be here. Took me by surprise when you hollered at me outside there, a while ago." Travers scratched his jutting chin. "You was inside here, holed up, waiting for him to show?"

"Something like that. The girl sent us a letter, up in Denver."

"Um. Well, I guess you can leave Blount to us, Longarm. Any ranger-killer's rightly our meat."

"Just happens I can't do that, Travers. He killed one of our men too. And that was before he gunned yours, so we're first in line."

"Your man was the one riding shotgun on that shipment of money Blount tried to grab off?"

"McClintock. A special friend of my chief, Billy Vail."

"So Vail sent you to bring Blount back?"

"That's the whole story. It's my case, and I don't plan to step aside in your favor. How'd he get to your man, anyhow?"

"You know our way, I guess, when we're bringing a man in? We give him a choice—the hard way or the easy one. If he takes the hard way, we bring him in cuffed, maybe wearing leg-irons too, and roust him every step of the way. If he wants it easy, all he's got to do is pledge he won't try to get away. Of course, he knows that if he busts his pledge, he's a dead man."

Longarm nodded. "I've heard about that deal your men make. Usually works out though, don't it?"

"Most of the time. It didn't with Blount. He pledged, and poor old Joe Rambold took his word. Then, when Joe let his guard down for a minute, Blount grabbed his gun and backshot him."

"Which means you men have got to take Blount, or everybody else on the wrong side's going to get the idea they can do the same thing he did."

"That's about the size of it," Travers admitted. "So you see why I can't let you have Blount, no matter how bad your chief might want him."

"Well, now." It was Longarm's turn to scratch his chin. "Looks like we got the same problem, don't it, Travers?"

"I haven't got a problem. I'd say you have, though."

"Meaning what?"

"Meaning that even the U.S. marshal's office ain't big enough to take a man we want away from us." There was no bluster to Travers's statement; it was simply an even-toned summary of fact.

Longarm looked at the empty brandy bottle on the floor of the cavern. "You know, Travers, I think what we better do is hold up on talking about this right now. Let's put it off till we can get to someplace where we can sit down and feel easy. Maybe split a bottle between us, sort of lubricate what we say to each other."

"That's not going to change anything, Long."

"I don't suppose it will. But it might help us figure out a way that'll satisfy us both."

"Damned if I can see how."

"Well, if it comes to that, I can't see how, either. But it won't hurt to try. Here we are, looking at a dirty job we got to do, and we're wasting time arguing about something that ain't happened yet."

"I guess you got a point, at that. You want to bury

57

her here, or carry her to town and let an undertaker do the job?"

"I don't suppose it matters much to her. From what I seen of her, Netta wasn't the kind of woman who'd put much store in ceremonies. Except I don't happen to carry a shovel around with me, and I don't imagine you do, either. We've got no chance of trying to start tracking Blount tonight, and it appears to me we're going to have to settle things between us before we do. So I'd say we go to town."

"It's probably the best thing." Travers poked the brandy bottle with the pointed toe of his boot. "Especially if all you've got here's this empty bottle. All right, Longarm. I'll stick with you until we've settled things about Blount. After that, I'd say it's going to be every man for himself, devil take the hindmost."

Halfway to Round Rock the rain stopped, and that made the rest of the ride easier, but still didn't ease the tension that hung between Longarm and Will Travers. Longarm rode with Netta's limp, blanket-wrapped body draped over his saddle horn, and he couldn't help thinking, every time the claybank's hoof slid on a patch of soft mud and the corpse rolled against his knees, of Netta alive and enjoying the pleasures they'd shared for a few brief hours. Carrying her to the undertaker to be put away forever in the earth didn't give him much desire for idle chatter.

After the necessary business had been finished, it was too late to go to bed and too early to find a dining hall open for breakfast. As they munched on the soft local longhorn cheese that was Round Rock's chief claim to fame, Travers growled along with Longarm about the lack of hot food at the free lunch counter of the saloon they found on Main Street. Longarm growled because Texas was bourbon country, and the best rye the barkeep could offer was a cut below that to which he'd become accustomed. Still, the mutual growling gave the two a sort of left-hand kinship, and the chill that had been between them when they left the cave had diminished by the time the growling of their bellies had been stopped by food and drink.

"Well?" Longarm asked Travers as they leaned

back in the heavy saloon chairs. "You ready to do a little palavering about who's going to take Blount in?"

"I've got nothing to say that we ain't already said," the ranger replied. "You go your way and I'll go mine, and whoever gets him first keeps him. Or tries to," he added. "Like I told you, if you grab Blount first, you sure as hell ain't going to get him out of Texas alive."

"You mean him alive, or me?"

"Take it any way you want. Any outlaw that kills a ranger answers to Texas law and nobody else's."

"I might feel like going along with you, Travers, except for one thing. In the marshal's office, we feel just as strong as you rangers do about a bastard who's gunned down one of our men."

"Looks like a standoff, then."

"No. It don't have to be," Longarm answered. "You know, it strikes me as being pretty silly if we didn't work together to bring Blount in. You know the old saying about what the barrel said to the box."

"Two heads are better than one?" For the first time since they'd been together, Travers grinned. "That's what my old daddy used to say when I'd go to him with some kind of a question that was stumping me. 'Will,' he'd say, 'Let's you and me work this out together.' Then he'd tell me about the barrel and the box."

"And it worked out pretty well for you and him, didn't it?" Longarm asked.

"Seemed to. I guess he really come up with most of the answers, but I put in my two bits' worth too."

"Then why the hell can't it work out for us?" Longarm demanded. "It don't make any difference how slick and smart Blount is, he's just one man. It stands to reason we'd be better than him, if we can figure out a way to work together."

Travers said thoughtfully, "Two heads against one."

"It'd work, if we can get our two heads together." Longarm tossed off the remark with a casualness he was far from feeling. "If we don't manage to, we're going to get in each other's way. You'll follow the same trail I'm on, we'll cross each other."

"I'm pretty near to agreeing with you," Travers admitted. "The thing that holds me back is, what's my

59

captain going to say when he finds out about it?"

"Might be he'd say the same thing my chief would. Pull as a team, settle whoever gets Blount for keeps after we've brought him in."

"All right, Longarm," Travers said. He spoke fast, as thought he might be tempted to change his mind if he hesitated. "We'll make ourselves a deal. We'll go after Blount together, and settle who gets to keep him after we catch him."

"Suits me fine."

Privately, Longarm had reservations about the deal. Travers and the rangers outnumbered him a hundred or more to one, and he was operating in their home territory. He'd suggested the deal with the ranger chiefly because of that. If he had to fight the Texas Rangers while he trailed Blount, he'd be fighting a losing battle. But Travers knew the country. He knew the local hideouts, knew where outlaws congregated, and knew, too, the back-trails a fugitive running hard would be most likely to use.

As for who's going to keep Blount once he's been taken, Longarm told himself, *that's going to depend on who can outfox the other the best. And I'll put my money on my own back, instead of on a horse I don't know about.*

Aloud, he said to Travers, "The way I feel right now, I'd like to get a couple of hours of shut-eye before we ride out. Does that jibe with the way you're thinking?"

"It sure does, even if it means giving Blount a longer start on us. Of course, we got no way of knowing how much country the rain's covered. We know he's heading east, I'd say either for the Red River and Louisiana, or for the Piney Woods on this side of the river. Either way, all we'll have to do is head east and fan out until one of us crosses his trail."

"He won't be making good time, as long as the bad weather holds. Is there a hotel here where we can get a room and sleep awhile?"

"There's a hotel, but I got a better deal." Travers stood up. "Come on. We'll go find a shakedown at a place I know about."

Longarm followed the ranger to a small house on a

60

back street off Round Rock's town square. Travers seemed to be completely at home. He rode into the yard and back to a dilapidated and obviously long unused stable, where they dismounted and let their horses stand. Going to the back door, the ranger tapped with a triple knock that Longarm took for some kind of private signal. They waited a long time, it seemed, before a middle-aged woman wearing a faded flannel wrapper over an ankle-length muslin nightgown opened the door. Her hair was disarrayed; obviously, Travers's knock had awakened her.

"Will!" she said. "It's nice to see you, even at this uncivilized time of night. Come on in, you and your friend, and I'll hotten up the coffee."

"I hope you don't mind me rousing you this way," Travers apologized. "But me and my friend here—this is U.S. Marshal Long, Mrs. Grady—" Longarm doffed his hat and Mrs. Grady nodded— "the fact is, me and him been up all night, and we need a place to spread our bedrolls for an hour or two before we hit the trail again. Would it bother you too much—"

"Laws, no!" she said cheerfully. "Come on in. I'll stir up some breakfast for you; I suppose you're hungry too. And you'll sleep better on a full stomach."

"Now, we don't need—" Longarm began.

Travers interrupted him. "Thanks, Mrs. Grady. We've got to tend our horses first. But we'll be right in, if you're sure it won't put you out too much."

"You know it won't. Nothing's too good for my ranger boys. I'll leave the door on the latch. You just walk on in, when you've done your chores."

While they unsaddled their horses in the tumbledown shed, Travers explained, "She's a ranger's widow. Jim got killed about five years ago, and she's sorta adopted the whole ranger force. Gets mad if we don't stay with her, or at least visit, when we pass through."

"I see. Makes it real handy to have a place like that, where you can get a shakedown when you need one."

"She's a nice lady, Long. Of course she gets lonesome, and she'll talk your arm off if you let her, but all of us try to keep on visiting her, because of Jim."

They carried their bedrolls into the house. Mrs. Grady was frying thin slices of country ham, and a bowl of brown-shelled eggs stood handy, to be broken into the skillet at the proper time.

"You know the way to the sitting room, Will," she said. "You and Mr. Long make yourselves as comfortable as you can, and I'll have you some breakfast in just a minute."

Travers led the way into a shabby-genteel sitting room, crowded with furniture. The shades were drawn, and Longarm judged from the look of the room that they stayed drawn except on such rare occasions as a call by Mrs. Grady's minister, or a once-a-year tea party for her women friends. They shifted chairs and tables until they'd made space on the floor for their bedrolls, and went back into the kitchen. The widow was dishing the ham and eggs onto the plates, and the aroma of coffee mingled with the scent of the ham fat.

Longarm said little during breakfast. Mostly he listened to Mrs. Grady's questions about one or another of her ranger friends, and Travers's answers. When they'd finished eating, the ranger said, "Now, Mrs. Grady, I'll ask you to rouse us in about three hours. We're hoping the weather will break by then, but rain or shine, we've got to get on the trail before too long."

"I'll do that, Will. You men sleep good, now. I know you need your rest."

They didn't undress, just skinned off their boots and took off coats and vests and gunbelts before stretching out on their bedrolls. Longarm fell asleep almost instantly. He woke up once, brought from his habitually light slumber by some noise nearby. He lay quietly, listening. From somewhere in the house, he heard a woman's moans, accompanied by creaking bedsprings. He looked over at Travers's bedroll, and saw that the ranger was gone. Grinning, Longarm lay back down. *Looks to me like the rangers take pretty good care of widows,* he thought, as he closed his eyes and went back to sleep.

Travers was back in his bedroll when Mrs. Grady knocked on the sitting room door in midmorning to wake them, and Longarm said nothing about what he'd heard. They refused the widow's offer of a second breakfast, saddled up at once, and rode out. It promised to be a warm day; Longarm took off his coat and folded it, then added it to his bedroll. In town, they stopped at one of the stores on the square to buy provisions; neither of them was traveling with full saddlebags. By noon, they were in the saddle again, riding toward the limestone cavern, where they hoped to be able to pick up Blount's trail.

Sleep, together with whatever relaxation he'd shared with the widow Grady, had relaxed Travers. Maybe it was because the weather had broken and the sun was shining. Whatever the reason, the ranger was a lot friendlier than he'd been the night before.

"I figure Blount's going to head for the river instead of the Big Thicket," he told Longarm as they rode. "It's closer, for one thing. And from what little I know about the son of a bitch, that little corner of east Texas is one of his favorite stomping grounds."

"Might be you're right," Longarm agreed. "That train job he tried to pull was up there, wasn't it, now? Well, all we can do is see if we can pick up a trail, and stay on it."

Picking up the trail was easy enough, but staying on it proved harder. They cast around in circles after they got to the creek that ran below the cavern. Longarm circled to the north, Travers to the south, until the ranger came across the deep hoofprints left in the still soggy ground by the fleeing outlaw's horse. The trail was easy to follow for the rest of that day and the morning of the next. It led across as yet unsettled country, raw land waiting for the plow after it had been grazed clean through the years by the cattle herds that had moved when the big ranges of the north and west had been opened after the War.

Late on the morning of the second day, the trail ended at a road. It was really more of a trace than a road, twin wheel ruts of sandy red earth that meandered around boulders and wandered along the banks of small creeks until it reached a sandbar that served as a ford. For a backcountry road, it was well traveled. The prints of Blount's mount were lost in a maze of other hoofprints, of wagon teams and riding-horses.

"There'll be farms both ways along the road,"

Travers told Longarm. "You go that way, I'll go the other way, and we'll ask wherever there's a house."

"And meet back here how long from now?" Longarm asked. He was perfectly willing to let the ranger call the shots; it was country that Travers knew better than Longarm did.

"Oh, halfway through the afternoon, I'd say. Blount's got to've stopped someplace, or somebody's seen him going by. I'd sure like to know what kind of nag he was on, though. It'd make it a lot easier. Folks around here look at the horse first, then at whoever's riding it."

"I got a notion we'd be safe in asking about a fellow on a gray, or maybe a dapple," Longarm said, pushing his Stetson back from his forehead. "That place just a few miles before we got to the road here, where he pushed through that willow thicket on the sandbar in the creek, there was some gray horsetail hairs caught in the willows."

Travers blinked and sat bolt-upright in his saddle.

"Hell you say! Why didn't you mention it to me?"

"Why, I just figured you'd seen 'em too," Longarm replied guilelessly.

"Guess I must've missed 'em. I was watching to see where he left the creek," Travers said curtly. "All right, I don't suppose there'd have been two men making that trail we were on. We'll ask about a gray, then."

It was Longarm who picked up the trail this time. He'd ridden eight miles and stopped at two farmhouses without any results when he turned the claybank gelding into the third farmhouse and saw a dapple-gray stamping in the stableyard. Beyond the horse, behind the barn, a farmer was working down a pile of sweepings with a manure fork. Longarm dismounted and walked back to where the man was working.

"Howdy," he called when he was still a dozen paces away. "Wonder if you can help me a little bit?"

"Depends." The man drove the fork into the ground and leaned on its handle. "What kind of help you looking for?"

"My name's Long. "I'm a deputy U.S. marshal, and I'm trying to track down a man who might've passed this way last night or real early this morning."

"Is he some kind of robber or something?"

"Some kind of bad one, yes, sir. You see anybody go by, or have anybody stop in and ask for a meal or to water his horse?"

"How'd you figure that out? Fellow did stop, right after I got up this morning, just at daybreak. Only he didn't want to water a horse, he wanted to trade one." The man's eyes widened and he asked, "This fellow you're after's not a horse thief, is he?"

"No. Why? Did you trade with him?"

"I sure did. Took that dapple over there and a double eagle to boot for a half-broke critter I picked up last week at a horse auction."

"What'd this fellow look like?"

"Well—" The farmer frowned thoughtfully. "He was shorter than me. Needed a shave. Awful muddy. Said he was a commercial messenger, whatever that is. I never heard of one before."

"Did he say where he was going?"

"Not right out. He asked me if there was another ferry he could take across the Red River. South of Shreve's Ferry, that is. Seemed to be in a right smart hurry to keep moving, after we'd done dickering. Wouldn't even stop for breakfast."

"What'd you tell him about the river crossing?"

"Told him I didn't know, a'course. Hell, Marshal, that's a long ways from here. I never been closer to the Red River than Fort Worth, and I only been there three or four times."

"But he headed east when he left here, did he?"

"Sure did." The farmer grinned. "I guess he got along all right with that mustang I traded him. I told him the critter wasn't broke good, but he didn't seem to mind. He was holding on for dear life when he took off along the road."

"Thanks Mr.—"

"Henshaw. I hope I helped you some?"

"You sure did, Mr. Henshaw. Maybe a lot more than you'll ever know. I'm real obliged."

Longarm wasted no time getting back to the place where he hoped he'd find Travers waiting. He'd formed a theory based on the farmer's story that he wanted to test against the ranger's knowledge of the country.

Old son, he thought as he kicked the gelding to a slightly faster walk, *you might not know much about Blount, but you do know how crooks think. And if Blount planted the idea that he was heading for the Red River and Louisiana, it's a pretty safe bet that we better go in the other direction if we aim to catch up with him.*

Chapter 6

A half-hour later, when he and Travers had made their rendezvous, Longarm found himself arguing with the ranger in support of the theory he'd formed about Blount's plans.

"Don't be a fool," Travers snapped. "He'd go for the place he knows best, and that's just where the farmer said he was asking about."

"I ain't as sure of that as you seem to be, Travers," Longarm said. "I'll grant you, Blount favors that part of the country, but I'd say that's a good reason for him to steer clear of it. Too many people might recognize him."

"Shit!" Travers snorted. "The ones who'd know him are the ones who'd hide him. He'd be moving among friends."

"Maybe. But I'd give Blount credit for being smarter than that. On the prod the way he is, with us right behind him, I'd bet he'd lay down a false trail to the northeast and then cut southeast. Or southwest, or west, or due north."

"He wouldn't have no way of knowing we'd find that farm where he swapped horses," the ranger objected.

"He wouldn't know for sure, but he'd figure it's a pretty good bet we would. This is the first place we've come to where there's any farms or houses. He'd know we'd be bound to stop along the way and ask about him."

Travers shook his head in disgust. "All Blount's interested in right now's getting clear of Texas. And the Louisiana border's the nearest place he can do that."

"Nearest ain't always safest, when you're running and you know there's somebody right on your tail.

67

Besides, I sort of get the idea that if he headed the way he wants us to think he's going, he'd be running into a bottleneck."

"A bottleneck might look better to him than trying to cross the desert into Mexico. Or the bareassed prairie between here and New Mexico. And he'd be a fool to try for the Indian Nation. The Red River's in flood at this time of year, and that border up there's the closest-watched one in the state."

"Which leaves the southeast," Longarm pointed out. "The Big Thicket, as you called it, lays that way. So does the Gulf, where he could get on a boat for just about anyplace. And they're both a damn sight closer."

For the first time, Travers seemed to be uncertain. "You might've hit on something, now. Down in the Big Thicket and on east of the Piney Woods, there's a thousand places a man like Blount could hole up. Places where we'd never think about looking for him."

"And if he should get flushed out, there'd be the coast not too far away. Ships to the East, to Mexico, South America." Longarm saw that his companion was wavering. He decided he could push a little harder without a risk of breaking the thin thread that held him and Travers together at this point. "There ought to be somebody from your outfit who could keep an eye on the road to Shreve's Ferry, and then we could see if I'm right in trying to pick up Blount's trail to the southeast."

"There is, sure. If I could get word to 'em," the ranger agreed. "There's a man from D Company on station at Nacogdoches, which ain't too far off the road Blount would have to take if he's cutting a shuck for up there. Thing about it is, there's no way to get word to him to keep his eyes peeled for Blount."

"He'd know who Blount is, though?"

"You're damned right he would! Every ranger in the outfit's got Blount's description and all the rest of it. I told you, he killed one of our boys."

"This place Naco-whatall, is there a railroad that runs through it? Or close to it?" Longarm asked.

"It's on the T&P. Which won't do us no good, Longarm; the T&P's only built as far as the Gulf. If you're thinking about us taking a train there, or some outlandish notion like that, put it out of your head. Hell, we'd have to get on the I-GN and go damn near to Indian Territory before we could change to the T&P."

The tall deputy marshal shifted his weight in his saddle. "That's not exactly what I had in mind. How far are we right here from the I-GN? Or just about any other railroad?"

"The I-GN mail line north is only about ten miles from here, eastward. What the hell you figuring?"

"A way to put your man in Naco-something-or-other on the lookout for Blount, in case he does go that way. Which I don't believe he will, but when you got a shaky bet on the layout, the thing to do is copper it."

Travers shook his head. "I guess you know what you mean, but I sure don't."

"Never mind; you'll see what I'm getting at. Let's head for those I-GN tracks. It's the way we'd have to go, whether Blount happens to be heading north or south, ain't it?"

"More or less."

"We ain't losing a thing, then, are we?" Longarm asked. Then he added, "Tell you what, Travers. We'll stop at a few places and see if anybody's noticed Blount going by, or if he's stopped off, maybe for a meal or something. The man's got to eat, I figure. If we get any hint which way he's planning to move, we can swing that same way. If we don't, then we'll send word for your man in Naco-something-or-other to watch the road for him, and we'll start off in the direction I figure he's taking."

Travers considered Longarm's suggestion for a moment, and nodded his agreement. He said, "Now that makes more sense than anything you've said yet, Long. All right. Let's go. But I still don't see how you're planning to get word to Nacogdoches."

"You will, when it's time. Right now, let's get moving!"

It was rich country through which they traveled for the next several hours. There were farmhouses every few miles, set in fields where the green of summer's crops was just beginning to push through the soft, moist loam of the brown furrows. Longarm's farm-boy days were far behind him, and he didn't recognize many of the shoots that were surfacing. Travers did. He ticked them off as they rode: peanuts, cotton, potatoes, watermelons, muskmelons, beans, okra, cabbage. Only those vegetables that required very wet conditions, or the grains—wheat and corn—which needed long spells of dry, hot weather to mature, were missing from the list.

They stopped at several of the farmhouses, more during the first few miles of the ride than later, to ask about the fugitive they were following. All their inquiries drew blanks until they were close to the railroad line, where, at one farm dwelling, they learned that Blount—it could only have been him, from the description of the farmer and his wife—had stopped and offered to buy a meal.

"Well, we didn't charge the pore fellow nothing, a'course," the farmer said. "Him being so sad 'cause he was traveling to his wife's funeral up by Longview. And we told him the shortest way to go, trying to help him all we could."

In the saddle again, Travers went back to his original idea. "Blount's got to be heading for Shreve's Ferry, Longarm. Else why'd he tell them folks back there he was going to Longview?"

"Damn it, because he figured they'd tell us, if we happened to stop and ask about him. A blind man could see that!"

"Well, I ain't noticed anything wrong with my eyesight," Travers retorted. "And I'm beginning to think your idea about him heading down to the Gulf ain't so good after all."

"You going back on our bargain?" Longarm demanded. "I won't hold you to it, if you feel all that strong that I'm wrong. But I won't tag along with you, either, if you cut north. I'll go on the way I figure makes the most sense, and I'll bet you a brand new John B. Stetson that I'll wind up taking Blount back to Denver while you're still waiting for him at the ferry."

"Now, hold on—"

"Ain't no reason why we got to agree," Longarm reminded the ranger. "No reason why we got to stay together, either, if it comes down to that. Say the word, Travers, and we can split up right here, or when we hit the railroad, or whenever you take a notion to."

Travers was silent for a long while. Longarm was sure his companion was thinking about the alternatives. If they separated and Longarm captured Blount, it would be a blow to the Texas Rangers' pride. He'd figured Travers would choose to stay with him rather than risk having Longarm capture Blount alone.

"All right," the ranger said at last. "I'll stay with you, at least for now. And if you manage to get word to Nacogdoches to watch the trail northeast, I might go on with your scheme."

"Fair enough," Longarm agreed. He felt a bit mean in holding from Travers his plan for alerting the ranger stationed in Nacogdoches, but decided that his companion had earned a little unease of mind by being so damned stubborn.

Longarm kept Travers in suspense until they reached the I-GN tracks. Then he produced his telegraph key from his saddlebag and held it out for the ranger to inspect.

"There it is," he said. "If you'll give me a hand while I shinny up that pole yonder, I'll get word to your man in Naco-whatever in about three jerks of a jackasses' tailbone."

"Over the railroad telegraph line?"

"Sure. Don't matter where you go these days, the way they're laying rails all over, from hell to breakfast, you can send a message to some railroad's division point. And if you let them know it's official federal business, they'll relay it to any other railroad you ask them to. All the roads in the country have got some kind of interconnection on their telegraph lines, you see. Places where two lines connect, or where they do a lot of switching. Sooner or later, your message gets to the man it's meant for."

"You mean you know how to send with one of them keys?"

"I damn sure don't carry this one just because I think it's pretty to look at. If I couldn't use it, it'd just be something else to clutter up my saddlebags."

"Where'd you learn?"

"Picked it up during the War, along with a few other bad habits, like smoking cigars."

"Well, I'll be damned! You federal men have got a few tricks you ought to pass on to us rangers. After all, we're in the same line of work."

"All right, you know about it. Pass the word along yourself. But if I'm going to send that message, make me a hand-stirrup to get me started up that pole. Then, when I've sent it, we'll cut on to the southeast, and see which one of us is right about the way our man's headed."

With a boost from Travers, Longarm had no trouble climbing the rest of the way up the telegraph pole; it was only fifteen feet high from base to insulator. Wrapping his legs around the rough pine pole, he snapped the alligator-clip leads to the telegraph wire and began tapping the key. Within a few moments, it clicked rapidly with a reply from the I-GN telegrapher at the Tyler division point. Longarm explained what he wanted in short bursts of dots and dashes, and the other telegrapher replied with an agreement to relay the message to the T&P telegrapher at Jefferson, who in turn would send it on to Nacogdoches for delivery to the Ranger there.

At every stage of the procedure, Longarm called the substance of the coded transmission down to Travers, who watched from the ground. The whole thing, including waiting for confirmation of receipt of the message at Nacogdoches T&P depot, took little more than ten minutes. Longarm removed the key's clips from the wire and swung himself down.

"That's all there is to it," he told Travers as he carefully rewrapped the lead wires around the key and picked wood-splinters out of his trousers. "Now, if Blount was really headed for where he let on, we've shut his bolthole. But I still think I'm right. You'll see, after we've moseyed along a while going toward the Big Thicket and the Piney Woods."

"Maybe you're right, maybe you ain't. But as long as we've cut him off up north, I'll take my chances and go along with you," Travers told him.

"Good enough. And seeing as how there's not much

use in us hanging around here, we might as well mosey along."

The two lawmen turned their horses due east. They pushed on with the sun at their backs, stopping at one farmhouse after another just long enough to ask if any strange riders had been seen passing by, if any strangers had stopped in to ask directions or in search of a meal. As far as they could learn, they were the only newcomers the residents along the way had seen in recent days.

As darkness closed on them, they debated the wisdom of losing time by stopping, or perhaps closing the gap between themselves and the fugitive by pushing on in the dark. Longarm favored moving on; Travers, whose uncertain belief they were moving in the right direction had diminished with each unproductive inquiry, wanted to stop.

"It ain't like we're sure Blount's running in front of us," he told Longarm. "Damn it, if he come this way, somebody would've seen him, sure as hell."

"Not if he didn't want 'em to," Longarm retorted. "You just ain't thinking the way a man on the run does, Travers."

"I don't follow you."

"Look here, if you was Blount, trying to shake us off, how many people would you let catch sight of you?"

"Why, nobody I could keep from seeing me, I guess."

"That's the whole thing I been trying to get across to you. Now, Blount might've felt like it'd be smart for him to get a fresh horse, but he didn't have to. I saw that dapple he was riding when he left the cave last night. There wasn't anything wrong with the animal, it wasn't lamed or blowed or anything like that. So why'd he stop to make a swap?"

Travers knitted his brow in concentration. After a moment, he said slowly, "If he didn't really need a fresh horse, he must've had some other reason."

"That's it. And his reason was to plant the idea with us that he was going a different way than the one he took. You say Blount's spent a lot of time up in the northeast corner of Texas. Well, hell, he didn't need to ask about Shreve's Ferry. That's something he'd already know."

"Sure he would. That never occurred to me."

"It did to me. And if he was asking about that ferry, my bet is that he didn't have a notion in the world of going anyplace close to it. Not even in the general direction of it."

"So you figured it all out from that, did you?"

"I think so. My hunch is strong enough so I decided right then and there that if we want to catch him, we better look in another direction. You figured out why he wasn't likely to double back and head west or north. Well, that didn't leave but one way for him to move. That's the direction we're traveling now."

Travers rode thoughtfully for several minutes before admitting, "I guess I been wrong about which way he was aiming to go, Longarm. Right now, you've pretty well convinced me that what you figured on him doing holds water pretty good."

"I'm glad you came around," Longarm replied. "Now let's see if we can't agree on whether it's better to stop or keep on moving tonight."

"Well, I ain't changed my mind about wanting to stop. We can't go on all night without feeling it tomorrow, and neither can Sim Blount. Hell, he'd be tireder then we are right now. He took off from the cave last night and didn't get no rest at all, the way it looks. Maybe he stopped for an hour to doze, something like that, but we had a pretty good sleep. He must be beat by now. He won't gain enough ground on us to make much never-mind if we stop and get a little bit of shut-eye."

"Except if we didn't stop, we'd close the gap a lot faster than if we did," Longarm pointed out.

"Well, that's certain sure. But we might pass someplace in the dark where he's stopped, might miss somebody who'd be able to tell us whether we're on the right trail or not."

"There's that, of course. I guess it don't matter all that much. We'll stop, then. First house we come to that's still showing light, we'll knock and ask can we have a shakedown in their barn or something like that."

"We don't have to sleep in a barn. When folks find out I'm a ranger, they'll put us up in the house."

"Oh, I don't doubt that. But if we sleep indoors, we're going to lose a lot more time than if we just spread our bedrolls in somebody's hayloft, and took off when we felt like it. We go to sleeping inside, they're going to want to have us stay for breakfast, and visit and all."

"I don't see anything wrong with that. It'll stretch out our rations, if we eat with 'em."

"No. Let's just settle for the barn. Then, if our bellies start to growl around daybreak, we can stop at a farmhouse and get a meal. Which I'll pay for, for both of us."

"You federals must have a lot more money to spend than us rangers. Hell, when I get offered a free meal, I grab it."

"Well, I guess I've grabbed my share. But my chief's told us we got to offer to pay, and offer twice. If they don't take our money the second offer, then it's all right, he says, they really mean it."

They found the shakedown they were looking for a few miles farther on. True to Travers's prediction, when the occupants discovered the pair's identities, they refused to accept payment, and then fulfilled Longarm's conditions by repeating their refusal to accept payment. It took a great deal of persuasion to convince their impromptu hosts that the lawmen really wanted to sleep in the barn, but Longarm's perseverance finally put an end to the objections, and he and Travers bedded down for the night on fragrant straw in the farm's hayloft.

Before daybreak they were on the trail again, and shortly after dawn decided to stop for breakfast at the first farmhouse they came to that showed signs that the family was up and around. They rode into the farmyard and knocked at the back door of the house, but got no response, although through the window they could see quite clearly a kerosene lamp burning on the kitchen table.

"Maybe it's too early for them to be eating," Travers suggested. "Let's look around a little bit, out by the barn."

They walked their mounts to the barn, but it too was

deserted. A smaller building with an open door a dozen yards from the barn caught their eyes.

"Looks like whoever lives here might be over in that shed," Longarm said. He turned the claybank and rode over to the structure. Just as he reached it, a woman came thorugh the door, wild-eyed. She was carrying a shotgun, and leveled it at Longarm, who'd reined in a few feet from the door.

"Now you stop right there!" she called. "Don't think I don't know how to use this gun just because I'm a woman, or that I won't use it if I have to!"

"Now, ma'am, we don't mean you no harm," Longarm assured her, holding his hands open and away from his body. "We were just riding past, and thought we might buy our breakfast from you."

"Hmph. Which way'd you ride up from?" she asked, keeping the gun's muzzle pointed at Longarm's midsection.

"From the west. Why?"

"Because I was hoping you'd come from the other way, and might be able to tell me whether you seen the skunk that broke into our smokehouse last night," she said. "My husband chased him away, and he took off toward the east. That's where my man is now, chasing after him." She lowered the gun. "I guess if you come from the other direction, you couldn't tell me anything."

Longarm motioned for Travers to ride over and join him. He asked the woman, "You want to tell us about it? We're law officers, me and my friend."

"Well, laws-ee! If that ain't lucky! Maybe you'll go after him too. My man might need some help, if he catches up with the varmint."

"We'll do that," Travers assured her. "But can you tell us what this robber looked like? And what he took? And how long ago all this happened?"

"I didn't get a good look at whoever it was, and I don't think Paw did either. What roused us up was old Tige raising a ruckus. Paw said it was likely a skunk or a fox that got him stirred up, but when Tige cut off short, right in the middle of a bark, he got worried and lit a lantern and come out to look. He seen this man jumping on a horse, and then he seen Tige." She pointed to the carcass of a brindle dog lying almost out of sight around the corner of the smokehouse.

Longarm took a quick look at the dead animal. Its throat had been cut. "Looks like Blount's work," he told Travers.

"Does to me too," Travers agreed. "He likes to use a knife, from what I've heard about him."

"You men mean to say you know who it was robbed us?" the woman asked.

"Might be we do," Longarm said. "What all did he steal?"

"That's the strange thing about it," she answered. "All I can see's missing is a side of bacon and half a ham I been using off of. It don't make much sense to me for somebody to go to the trouble of stealing such a middling bit as that."

"No it don't," Longarm agreed. His voice was sober. "You said your husband took after the robber, going east. How long ago was that, ma'am?"

"A long time, it seems like. Tige started barking about midnight. It all happened right fast. Paw's been gone four or five hours now, and I'm getting worried."

"Did he have a gun?" Travers asked, then added quickly, "Your husband, I mean."

"He took the rifle, left me this shotgun. He didn't waste a minute taking after the robber, either, just long enough to pull on some pants, then he jumped on the plowhorse bareback, didn't stop to saddle up."

Longarm and Travers exchanged quick glances. Longarm touched the brim of his hat and said, "We won't waste any time either, ma'am. Like you said, your husband might need some help. We'll go right on and see if we can give it to him."

They wheeled their mounts and rode off at a run, leaving the woman staring after them.

Chapter 7

Although they galloped all the way, Longarm and Travers didn't catch up in time. Less than four miles from the farmhouse they saw a barebacked, heavy-hoofed plowhorse coming toward them. The animal was plodding in an aimless zigzag along the narrow dirt road. They pulled up, and Travers leaned out of his saddle to grasp the horse's loose reins. Both he and Longarm saw the bloodstains on the horse's back at the same time.

"You was right, Longarm," Travers admitted soberly. "Blount laid us a false trail back where we started out. This has got to be his work. I don't know many outlaws who'd kill a harmless farmer for a side of bacon and half a ham."

"It wasn't the meat. It was the farmer seeing him. Blount knew he'd set the law on him, if he let him get away," Longarm answered, his voice as sober as the ranger's.

"He must've caught on that we're close behind him," Travers said. "Otherwise—"

Longarm interrupted, "No, I don't think that's the way of it. He just wasn't about to take any chances at all."

Knowing what they'd find, they rode on down the road until they reached the body. The dead farmer was lying facedown in a clump of milfoil beside the road. He hadn't stopped to dress fully before taking out after the outlaw, just pulled on jeans over his nightshirt, and the white fabric of the garment was stained with blood.

Longarm was out of his saddle first. He bent over the recumbent figure and felt for a heartbeat, then shook his head. "He's gone, all right. Been dead long enough to start cooling off, too. That'd mean he caught up with

Blount pretty quick. The woman said he left at midnight. It's close to six o'clock now."

"Looks to me like he was backshot," Travers commented, pointing to the bloodstained back of the dead man's nightshirt. "How you figure Blount brought that off, if this fellow had a rifle?"

"You and me both know having a gun don't always give a man enough sand in his craw to use it, when the chips are down. Happens all the time to folks like this poor devil. They'll start out hollering fire and brimstone, then when the time comes that they ought to be pulling the trigger, they panic or something."

Longarm bent over the body, and pulled the tail of the nightshirt up out of the dead man's pants to bare his back. Two small bullet holes could be seen amid the coagulating blood. He pointed to the wounds.

"Small-caliber cartridge, wouldn't you say?" he asked the ranger.

Travers inspected the bullet holes and nodded. "Sure wasn't no .44-40 or .45 that made them. More like a .32-20, or maybe a .31 pocket pistol. Only way to tell for sure'd be to dig out the slugs and look at 'em."

"I don't think there's much need to. Only reason I was curious, Blount killed the woman back at the cave with a light-hitting pistol. He wasn't but a few feet away when he shot her. If he'd been using a .44 or .45, the slugs would've gone clear through her, little as she was, and plowed into me."

"That's about all we need, then, to be sure it was Blount who killed this one too," Travers said with a thoughtful crease appearing between his eyebrows. "That'd mean he's not more'n five or six hours ahead of us."

"Looks that way. Too bad we got to lose time here."

"What do you mean?"

"We'll have to load this poor devil on his horse and take him back there to his wife. By the time we do that, and get on Blount's trail again, he'll have gained an hour or two."

"I don't see any reason why we'd have to lose that time, Long," Travers said. "I'd favor taking on after

79

Blount right away, now we know it's him up ahead of us."

Longarm shook his head. "Damn it, we can't just leave this body laying here in the road, you ought to know that. We'll have to take him back, tell his wife what happened. She'd be crazy from worry if we just hauled ass out of here and didn't do that."

"Catching up with Blount's a hell of a lot more important than messing around here," Travers said.

"I want to catch him as bad as you do," Longarm snapped. "But I'm damned if I can be cold-blooded enough to leave that poor woman wondering what's become of her man, and worrying about him."

"You take him back and tell her, then," Travers suggested. "I'll go on after Blount."

"Like hell I will!"

"It's your idea. You go ahead and do it, then," Travers said curtly.

Longarm looked hard-eyed at the ranger. "That ain't the way we agreed it'd be, when we set out. We said we'd go after Blount together, and after we caught him—if we caught him alive—we'd wrangle about who gets to keep him."

"That's what I still want to do. I just don't want us to shit away a lot of time doing something we don't have to."

"In my book, it's something we have to do."

"Maybe it is in your book. It sure ain't in mine," Travers shot back. "The most important thing we're looking at right now is to catch up with the man we're after and bring him in."

Longarm shook his head. "No. It's all part of the same job. We run onto a mess like this, we're obliged to clean it up. If it meant we'd lose a day or more, I might feel different, but it won't take more than an hour or so to do what we got to here."

"Blount can cover ground, maybe change the way he's going, in an hour or two," Travers said angrily. His lips were compressed into a thin line and his lantern jaw jutted out stubbornly.

"It won't make that much difference," Longarm insisted. "A half-day or a day might, but an hour or two ain't going to change things all that much."

"If you're so damned certain it won't, then do what I said a minute ago. You stay here and do whatever you feel like you got to do. I'll keep on following Blount."

"Look here, Travers, you gave your word on this deal we made, just like I gave mine," Longarm said quietly. He was getting angrier by the minute, and making a real effort to keep it from showing. "Now, I always heard that a Texas Ranger's word's as good as his bond. You going to go back on yours?"

"No, by God, I'm not! It's not me that wants to change anything. It's your idea, damn it!"

"It's my idea to do what's right and decent, and what we got a responsibility to do. Ain't a damn thing you can say that's going to change my mind about that. But we agreed we'd stick together until we took Blount, and here it is—you want to go off by yourself, I say we got to stay together."

For a long moment, Travers stood silent, thinking about what Longarm had said. Finally, and with obvious reluctance, he nodded. "I guess you got a point. We'll stay together. But let's cut what you feel like we're obliged to do just as short as we can."

"I never said we wouldn't. I don't like the idea of wasting time any better than you do, but cleaning up this mess here's part of a lawman's job. Now let's haze that plowhorse to where we can grab his reins, and load this man on it, and get moving. The time we've spent jawing, we could've got the job finished and be on our way by now!"

They made as short work of their unpleasant task as was decently possible, but an hour or more passed before they could leave the newly widowed farm woman and take up the trail again. It was still early morning, though, with the sun not yet high enough to dry the dew that had collected overnight on the growing crops in the unfenced fields that lined the dirt road over which they traveled. The interruption had driven all thoughts of breakfast from their minds, and, by the time they'd been riding for a half-hour, both men became aware of their growling stomachs.

"I'm hungry as a bitch-wolf with a pack of fresh cubs," Travers told Longarm as they rode along. "What we need right now is another breakfast. We've covered a lot of miles since we set out."

"Any towns up ahead where we can stop for a bite?"

"Oh, sure. There's towns along all these back roads, about a wagon-haul apart. About all most of 'em's got is a boardinghouse, though, not any real restaurants. We'd do better stopping at farmhouses."

"You're right about that, I reckon. Blount'd ride around any towns he might come to. Wouldn't want to risk so many people catching sight of him. But I hate to beg breakfast from these farmers along here."

"Shit, don't feel that way, Longarm. They're glad to have the company. Most of 'em don't see nobody but their own families for two or three weeks running."

"We'd have to stay and visit, though. That'd take a lot of time. Seems I recall you're the one who was in such an all-fired hurry just a little while ago."

"I was, and I still am. But we got to stop and ask along the way. And I keep thinking about how good a cup of hot coffee'd go down right about now."

Longarm judged, from the tone of his companion's reply, that Travers had cooled down after their argument and wanted to get things back on a friendly footing between them. He said, "Tell you what. Let's agree right now that we won't waste time stopping in every little jerkwater town we come to. It was dark when Blount passed through those we'll run into before noon, but farm folks keep early hours, and there'd be a better chance some of them might've noticed him."

"Makes sense," Travers said, nodding.

"All right. We can chew jerky until we get to the next farmhouse. We'll stop there and ask about Blount, and see if we can rustle up a cup of coffee while we're asking."

As they rode, they sliced slivers off the strips of leathery jerky from their saddlebags and chewed the tough meat with a few stone-hard corn kernels, moistened with a sip of water. A little bit of this rough chewing went a long way. Their jaws were tired long before their stomachs felt satisfied, but by the time the next farmhouse came into view, they'd taken the edge off their hunger and were ready to stop for the coffee to top off their coarse meal.

Their inquiries, made while they sipped the coffee that had been offered them the minute they dismounted, brought no results. They hadn't really expected any. Blount's passing must have been before sunup, and like the inhabitants of the towns they'd agreed to pass by, the occupants of the farmhouse must still have been sleeping. They wasted little time in gulping their coffee and getting back into the saddle.

Again and again as the day wore on, they stopped to inquire, and again and again got no information for their asking.

Sunset found them between towns, with cultivated fields both behind and ahead. Distantly, a glimmer of light showed at one side of the dirt road.

"You want to stop at the place up ahead, or push on?" Travers asked.

"I'd say to stop. Blount might be pushing harder than we are; he don't have to break his pace by stopping to ask questions. If he's sure where he's heading for, that is. But we ain't all that far behind. And I'd rather ride fresh than tired, tomorrow."

As before, they had to refuse accommodations in the farmhouse itself in favor of a shakedown in the hayloft, in order to get an earlier start than would have been possible if they'd waited to eat the breakfast to which they were also invited.

"But I'm not going to let you men start out on empty stomachs," the farmwife said with finality. "I'll tell you what. I'll bank up the fire good before I go to bed, and I'll leave a pot of coffee on the back of the stove and some ham and fresh-baked bread in the oven. You men come in when you get ready, and don't bother about disturbing us. You make yourselves a good, hot meal before you leave my house. And don't argue with me, either of you, because I won't have it any other way!"

They didn't argue, and didn't ignore the hot food and fragrant coffee either. They felt fresher than they'd been the day before when they rode out of the sleeping farmyard and turned in the false dawn down the dew-moistened dirt road.

In midmorning, Travers's doubts returned. "Damn it to hell!" he swore. "I'd sure like to feel we wasn't off on some kind of wild-goose chase! Here we are, not knowing whether we're on the right track or not, when Blount might've veered off and headed some other way."

"Well, this is your home territory," Longarm said. "You got any better ideas about what we ought to do?"

"No I haven't!" the ranger snapped. "And that's what makes me so mad! Stands to reason somebody would've seen that son of a bitch, if he'd passed this way!"

"That don't necessarily follow, if he was making work of keeping out of sight. Which I'd be doing, was I in his boots."

"Sure. But I tell you, Longarm, it's a mighty uncertain feeling."

"Couldn't agree with you more. Except it's like the crooked poker game the fellow got warned about. It's the only game we got to play in."

To ease their discouragement, they began stopping more often. At last they got the clue they needed, at the most unlikely of all places, one they'd almost passed by as being a waste of time. They'd already gone a dozen yards beyond the schoolhouse when Longarm reined in.

"What's the matter?" Travers asked.

"I just had a hunch. That schoolhouse—maybe we ought not to ride by it without stopping."

"But we both said it'd be—"

"I know what we said. But I remember something. When I was a kid in school, we spent more time looking out of the windows, wishing we was outdoors, than we did listening to the teacher. Let's go ask, Travers. We wasted so much time already that one more stop ain't going to make all that much difference."

At Travers's request, the teacher interrupted a spelling lesson and let the ranger ask the class if they'd seen a lone traveler or a raw mustang ride by that morning, or late the day before. After a long wait, a boy sitting beside one of the room's two windows hesitantly raised a hand.

"I seen—" he caught the teacher's frown— "I *saw* a man like that go by just before last bell yesterday," he said.

"Did he act like he was in a hurry?" Longarm asked.

"Well, he wasn't wasting much time, mister. Had his head down and his hat pulled low. You think he might be the man you're after?"

"Might just be," Travers replied. "What'd he have on?"

Frowning, the boy thought for a moment. "A suit of clothes. Maybe that's why he caught my eye. He sure didn't look like anybody I seen—I mean, I *saw,* around here before."

"Thanks, son. You been a big help," the ranger said, smiling.

When they were in the saddle once more the ranger said to Longarm, "I feel a lot better now. It's not much to go on, but at this time of year, with crops just coming up good, there's not going to be many farmers traveling anywhere."

"You feel like we're going right, then?"

"A lot more than I did. And if it was Blount, and he stays on this road, there's only two places he can be making for. One's the Piney Woods, the other's the Big Thicket."

"Which one you think's most likely?"

"I'd say the Thicket. And if I'm right, if we let him get in there, it's going to be one hell of a job to find him."

"You've mentioned this Big Thicket before. What's it like, anyhow?" Longarm asked.

"Just about what the name sounds like. Wild as hell and just about as mean a place to be in."

"You don't make it sound very inviting," Longarm said dryly.

"It ain't. Blount oughta feel right at home there."

"Got any people living in it?"

"Some. I don't guess anybody knows how many. It's a robbers' roost, of course, has been since the days when Mexico owned Texas. And the type of folks who live there ain't improved much since then."

"You talk like you've been there."

"Oh, I have. One time, about six years ago. Got out with a whole skin and swore I never wanted to go back. Now it looks like I'm going to have to."

"You think Blount might know his way around in it?"

"Hard to say. But there's enough crooks and near-to-crooks in it so's he'd get a welcome. You see, Longarm, the Thicket was took over by the Indians first, when the settlers commenced staking out homestead claims in the real early days. Then, during the War, the jayhawkers moved in. Fellow by the name of—" Travers frowned, trying to remember— "Klein, I think it was, tried to burn 'em out, but it didn't work. All he did was burn up a lot of trees and brush, and most of the jayhawkers got away. Now they've bred with the Indians and the Mex and I guess the blacks too, that hid out in there."

"Will we go in on foot? Or can we take our horses?"

"Hell, we'll take our horses and keep on 'em as much as we can. Times we'll have to go shank's mare, though." The ranger turned in his saddle and glared at Longarm. "Now do you see why I was so hot to get back on the trail when Blount killed that farmer? He gets into the Thicket, it's going to take a while to flush him."

They rode in silence for a while. The character of the land had already changed once since they'd begun their pursuit, and now it was changing again. From their starting point at the cavern, they'd dipped down a long slope from the hill country's fringes into the sprawling, shallow Brazos River valley. They'd crossed the Brazos at a gravel-bottomed ford on the road, but Travers hadn't thought it important enough to mention. Then they'd climbed up the low, gentle slope of the valley's eastern side, topping it a short distance after leaving the farm where Blount had murdered the farmer who had pursued him. Now they were on the long, gradual slant that led into the Trinity River valley.

There had been nothing abrupt about any of the changes. Stone and stone-and-adobe houses had predominated where they'd started, and these had given way to houses built of boards. Now the lumber-built houses had gradually disappeared, to be replaced by dwellings and outbuildings of logs, with yellow clay-plastered chinks. The style of construction and the buildings' outlines had stayed much the same. The dogtrot type of dwelling persisted: two small, rectangular cabins built eight or ten feet apart, connected by a roofed-over space that was open on one or both sides—the "trot."

There had been other transitions. Though the vegetation had stayed constant, the soil had changed. Around Round Rock, the earth had been a rich brown, studded with stones and pebbles of gleaming white and cream. In the Brazos Valley itself, the dirt grayed out to a lighter brown, from silt brought to it by the flooding of the creeks and rivers mingling with the loam. Now the soil had deepened in tone until it was a uniform deep black loam. The row crops here had been planted earlier in the year than had those farther to the west and north, and the green shoots rose higher over the earth.

This was Old Texas through which the two men rode. This was the Texas settled in the first wave of immigration from the East, by members of the Austin colony and those who came immediately after them. The colonists had fanned north, following the rivers, to escape the sandy, flat coastal plain with its perennial heavy rains, staking their homesteads when they reached good soil, building their houses, planting their crops. Later arrivals had found land farther west, on the grass-rich llanos that swept level to the Gulf from the base of the Owens Plateau. The crops the late-comers grew at first had been longhorn, and later on, Hereford cattle.

As Longarm and Travers rode on, they noticed that the farmhouses were spaced closer together, a result of the original homesteaders passing on parts of their land to sons, and the sons to grandsons.

Longarm observed, "There's more people living along here than there were where we set out from. Ought to make it easier to pick up some trace of Blount."

"Yeah. We better make more stops and ask," Travers agreed.

They did, and felt better after they'd found two or three farmhouses where the fugitive had been noticed when he passed. "He's ahead of us, all right," Longarm told Travers as they continued along the dirt road that now curved consistently toward the south.

"Seems like you was right. Well, I'm just as glad. Only I'm wishing he'd picked some other place to run to."

Longarm saw why Travers had made the wish when he looked across the Trinity River late the next morning and saw a tangle of trees and brush lining the far bank.

"There it is," the ranger said. "The Big Thicket."

Chapter 8

Longarm lit a cheroot as he surveyed the wall of living green that rose abruptly from the water on the river's opposite side. "I don't see any land," he told Travers. "Looks from here like it's just a great big tangle of bushes and trees growing out of the water."

"There's land, all right," Travers assured him. "And that big tangle of brush is a hell of a lot worse than it looks from here. Wait'll we get across the river, and you see it up close."

"Do we cross here, or someplace else?"

"We better go downstream a ways. There's a little settlement on this side where there's a store. We can buy vittles there. It's either carry what we want to eat, or depend on what game we can shoot."

"With all that cover, there ought to be plenty of wild animals that a man could eat without gagging on 'em. Hell, times when I've been right hungry I've et rabbit with warbles, and rattlesnake, and a lot of other things that didn't taste real good."

Travers grinned. "If you fancy rattlesnake, you'll find plenty of 'em in the Thicket. There are water moccasins in there too, and a few copperheads, and a lot of snakes that won't bite back at you."

"I said I had to be pretty hungry before I'd relish snake," Longarm retorted. "What about deer and squirrel and rabbits?"

"Plenty of all of 'em. Deer, red and gray squirrels, if you're choosy. And skunks and Texas red wolves and a few stray lobos and bobcats and cougar. But I wasn't thinking about eating game. We start shooting, it'll bring too many visitors we might not want, and could scare Blount off."

"Makes good sense," Longarm agreed. He was still

studying the green wall on the opposite bank. "I can't say I fancy the way that looks, over there."

"Like I said a minute ago, it's worse than it looks from here. You'll find out. Them trees grows so high and stands so close together it looks at noon like the sun's about to go down. The brush under them trees don't look so bad from where we are now, but it's head-high and you can't see over it. You damn near can't even see *through* it, when you're on foot. There's lots of little springs and creeks you can't see too, because the ferns and moss around them is so thick. You'll find places where the ground turns soft so fast you'll sink knee-deep and get your boots full of mud before you know what's happened to you. You start out walking, and there's a thorny haw-brush that'll grab your shirt, and devil's walking-stick plants that'll try to pull your pants off. Oh, it's a hell of a place to get around in."

"If there's people in it, there's got to be trails," Longarm said.

"Sure. A few. Never know where they'll take you, of course." Travers nudged his horse with a bootheel. "Well, you got your first look at the Big Thicket. Let's go on and find the store and stock up on grub. We want to get across the river before it gets too late. There's a ford right by the store we can use."

"If we ask just right, we might find that Blount stopped at that store before he went in," Longarm suggested as they followed the road along the riverbank.

"Let's hope so. Because if we don't get some trace of him before we dive into that mess, we could spend the rest of our lives in there looking for him."

They reached the settlement Travers had remembered. It was not much more than a couple of dozen ramshackle shanties strung out along the shore, most of them with boats beached near their doors. The houses stood between the road and the river, about equally divided on either side of a rambling, unpainted building of cypress boards that could only be the store. They pulled up at the hitch rail that was on the side of the building.

Before they dismounted, Longarm said, "Suppose

we handle this just like I would if I was in Blount's home territory."

Travers frowned, puzzled. "For all I know, it *is* his home territory. Only I don't see what you're getting at."

"Here's what's in my mind, Travers. We don't know who his friends are, who our friends are, or even if we got any friends hereabouts. So suppose we don't let on we're after Blount to bring him in. Let's say we're friends looking to join him."

"That strikes me as a sorta sneaky way to do, Long."

"You can call it that, if you're of a mind to. But I've found out that a little bit of sneaking now and again can save a hell of a lot of shooting."

"You still think I'm trigger-happy because I tossed a couple of blind shots your way, back there at the cave?" Travers bristled.

"Now I didn't say that. And I wasn't making any hints. All I want is to get on Blount's tail the fastest way there is, and this trick's worked for me before."

"All right. You go ahead. I'll back whatever play you make."

They dismounted and went into the store. The interior was dim and cool, and Longarm and Travers had been riding with the bright sunlight reflected into their faces from the surface of the river. For a moment they thought the place was deserted, until they saw a thin-faced, bald-headed man dozing in a chair that was propped back against a side wall. He was snoring gently, and his oval gold-rimmed spectacles were about to slip from the tip of his nose.

Longarm and Travers looked around the store. It was like most stores they'd seen in similar places. Kegs of pickles and sauerkraut, pickled beef and pork, stood at one side of a long wooden counter. A flour barrel occupied a spot near the scales. There were wooden boxes leaning against the wall, displaying prunes and dried apples. A few hams and bacon sides hung from the rafters. Along one side there were racks on which hung overalls and calico dresses and men's shirts of flannel and denim in no particular order or arrangement.

Bolts of yard goods were stacked on a table in the

center of the room. Toward the back they could barely make out piles of tools, leather harness fittings, and a stack of saddle blankets. On the counter, a plug-cutter stood beside a box of chewing twist and, next to it, a huge round of cheese, partly cut, rested on its cutting platform. A glass display case inside the door held a meager assortment of candies: peppermint sticks, jaw-breakers, and jujubes. On shelves behind the counter, some tins of peaches and tomatoes rested, their labels gaudy in contrast to the unpainted wall behind them.

When the man in the chair showed no signs of stir-ring, Longarm cleared his throat loudly. The man woke with a startled jump that sent the chair's front legs dropping to the floor and jarred his glasses free. He grabbed for them and groped for a moment, adjusting them. Then he stood up and peered at the newcomers.

"Howdy," he said. "What can I do for you men?"

"If you got beer in one of them kegs, a cold glass of it sure would go down good right now," Longarm replied.

"Can't give you barrel beer," the man told him. "But I got bottle beer back in the springhouse. There's whiskey in the keg back by the sorghum barrel, and it's cheaper. Dime a dip. Beer'll cost you fifteen cents a bottle. I got to have it shipped clear from the Pearl brewery in San Antonio."

Longarm looked questioningly at Travers. "I'll take the beer," the ranger said.

"Make it two, then," Longarm told the storekeeper.

"Dovey!" the man called, peering toward the back of the store. Then, louder, "Dove!"

There was a stirring in the dimmest area at the back of the store where the harness and saddle blankets were stacked. A slim young girl jumped off the piled blankets and came hurrying toward them. "You was calling me, Pap?"

"If you heard me, you don't need to ask. Go back to the springhouse and get these men a bottle each of Pearl."

"Have one with us," Longarm invited.

"Thanks, but I wear the white ribbon," the man re-plied. "If it's all the same to you, though, I'll take a cigar instead."

Longarm nodded. "Do. While you're picking yours out, I better get some too. I'm running low." He had more than a hunch that when they'd gone, the store-keeper would replace the cigar in the box and transfer its price from the till to his own pocket. "Might as well get me a box," he added, "seeing as we're going to be in the Thicket a while. That is, if Sim shows up like he promised he would. You seen him lately?"

"Sim?"

"Sim Blount," Longarm replied. "He's supposed to meet us here, but I didn't see his horse outside." As soon as he'd said it, Longarm realized the mistake he'd made from the way the man looked.

Travers hurried to correct things. "I guess you forgot, partner. Sim told us he'd likely row over, so we'd have the boat to tote our provisions back across the river."

"That's right!" Longarm exclaimed. "Guess I just disremembered." He turned to the storekeeper, but before he could go on with their conversation the girl, Dove, came from the rear of the store carrying two dripping brown bottles.

"Here's your beers," she said, handing one bottle to Longarm, the other to Travers. "You want me to pop the caps for you, or do you know how these new tin tops work?"

"I'll manage, thanks," Longarm told her.

As he bent up the serrated lip of the tin bottle cap, he took his first good look at the girl. She was older than he'd thought from the fleeting glimpse he'd had of her in the shadowed dark end of the store. He judged that she was in her late teens, perhaps even just out of them. Her dark hair was done up in twin braids, one braid brought down over each shoulder. The arrange-ment pulled the hair on the top of her head back, skullcap-style, and showed a high brow, unlined and unmarred. She had high cheekbones under large brown eyes, a saucy, uptilted pug nose, and a wide mouth over a wide, rounded chin. Longarm didn't think it was good business to inspect the rest of the girl as he'd have liked to; he limited himself to a quick glance at her generous, upthrust breasts and spreading hips that the shapeless, wrinkled dress she wore couldn't hide.

He returned to his conversation with the storekeeper. "Old Sim didn't leave word for us with you, did he? About when he'd be back to meet us?"

"Now hold on," the storekeeper said. "I thought you were talking about *young* Sim. *Old* Sim doesn't come over here more'n once a year; I haven't seen him since the middle of summer."

"Oh, sure, it's young Sim we're talking about," Travers said quickly. "My partner just talks that way, you know. Old man, old Bob, old Jim—you know, just a way of talking."

"I see. Well, I don't—"

Dove broke in. "Maybe Sim just forgot to say anything to you, Pap."

"That's enough from you, Dove," the man said severely. "You know not to interrupt when your elders are talking."

"But he could've forgot to tell you these men were coming to meet him," Dove insisted. "Sim was in a real big hurry when he passed by yesterday evening."

With a sigh, the storekeeper gave up. "He was rushed, for a fact. Likely he did forget, like Dove says. It seemed to me he had a lot on his mind."

Travers nodded. "Sounds like Sim, all right. Well, Sim wasn't real sure we'd get here today, of course. He might not be looking for us until tomorrow. He knew we had a long way to travel."

Longarm hurried to support Travers's fiction. He asked the ranger, with a concerned half-frown, "You figure we ought to wait for him? Sim's been traveling too; he might've got his days mixed up. Or maybe it's us got the day wrong. Think we got here a day earlier than Sim figured we would?"

"Oh, I don't see that it matters all that much," Travers said to Longarm. Both of them were now acting as though the storekeeper and his daughter weren't there. "Sim knows we'll be waiting. He'll come after us, today or tomorrow."

"I ain't much of a mind to lose a day waiting for him, you know," Longarm replied. "I guess this gentleman could tell us how to get to wherever Sim's at in the Thicket. Then we can just go on across the river, and tomorrow or next day we can come back with Sim and buy the things we'll need."

"Now, that's a prime idea!" Travers exclaimed enthusiastically. "We'd sure save time that way."

"Now look here, you men—" the storekeeper began.

Longarm ignored him. "You heard what my partner said, Mr.—Mr.—"

"Tews," the storekeeper supplied. "Herman Tews."

"Of course, Mr. Tews. Now you sure ought to be able to tell us where to find the starting of the trail that'll take us to Sim's place."

"I'm sorry, but I can't," Tews replied firmly. "I'm not even sure I could tell you where to find the start of the trail that'd lead you to the trail that goes there. I don't think it'd do you any good if I could. The Thicket's not a place strangers can find their way around in all that easy."

"That's right, Pap," Dove put in. "If you don't—"

"Dove!" Tews said sharply. "I told you not to interrupt! Now that's enough out of you!"

"I'm sorry, Pap," Dove said, though there was no tone of apology in her voice. "But I know where Sim's folks live. You remember, before she grew up and started acting so stuck-up, Francy used to take me there to play."

"I'm sure these men aren't interested in what you and Francy did," the storekeeper told her severely. "Besides it's been quite a few years since you and Francy played together."

"That wouldn't make any difference," Dove retorted. "I still know where they live. Of course, I know lots of other trails in the Thicket besides that one." She turned to Longarm and Travers. "Pap's right about you not being able to find your way over there. If you don't know just exactly which fork of every trail to take, you'll sure get lost."

"Let's see now." Longarm frowned as though trying to remember. "Sim never was one to talk much about his family. Francy, she'd be—?" He paused with his voice rising in inquiry.

"Sim's stepsister," Tews volunteered. "His stepmother's girl."

"Of course. I recall him mentioning her, but I never

95

did get the family straight in my mind," Longarm nodded.

Dove grinned. "Not much family to get in mind. Just old Sim and Ma and Francy, besides young Sim. Even if he's not so young anymore."

"Dove—" her father began.

She paid him no attention, but went on, "Now, I could guide you to their place, slicker'n slick. I know just which turn to take at every trail fork."

"Dove!" Tews's voice rose, outraged. "You can't mean that! Why, if your poor dead mother heard you offering to go into the Big Thicket with two strange men, she'd turn over in her grave!"

"I bet she wouldn't! Ma'd know I'm grown up, and able to take care of myself! You're the one who tries to keep me a baby! She never did!"

Tews was obviously exercising all his self-restraint when he answered, "That's as it may be. Now you get on about whatever chores you've got to do, and leave me and these men to talk." After the girl had flounced off with a pout, he told Longarm and Travers, "Dove's a good girl at heart. She just doesn't understand about things like this."

"Sure," Longarm replied. "Now look here, Mr. Tews, you sure wouldn't want to see us waste valuable time waiting around for Sim to remember he's supposed to meet us here. If you can just give us an idea of where to find his place in the Thicket, we'll do the rest."

"I wish I could help you," Tews replied. "But I don't really know where Sim's folks live in the Thicket. I've heard them talk about a creek that runs by their place, but I can't recall ever hearing them name it."

"I guess there's lots of creeks in there too," Travers commented.

"Hundreds, I'm told," Tews said. He shuddered. "I don't like the Thicket myself. I never go in there. It gives me the creeps."

"Now, Mr. Tews, Sim's folks' place has got to be on some kind of trail," Travers said patiently. "And that trail's got to begin someplace, and lead north or east or south. At least you oughta be able to get us started."

"You don't mean you're planning to go in to look for Sim by yourself, just the two of you?" Tews asked incredulously. "Oh no, I wouldn't advise that at all."

"Why not? We're used to looking out for ourselves," Longarm said. "We've both us been out in wild country before now."

"You haven't been out in any country as wild as the Big Thicket," Tews told them very soberly. He dropped his voice to a hoarse whisper and added, "Big Thicket folks don't take kindly to outsiders. In fact, there've been stories about strangers just dropping out of sight over there across the river. Oh, I'd certainly suggest that you wait for Sim to come and meet you."

Longarm said, equally soberly, "Well now, we appreciate your advice, Mr. Tews. But all the same, I think we'll strike out on our own. It sure won't hurt anything if we go over and look around. We might follow a false trail a time or two, but sooner or later we'll wind up where we're headed for."

"Do you men have any idea how big the Thicket really is?" Tews asked.

Travers answered for both of them: "Can't say we have. It can't be all that big, though."

"It's just a about a hundred miles from here to the Nueces River," Tews said. "And the Big Thicket fills the space for fifty miles along both streams."

Longarm and Travers exchanged looks. Neither of them had realized what a big chunk of country was involved. Finally, Longarm said, "Well, big as it is, we'll take our chances. I guess it's safe to cross here. No quicksand, or anything like that?"

"No. There's no quicksand I know of for a dozen miles on either side of us here. And the river's shallow, all shoalwater except for a hundred yards or so at midstream, and then it'll only come chest-high on your horses. Crossing will be easy. That's more than I can say for what you'll find when you go ashore on the other side."

"We'll settle up then, and be on our way." Longarm took a half-eagle from his fob pocket and handed it to Tews. "Will that cover the cigars and the beers?"

"Of course. It'll be two dollars for the cigars, thirty cents for the beers. I'll get your change."

Longarm and Travers waded their horses into the stream. Tews stood outside the store watching them. Before they'd gotten more than a dozen yards from shore, he called, "I forgot to ask you! What shall I tell Sim if he comes to meet you?"

"Just act like we're deaf," Longarm advised the ranger.

They turned and waved, as though they hadn't understood the storekeeper's question. Then they put their attention to the crossing. The river flowed sluggishly, with an even sweep. The bottom was smooth, and the water shallow, until they were almost in midstream, where it deepened gradually for a hundred yards before the bottom shelved upward again. In this part, they had to slip their feet from their stirrups and ride with them held high to keep their boots dry.

Both men were watching the opposite shore as they approached it. The closer they got, the worse tangled the vegetation on the banks looked to be. Willows grew with their roots in the water, and over the tops of the willows, the wispy-leafed branches of cypress trees bowed almost to the surface of the stream. They could see nothing past the cypresses.

"There's got to be a place to get ashore," Travers called to Longarm.

"Sure. The trick is to find it! We better split up before we get too close to shore; you go upstream and I'll go down, and we'll see if we can't spot a clear place to go through."

Within a few moments after they parted, Travers called, "Up this way, Long! There's a creek flowing in here. We can wade the nags up it."

A short distance from the creek's mouth, there was a small, fern-studded clearing where they could get to dry land. They let the horses stand while they looked around.

"No sign of a trail," Travers said. "Which way you think we better go?"

Longarm had been surveying the vegetation ahead of them. Wherever he looked, the cypresses grew so close together that their drooping branches intertwined. It was impossible to tell where one tree left off and the next began. Inland from the cypress belt, the boles of sugar pines stood almost as closely spaced, the tops of the conifers invisible through the screen of foliage that cut off the sunlight and turned the Thicket into a world half-shaded, a hazy green.

"I don't think it makes much never-mind," he told the ranger. "Whichever way we go, we're going to be winding in and out of those trees till we ain't going to know which way we been or which way we're headed."

"We can't just stay here."

"No, we can't. But I don't think we ought to get too far off from here." Longarm pointed to their right. "Seems like that way might be the best one to try. What we need to do is get a little clear spot right across from the store and stay there till morning. Keep our eyes peeled, and see if anybody goes across from here or comes across from there."

After thinking this over for a moment, Travers nodded. "I see what you got in mind. If anybody comes across from there, they're going to bring word we're in the Thicket. And they're going to be looking for Blount. All we'd have to do is trail 'em and we got him."

"That's about the size of it. Only way I can think of to find anything in this mess is to follow somebody who knows his way around."

"Let's do it, then."

With their horses high-stepping among the ferns and weedy brush that grew everywhere, with the two of them ducking low-hanging branches from the trees that made detours the rule rather than the exception, they worked their way slowly along the short until they struck a well-defined trail.

"This is where we ought to've come ashore, I guess," Travers said. "Well, we didn't miss it very far. Now all we need is a clear place big enough to tether the horses and to spread our bedrolls."

After a few minutes more of looking, they found a vest-pocket-sized clearing that would fit their needs. By pulling some of the lazy twigs off a few cypress branches and chopping off the tops of some willow shoots with their knives, they made a loophole through which they could see Tews's store.

"After all the ground we covered, it feels good just

being off a horse," Travers commented as he stretched out on his bedroll.

Longarm gestured at the thick growth surrounding them. "I'd say we won't do a lot of riding in here. By the time we catch up with Blount, we'll be tired of shanks' mare."

"You think we need to share watches tonight?"

"Not unless you sleep a lot sounder than I do. Not even a ghost could sneak through this brush without making noise enough to rouse me."

They watched the store, and the sunset beyond it, while they made a fireless supper. By dark, they were both asleep.

Longarm heard the brush rustling before Travers did. He picked up his Colt, which he'd put at the head of his bedroll, before stretching out a foot to arouse his companion. Travers awakened at once, sitting up in his blankets. He said nothing until he saw the gun in Longarm's hand.

"What's the matter?" he whispered, a breathed question that could not have been heard two yards away.

"Ain't sure yet. Something's moving."

A moment later, Travers whispered, "I hear it. Off toward the trail."

Neither man had taken off his boots. They rose and moved as silently as possible in the direction of the sounds. They'd gone only a few feet when a light voice in front of them said in a conversational tone, "I hear you. Don't get upset, it's only me. Dove."

Chapter 9

"Dove?" Longarm couldn't keep the surprise out of his voice. "What in tarnation are you doing here?"

"You need somebody to show you the way to Sim's place. There wasn't anybody but me to do it, so I decided I'd better."

Travers said, "Your daddy told you to stay clear of us. He'll hide you good for sneaking off this way."

"Pooh!" Dove tossed her head. "Pap thinks I'm still a little bitty baby. And I'm not."

"You're not much better'n one," Longarm said. "Now why don't you just go right on back home and leave us to worry about finding Sim Blount. We don't want you to get into trouble on our account."

For a moment the trio looked from one to the other in the dim greenish light of the full moon, filtered through the leaves of the overhanging trees. Dove still had on the long, nondescript dress she'd been wearing when Longarm and Travers first saw her at the store, but now the dress was wet after her swim across the river, and it did not conceal her body anymore. Rather, it clung revealingly to the bulges of her high, youthful breasts, the incurve of her slim waist, the spreading of her hips, and the long, smooth taper of her thighs and legs.

She's right about one thing, old son, Longarm told himself. *This one sure ain't a little bitty baby anymore. She's a woman full-grown, if ever I looked at one.*

Dove said, "You can tell me to go back across the river, but there's not any way you can make me do it. I guess you can tie me up and carry me back, if you're a mind to, but you'd have to catch me first. And it'll be a lot easier for me to hide in the Thicket than it will be

101

for you to find me, because I'll know where to go, but you won't know where to start looking."

"What makes you think we'd bother to look for you?" Travers asked. "Suppose we just go on about our business, and don't pay any mind to you?"

Dove smiled. "Oh, I don't think you'll want to do that." Her smile had nothing babyish about it. In the almost smugly self-possessed curving of her full, red lips they could see the certainty of a woman who knows her own mind and isn't shy about revealing it. She went on, "If you try to just walk away from me, I'll dog you men everywhere you go. You won't be able to get shed of me, and I'll make so much fuss that the Thicket folks will think you're hurting me. They're my friends, you know. How'd you explain that to them?"

Travers thought about her threat for a moment, then admitted, "I guess there wouldn't be much way to."

Longarm asked Dove, "How come you've been so all-fired set on helping us, from the first minute back there in the store, when you heard us say we were looking for Sim Blount? We never done you any favors, Dove. Why are you wanting to do us one?"

"Because I hate Sim."

Dove's statement, delivered in a flat, calm voice that held no emotion whatever, was more impressive than if she'd shouted it angrily. It had all the effect on Longarm and Travers that would have resulted if she'd produced a shotgun from under her dress and fired both barrels into the still night air.

For a moment both men were speechless, then Longarm said, "Maybe you better explain what you mean."

"All right, but it's going to take some time, and I'd like to hang my dress up to dry. The night's getting chilly."

"Well, sure. Come along. It's only a few steps to where we spread our bedrolls. You can wrap up in a blanket while we talk about all this."

Longarm yanked the folded blanket he'd been using as a mattress out of his bedroll. Dove didn't wait for him to get it. She pulled off her dripping dress the moment they stopped where the lawmen had made camp, and spread it on the low-hanging limb of a spreading cypress tree. She was barefoot, and under the dress she was wearing nothing but a thin shift. She proceeded to slip this off too, and hang it beside the dress.

Neither Longarm nor Travers made any effort to avert their eyes, and Dove didn't seem a bit upset by their undisguised stares. She seemed unperturbed as she walked over to Longarm to get the blanket he was holding. Her darkly rosetted breasts were large but firm, so firm that they bobbled only a little bit as she moved. Her skin glowed in the odd green moonlight, its flawless whiteness set off by the deep indentation of her navel in her flat stomach, and by the dark thatch of pubic hair below it. A fluff of dark hair showed in her armpits when she reached for the blanket and draped it around her shoulders.

"I guess we'd better sit down," she suggested. "It'll take me a little while to explain."

She settled down on Longarm's bedroll, scissoring her legs to sit down in a single graceful movement, and pulled the twin braids of her dark hair over her shoulders. Longarm and Travers sat on the other bedroll, still too amazed to do more than look at her.

"Well," Dove began, "It goes back a long time, the way I feel about Sim. I guess you remember what I said to Pap today, about how I used to play with Francy?" They nodded, and she went on, "Francy's older than I am, three or four years. And Sim's a lot older than Francy. It don't sound like much, but when you're eleven or twelve years old, it's an awful lot. Francy always knew more about things than I did. Men-and-women things, I mean. She was always saying things I didn't quite understand when we played with our dolls, but after a while, she started to explain. I didn't know then that Francy and Sim were already doing the things she talked about, and I didn't have any idea of doing them myself."

Dove paused, and a long, thoughtful sigh escaped her parted lips. She said, "I guess I was a lot more grown up than I knew. Anyhow, Sim started noticing me, and teasing me in that mean way of his." She set her jaw and looked at Longarm and Travers. "You know Sim's got a big streak of meanness, don't you?" When they nodded, she continued, "There never was more than three or four boys in the Thicket who'd play with him. He was bossy and always getting into fights and other kinds of scrapes. Stealing from fishtraps and trotlines and smokehouses. Sim liked to hurt people, as far back as I can remember."

Again she stopped talking, and sat quietly for a moment while the men waited for her to go on. "Well," she said, "I guess it had to happen the way it did. Sim came down to the playhouse Francy and me had made, a ways off from the real house where she lived. It wasn't much, I guess, just a bunch of branches stuck in the ground and propped up, with a sort of roof made out of cattail stalks and different kinds of leaves laid over them. But Sim came in one day, and took his thing out and started showing it off. I knew what he was after Francy to do, by then, but I didn't really know what to look for. Francy kept telling him it was her time of month, except I hadn't learned what that meant yet."

Now Dove began speaking faster, as though to finish quickly. "It was Francy that started him at me, but I know Sim would've been at me quick enough, even if she hadn't. Then when I said I wouldn't and kept on saying I wouldn't, Francy held me while Sim did it to me." She paused, still in that past day. "I didn't bleed much, but it hurt a lot. And Sim and Francy both said they'd get even with me if I told anybody, so I knew what that meant. Sim had already cut up a boy that he had a fight with. Didn't kill him, but it scarred him up. So I kept still."

"You didn't even tell your folks, I guess?" Longarm said when Dove stopped and had lost herself in thought again.

"Of course not! Because Pap was a lot younger then, he'd've gone to old Sim, and old Sim was as mean as young Sim, and old Sim might've killed Pap. But that's not the end of it, you see." She took a deep, sighing breath and continued, "Sim started laying for me, then. I stopped going to play with Francy. That didn't stop Sim, of course. The way it is along the river here, all of us had little skiffs or maybe just rafts that we'd pole across." She smiled. "I learned how to swim before I knew how to walk. Ma saw to that. She said she wasn't going to have any of her kids drowning."

"Sim kept giving you a bad time?" Travers asked, when Dove paused again and didn't seem inclined to say anything more.

"Whenever he could catch me away from the store," she said with a disgusted shake of her dark braids. "I guess I wasn't smart enough to stay close to Ma and Pap. I liked to go out, fish, watch the birds, maybe just walk. When I think about it now, I can see that Sim must've kept watch on me, spied on me, a lot of times. He caught me by myself an awful lot. He wasn't always by himself, either. Sometimes there'd be one or maybe two or three of his cronies with him. They'd all do it to me, one after the other, and maybe again after the first time. I stopped fighting them after a while. And it got so it didn't seem so bad. I got to where I'd enjoy it, and later on, I'd do it with boys I liked. But I never got to where I enjoyed it with Sim. I never did get a good feeling with him. And I never have stopped hating him, either."

"Well, we can sure see why," Longarm said. "But if you feel that way about him, why'd you keep quiet while we were in the store talking to your daddy?"

"Because Pap doesn't know how I feel about Sim. I never could tell him or Ma what had happened to me. They knew I stopped going over to play with Francy, but they thought there'd been some kind of fuss between her and me. Then Ma got the dengue fever and died. And after that, things changed between Pap and me."

"Changed how?"

"I'm all he's got left, you see," Dove said soberly. "Jimbob and Chester, my brothers—they're both a lot older than I am—they left home a long time ago, when I was still little. Ma and Pap both tried to keep me a little baby as long as they could. Pap still does. I guess you saw that."

"Won't he be worried if he finds you're gone?" Longarm asked.

"No. Not anymore. I get so worked up inside sometimes that I go out at night and walk. Or maybe go wake up one of the men I—well, one of the men I know—and when I go out that way, Pap just pretends it never did happen. He doesn't say anything or let on that he's noticed. But he still tries to keep me his little baby girl. You saw that when you were at the store."

"And you're sure you won't get in trouble, guiding us?" Longarm insisted.

"If I do, it'll be trouble I've made for myself. If you take Sim away, though, Francy and her ma and old Sim won't do anything to hurt Pap and me. I can handle Francy, and the old ones are too feeble now to do much."

"Wait a minute," Travers said. "What gives you the idea we're going to take Sim away?"

"You're after him, aren't you? Either you want to get even for something he's done to you, or you're lawmen come to arrest him."

"What makes you think that?" the ranger prodded.

"Oh, I could tell right off that you really aren't friends of Sim," Dove replied coolly. "You haven't got that ugly, mean look all his friends have. You're looking for him to do him some kind of hurt, aren't you? You fooled Pap, but you didn't fool me for a minute, with that talk about him going to meet you. If Sim had been going to meet you, he'd've been there waiting."

Again, Longarm and Travers exchanged looks, then they nodded at almost the same time. Dove's long story rang too true to have been fabricated for their benefit. They'd both heard enough liars' made-up yarns to recognize truth.

"We're after Sim Blount to put him away," Longarm told the girl. "This here's Will Travers, a Texas Ranger, and I'm Custis Long, a deputy U.S. marshal. We both want Blount for murder—and a lot of other things, too. So if you got any objections to helping the law, you'd best just go on back to the other side of the river."

"Not that we don't welcome your help," Travers added.

Dove's voice was clear and unwavering when she said, "If I hadn't thought you were after Sim to kill or arrest him, I wouldn't've come."

There was relief in Longarm's voice when he said, "Well, then, I guess we got that settled. The rest of it can wait till morning. Now, Dove, why don't you take my bedroll to sleep in? I'll just take a blanket and curl up over there a ways."

"No. I don't need anything but a blanket. Most of the time, when I stay out at night, I don't even have a blanket. The night's warm, and the sunset was clear, so it's not going to rain."

Dove stood up and moved a little distance away from the men. She spread the blanket, lay down, and pulled half of it over her. Longarm and Travers could think of nothing to say; they were still digesting the girl's surprising appearance and her story. They went back to their interrupted sleep. In a short while, the occasional slight rustling caused by one of the horses shifting position to graze was the only noise that broke the stillness.

Longarm didn't know how long he'd been sleeping when he was awakened by the pressure of soft fingertips on his lips. He was used to waking up quietly; he opened his eyes but remained motionless. The moon had gone now, and the starlight was not bright enough to penetrate the overhanging tree branches. The darkness was a tangible thing, something that could almost be felt, rubbed between his fingers.

Dove whispered in a voice softer than a dying breeze at sunset, "Is it all right if I come in with you?"

For answer, Longarm shifted to the edge of his bedroll to make room for her. Dove lifted a corner of the blanket that was covering him and slid under it. He was glad he'd taken off his boots when he'd returned to bed.

"Why'd you pick me instead of him?" he asked in a whisper as low as hers had been.

She knew who he meant; in the stillness they could hear Travers snoring softly a few yards away. "Because I like you better," she replied. "Your friend has a mean streak in him. Not bad-mean, like Sim's, but mean, just the same."

107

"You didn't have to come to either one of us."

"I know that. But I wanted to come to you."

Longarm let a hand wander over Dove's soft body. He slid his palm flatly down her back, along the thin layer of flesh that covered bones and vertebrae, feeling the bones under the smooth, unflawed skin. Her hips were wide, softly padded, and her buttocks firmly voluptuous. He felt himself getting hard.

Dove pulled her body to nest against his. He heard her utter a small sniff of dissatisfaction when she rubbed against his clothes, and then her fingers were busy on the buttons of his shirt, opening it to let her hands touch his chest. He shrugged out of the shirt and the top of his underwear, and her breasts pressed against his skin as she leaned above him. Her lips sought his mouth, her tongue pushing his lips apart. Longarm open his mouth to her, and her hands moved to his waist, to loosen the buttons of his pants. He arched his back and she pulled down his trousers, bringing his balbriggans with them. Clumsily, in his efforts to move silently, he freed his legs from the clothing.

When Dove's hand found his erection, he was fully hard. "Oh my," she whispered softly, "you're big." She trailed his erection up her thigh, up to her belly, and pressed against it, trapping it between their bodies.

Longarm's hands sought and found her breasts. He fondled her nipples for a moment, feeling them rise and harden under his touch. Then he bent to caress them with his lips and tongue. Dove cupped a hand under his chin and guided his mouth from one breast to the other and into the fragrant, woman-scented valley between them. She shuddered with silent delight when the stubble of his cheeks and the stiff hairs of his mustache brushed the tender tips.

She pushed her free hand between their bodies and found him rock-hard and throbbing. After running her hand along his shaft for a few moments, while Longarm continued to kiss and rub her budded nipples, Dove tucked his erection between her thighs, holding him there with muscles that were strong and firm under their covering of soft flesh.

108

A sudden worry invaded Longarm's mind. He said, "Maybe we better not let this go any further. I don't want to be responsible for gifting you with a woods-brat."

"You won't. There's a plant a Coushatta Indian woman showed me. They call it *melafila*. It keeps babies from getting started."

"You sure?"

"I've used it enough. I'm sure."

He stopped worrying then. There was combined in Dove a softness and a wildness, a breath of forests and rivers that clung to her skin, a sensuality in the movement of her lips on him, that was giving him a lifting excitement. He suddenly wanted to be in her.

Dove sensed his mounting desire. She shifted under him and Longarm raised his body to let her slip a thigh under his hips. She sighed as he went inside her, and he felt the soft, moist warmth that was engulfing him contract as she gasped with his entry. She pushed her hips forward, welcoming him. Longarm reached down to grasp her buttocks and drive fully into her.

For several moments they lay motionless, enjoying the sensations they were sharing. Then Dove began rolling her hips gently, and Longarm responded by meeting her rolls with a sharp forward thrust. Now she became all woman.

"Oh," she sighed breathlessly, "you're the most man I've ever felt inside me. I just want to go on this way forever and forever."

"I'll do my best," he whispered into her ear. Dove's head was tucked into the hollow of Longarm's shoulder, her tongue caressing his neck, her firm breasts crushed against the hard muscles of his chest.

Holding back, alternating long periods of gentle stroking with minutes of lying motionless, Longarm stretched their embrace until they both lost track of time. He reached the point when he could hold himself back no longer. He'd felt Dove shudder and stifle cries in her throat twice now, and from the shuddering of her body clasped to his, he knew she was again nearing the time when she'd reach the peak of her ecstasy. He said nothing, but pulled back farther and plunged deeper and faster until she began writhing and pushing against him. Then he rammed hard and deep as he let himself go, while Dove covered her mouth with a hand to keep her cries of pleasure from ringing out through the still night. Then the rapture ended and the frenzy died, and they fell away from each other limply as their muscles and nerves relaxed. And then they slept.

Chapter 10

Longarm was alone when he was awakened by a pleasantly discordant chorus of birdsongs. He sat up in his bedroll and looked around for the birds, but the sun was just rising and the ground below the trees was in shadow only a bit less deep than night's darkness. He'd felt Dove slip away from him in the darkness, but by then he'd lost track of time in sleep.

Travers was sitting up in his blankets, yawning and stretching. Dove had put on her shift and dress; she'd folded her blanket into a square pad and was sitting on it. She smiled pleasantly at Travers, then turned and smiled equally pleasantly at Longarm. Her expression betrayed no indication of anything that might have happened during the night.

She said to them, "I didn't want to dig into your saddlebags, looking for something to cook for breakfast." She indicated the bulging leather pouches, hanging on a limb above the saddles the men had tossed on the ground the night before when they'd stopped. "If you'll tell me where the food is, I'll fix it. It's too early for us to pick fruit or berries, so we'll have to eat just whatever you're carrying."

"That ain't very much," Travers said. "We got some pretty fair cheese and parched corn and jerky and soda crackers and a couple of onions and some prunes. And coffee."

Longarm volunteered, "I'll pick up some wood, and maybe you can get the coffee started right off." He spoke from behind a cloud of smoke. Missing his regular eye-opener of Maryland rye, he'd lighted his first cigar of the day. Privately, he looked on coffee as being better than nothing, but it took second place to a mouth-cleansing swallow of good whiskey.

111

"You won't need to get wood, I've already gathered some," she said. "I was just waiting to light a fire until you woke up."

Travers had already gone off, looking for a screening bush. Longarm followed him, and they stood side by side as they relieved their full bladders.

"I hope that tool of yours ain't too sore for you to piss with," Travers said sourly. "I heard you giving it a workout on that girl last night. How is she, a pretty good piece of tail?"

"Good enough. I'm not complaining," Longarm replied tersely; he took no pleasure from discussing his amorous encounters, believing such palaver to be ungentlemanly and, in any case, pale in comparison to the adventure itself.

"I looked for you to send her on over to me, when you was finished. Well, it'll be my turn tonight. You've had first crack at her, and fair's fair."

"Maybe Dove's got some ideas about that," Longarm said in his most deceptively mild voice.

"Maybe not! If you think you're going to hog her all to yourself, you got another think coming!"

"Listen, Travers. I didn't invite her into bed with me; it was her idea. And I don't aim to tell her who she's got to lay up with or when. She don't belong to me any more than she does to you."

"Just the same, if there's any ass handed around, I want my share. And I aim to get it, by God!"

"That's between you and her. You can ask her, but if she tells you she ain't interested, don't look for me to make her change her mind."

Longarm spoke levelly but emphatically. He wanted no misunderstanding between himself and the ranger at this stage in their pursuit of Blount, especially on the subject of Dove, on whom they were now depending to guide them to the fugitive.

Travers grunted angrily, but said nothing more. The Ranger's surly mood continued through their austere, quickly eaten breakfast: gruel made from crushed, parched corn, with slivers of jerky sliced into the pot as it boiled; uncooked prunes; cheese and soda crackers. He said little, reaching for what he wanted instead of asking for the pot or the scrag-end of cheese to be

112

passed to him. The only time he spoke was to ask Dove to pour him a second cup of coffee.

Once, when Travers was looking off into the distance, trying to locate the source of some real or imagined noise, Dove looked at Longarm and drew her brows together in a silent question. Longarm shook his head, and she nodded to show that she understood the need for silence. Breakfast was an uncomfortable meal, and all three of them were glad to get it over with.

As the men were putting the uneaten food into their saddlebags, Longarm asked Dove, "What about our horses? Had we ought to saddle up, or leave them here?"

"Yeah," Travers seconded. "When we come ashore yesterday, we'd of made better time walking than trying to ride, what with all these damn low-slung tree-limbs."

Dove shook her head. "If I'd only thought, I'd have come over in a boat, instead of swimming. Then we could pole right up the creek that runs past Sim's folks' house. But I just didn't think about it."

"Well, we sure can't fault you for that," Longarm said. "For all you knew, we might've been some of Blount's outlaw friends and cut your throat just to keep you from telling anybody we were here."

"What about the horses?" Travers insisted.

"It'll be uncomfortable riding the first half-mile, until we get to the main trail we'll follow," Dove said. "That trail will take us about three miles, to another little narrow, winding trail that runs along a swamp for part of the way. We'll be on it for less than a mile, but the horses would be sliding around a lot of the time."

"Well, that's all we need to know, ain't it?" Longarm said. "We'll lead the horses to the good trail and ride to the next little one, then we'll walk the rest of the way. That suit you, Travers?"

"I guess it'll have to. Too bad about the boat. It would of saved us some time."

As they left the little clearing and moved into the trackless undergrowth on the way to the trail Dove told them about, they moved into a different world.

113

It was a world such as might have existed on some impossible, unpeopled planet, for nowhere were there any signs of human life or use of the land.

On ground covered with a soft, hairlike moss from which footprints—even the hoofprints of their shod horses—disappeared almost instantly when the foot was lifted, trees, bushes, and flowers sprang up in wild, unlikely confusion, in a riot of shades of green. There was the soft emerald hue of moss, the deep black-green of dogwood leaves, the brilliant splash of lady's-slipper clumps not yet in flower. There was the pale, delicate touch of slim-budded lupine stalks with their narrow leaves, and the broad, dull blotches of bloodwort.

Where there were no shrubs growing, there were trees. Most of them were pines: big, honey-barked sugar pines with light green needles on their spreading branches, loblolly pines with deeper-hued needles and darker bark. Between the pine trunks, in the distance, the feathery foliage of cypress marked the locations of springs, the paths of creeks.

Birds, unafraid of the strangers passing below, were in most of the trees. The flashing red of the cardinal's wings caught their eyes occasionally, and more often, the dark iridescent sheen of the feathers of grackles and crows stood out on the branches or bushes where they perched. Sparrows darted everywhere, and the lighter hues of thrushes and thrashers and wrens and grosbeaks were almost as plentiful. Not until Dove, walking ahead of Longarm and Travers and the horses, was a yard or less from their perches, did the birds in her path take flight.

There were a few small clearings, no more than pocket-sized patches in the prevailing brush, and they had to push through a maze of thin, whippy limbs most of the time. The half-mile Dove had promised them took what seemed to be a long while to cover. At last they came to the trail. It was neither as wide nor as well-marked as Longarm and Travers had expected, but it was wide enough for a horse to pass along, and the trees it snaked between seldom had branches growing low enough to require them to bend double, as they'd had to do the evening before.

"You can ride pillion with either one of us you choose, I guess," Longarm said as they stopped to mount.

Dove looked from one to the other, and then walked to where Travers sat on his horse. He extended a hand, and she swung up behind his saddle, on the horse's rump.

"All we do is follow the trail?" he asked her.

"Yes. I'll tell you when we come to the fork where we're going to leave the horses."

With Travers leading, they started again. Now they were penetrating deeper into the Thicket, and on each side of the barely defined trail, the underbrush was thicker than it had been before. There were more big bushes, and fewer shrubs and flowers. Most of the trees here were loblolly pines, thin and spindly, with only a few small branches low on their trunks, but their small, scale-barked boles towered so high, and the branched tops of the trees grew so close together, that only an occasional, fugitive ray of light from the still-low morning sun penetrated to the trail.

Sunrise had brought out the squirrels, and their whisking, busy tails now joined the fluttering of bird's wings in the trees. Once a gray fox, scouting for a rabbit breakfast, came along the trail toward them. The fox stopped short when it saw Travers's horse, looked with its strange, slitted, vulpine eyes at the intruders, and, with a dainty dance-step move, vanished in the bushes bordering the track. The shadowed areas that had covered so much of the ground beneath the trees were slowly shrinking as the sun climbed higher in the nearly invisible sky. They never did see the sun itself, though, through the canopy of vegetation that met overhead. There was no way for them to tell in which direction they were moving, as the trail zigzagged sinuously between the trees.

When Dove at last signaled for them to halt, Longarm looked around for the fork in the trail that they would take on the final leg of their trip. He could see no sign of a new path leading off the one they'd been following, which, itself, had been growing imperceptibly fainter as they'd traveled. There was no path showing on the ground, no gap in the brush which grew thicker than ever between the trees around them. Travers, too, was turning his head slowly from side to side as he searched their surroundings.

Dove said, "The fork's right over there." She pointed, and now the men could see the suggestion of a new track branching off, which seemed to vanish in the shadows a dozen yards ahead.

"You think the horses will be safe here?" Longarm asked.

"As safe as anywhere else," she replied. "Thicket folks don't have much use for horses, and nobody's likely to pass this way for a day or two."

"Just the same, we better get 'em off the trail and into the brush," Longarm told Travers. "I'd just as soon not have to walk back to the river from here."

Dismounting, they pushed into the bushes, leading their horses, and tethered them in the thick brush where they could stand unseen by anyone who might be passing along the path. When they'd made their way back, carrying the rifles they'd pulled from their saddle scabbards, they saw that Dove had pulled up a partridge-berry vine and was plaiting its long, fibrous shoots into a strip. She pulled the back hem of her long skirt up between her thighs to her waist, then used the plaited vine as a belt to hold the skirt in place. Her legs were bared halfway up her thighs, and she looked as if she were wearing baggy bloomers.

"There's marsh and swamp along the trail ahead," she explained. "I can travel easier without my skirt dragging behind me."

"The going's pretty bad ahead, then?" Longarm asked.

"It'll be slick and muddy in places. There's one or two spots where we might have to wade ankle-deep."

Travers said gruffly, "Well, it won't get any better for us just standing here jawing about it. Let's get moving."

Dove led the way, with Longarm following her, his Winchester cradled in the crook of an elbow. Travers came behind them. Dove picked her way along by landmarks neither of the men could see. There were times when she turned abruptly to one side for several paces, then turned again in the direction they'd been

116

moving originally. They walked silently, concentrating on the ground, which was crisscrossed with exposed roots angling out from the ridged knees of the cypress trees that had quickly begun to take the place of pines after they'd left the main track.

There were vines too, threading here and there, some of them barely visible, others completely hidden under a thin layer of sandy soil, just buried deeply enough to snag the toe of a boot as it sank into the soft, moist surface. Where a foot had been planted, water flowed in to fill the depression, and Travers, in the rear, was forced to splash into the footprints left by Longarm. Dove, on her bare feet, and lighter than the men, left only the faintest impressions where she stepped.

A short distance after they'd taken up the new trail, they came to the beginning of the swamp. It started gradually, as moss-covered puddles spotted here and there beside the little hump along which the trail ran. Soon there were more puddles than dry land. The trail wavered from side to side and up and down, dipping into the puddles for a few feet before rising and becoming dry again.

Turtles' backs began to appear here and there in the opaque green water, their glistening, unblinking obsidian eyes showing as dark dots in their leathery, hook-beaked, serpentlike heads. There were no squirrels in the cypress trees, and few birds. The rounded ridge that marked the path grew steadily softer and more crooked as it wavered around the cypresses that grew closer and closer together. A vague sourness filled the air and became acrid in their nostrils, the rankness of vegetation rotting under the dark water and along its edges.

They made slow, tiring progress. Each step was a risk, and their nerves, already edgy with anticipation of what might wait at the trail's end, grew even tighter as they pressed deeper into the swamp. The cypress trees were older, taller, and more closely spaced the farther they went; their protruding knees sometimes jammed together and crowded the trail until it narrowed to a strip no wider than a man's foot, and sometimes narrower.

Dove, familiar with the path, had gotten a score of paces ahead of Longarm. She reached an unusually narrow spot where the three giant cypress knees had grown together to give the effect of three trees rising from a single set of bulging boles. She stopped and leaned, half-sitting against the knees, to wait for Longarm and Travers to catch up.

"It's not very much further," she said. "And the swamp ends just a little way ahead. It'll be easier going in a few minutes."

Longarm was about to answer her when he saw the water moccasin. The snake had been hanging on a branch six or seven feet up the trunk. Its dark, thick body blended with the cypress bark, and if it had not opened its yawning, white-lined mouth to strike just as Longarm looked at Dove, he would not have noticed it.

"Dove!" he called sharply. "Duck down, quick!"

There was no time for him to shift the Winchester and draw his Colt. He brought the rifle up to his shoulder and snapped off the safety as he was raising it. Less than a foot separated Dove's head from the moccasin's striking mouth, and he could see the snake's long, curved, venomous fangs gleaming ivory against the dead white of its mouth as it swayed before striking.

Sighting as the gun reached his shoulder, Longarm snapped off a shot. The slung tore through the moccasin's gaping mouth and thudded into the tree trunk, but the snake's small brain had sent the command to strike into its nerves and muscles, and its jaws stayed open as its head dropped toward the girl. Longarm levered in a second cartridge and fired again. His shot was echoed by the flatter boom of Travers's .45 as the ranger, spotting Longarm's target, drew and fired. The rifle bullet tore a second hole in the snake's head, and the heavier, slower-moving lead slug from the Colt completed the job, blasting the moccasin's thick body, tearing it apart. The snake glanced off Dove's shoulder as it fell, its fangs dripping venom, its tail snapping and flipping against the wet earth.

Dove's face was ashen under its tan when Longarm got to her. He planted a booted foot on the still-writhing snake, grinding the head and fangs into the dirt only inches from the girl's bare feet.

When Dove stopped shuddering, she said, "That was closer than I like to come to one of those nasty things. Water moccasins scare me blind, they're the one kind of snake I'm afraid of. Most snakes wriggle away when people come close, but a moccasin—well, they attack."

"You're all right now," Longarm told her. Then a fresh thought struck him and he asked. "Are we close enough to the Blount place so they'd have heard those shots?"

Dove's eyes widened. "Yes. We're real close to it now."

Travers frowned. "We better hump along then. I don't imagine there's too much shooting goes on around here. They'll be wondering who's afoot."

Sliding on the soggy, slick footing, they pushed as fast as they could through the remainder of the swamp. When they reached dry ground their pace increased, and Longarm and Travers moved up abreast of the girl as they trotted ahead.

"Blount's house is just ahead," she panted. "Past that next bunch of trees."

"Don't break cover, then," Longarm cautioned. "Sim Blount's cagey and suspicious. Chances are, he'll be waiting for us with a rifle ready after he heard that shooting we had to do."

Ahead of them, the underbrush thinned and the trees that had been so closely spaced diminished in number to a few that grew in a semicircle to their left. Through the suddenly scant vegetation, they saw the outlines of a house, with an outhouse and a shed behind it. They stopped at once, then started advancing again, picking their way carefully now, bending low to make the most of the little cover that the sparse growth now offered.

Longarm said, "Dove, you stay back. Duck behind one of them trees and don't show yourself while Travers and me ease up to where we can see better."

Obediently, Dove pressed herself to the safe side of the spindly loblolly pine nearest to them. Longarm and Travers dropped to the ground and belly-crawled un-

119

der the brush until they came to its end, where they could see the house clearly.

Only fifty or sixty feet of bare earth now separated them from the house. They lay flat and shoved their hats back on their heads to keep the broad brims out of their line of sight. The house was built of cypress planks. It was unpainted, and age and weather had striated the surfaces of the raw boards into long, thin ridges. The two windows on the side they faced had neither glass panes nor insect screens. The framed openings stared blackly at them, like square, sightless eyes.

To their right they could see the beginning of a veranda, posts and railing and warped floorboards, that Longarm judged must run along the front of the house. Only part of the porch was visible at the oblique angle from which they were gazing at it. If there was a door in the front of the house opening onto the veranda, it was hidden from their sight. At the back, a set of canted, sagging steps leds to the ground. The outhouse and shed rose beyond the steps to their left. Beyond the house, between its hidden front side and the brush that rose a few yards from it, the brown waters of a sluggishly flowing creek glinted dully. The creek, Longarm thought, must run very close to the side of the house they couldn't see.

"Sure is one hell of a looking place to live in," Travers grunted under his breath.

"That it is," Longarm agreed. "You want to try going on up to it? Or wait for somebody to show?"

Before Travers could reply, a blurred shape inside the house flitted past one of the yawning windows. The darkness beyond the window kept them from seeing more than the suggestion of motion.

"They've showed," Travers said so calmly he could have been telling Longarm the time. "Sim, likely, scouting to see if anybody's out here."

'Maybe he was moving too fast to notice us," Longarm said.

Without warning, a rifle muzzle appeared in one of the windows. It fired, and a puff of dirt exploded in front of the bushes where they lay. They rolled with the sound of the shot, Longarm one way and Travers the other, to get shelter behind the trees nearest them.

"He spotted us," Travers told Longarm. "You hold on here. I'll keep this tree trunk between me and the house and crawl back till I can circle around in the brush. I'll get to the back of the place; maybe there's an angle that'll let me see inside."

Longarm nodded. As the ranger moved, he divided his attention between watching the windows and keeping Travers in a corner of his eye until the other man vanished behind him in the brush.

A second shot came from the house, aimed higher than the first. It whizzed angrily through the brush until it was deflected by a twig, and its hornet-buzz ended in a *thunk,* as it buried itself in the dirt.

After the space of time that would be needed to lever a fresh shell into the rifle's chamber, a third shot followed. It plunked dully into the tree trunk that, until a few moments earlier, had sheltered Travers.

Longarm resisted the temptation to answer shot for shot. He hoped Travers would do the same. It was pretty certain that there were others in the house besides Sim Blount, and he didn't relish the prospect of cutting down anybody but the murderer they were after.

Minutes ticked past and no further shots came from the window. Longarm risked looking around the tree trunk, but no matter how hard he strained to see, he couldn't penetrate the obscurity of the room behind the window. He was beginning to wonder what Travers was doing when Dove called, "Quick! It's Sim! He's getting away!"

Longarm sprang from behind the trunk, but Dove's call had come too late. He saw a boat, unoccupied, cutting the water of the creek, heading from the house. It took him a second or so to realize that the pole extending from the stern of the skiff had been used to give the craft one hard shove before Sim Blount dropped to the bottom, out of sight.

Raising his Winchester, Longarm sent a round through the boat's stern. It splintered the wood above the waterline, but the skiff had good headway. Before he could shoot again, it was out of sight behind the sheltering bushes that grew on the banks of the creek.

Chapter 11

"Travers! The creek!" Longarm shouted before he broke cover and raced for the little stream. He didn't know how straight or how crooked the creek ran, but hoped he might get there before the boat was out of sight.

He covered the stretch of bare ground in a dozen strides and stopped just in time to dig in his heels and skid to a stop before he went into the water. The corner of the skiff's stern was vanishing around a bend, behind the bushes on the opposite bank. He'd already planted a foot in the shallows at the edge, planning to try his luck wading, when Dove called to him. He looked over his shoulder and saw her hurrying toward him.

"It's no use trying to wade after him," she said. "That creek's crooked as a corkscrew. He'd be gone around the next bend before you could wade to the first one."

Longarm looked in frustration at the little stream. Thick bushes grew to the water's edge; there was no chance of finding running-space along the bank.

He asked Dove, "Can we take the horses, ride cross-country, and cut him off before he gets to the river?"

Dove shook her head. "Not going through the brush. There's no trail down to the creek on this side, and none we can get to fast enough on the other side."

"Damn it! I sure hate to see him get away, after we got this close to taking him!"

Travers came up, panting from the run he'd made when he'd heard Longarm's call. He looked at their faces. "He got away, did he?"

"In a boat, down the creek. Pushed off from behind the house and then laid down in the bottom. I got off that one shot just before I yelled for you, but all I did was raise a few splinters off the ass-end of the boat." ·

Travers snorted disgustedly. "Just bad luck all around, I guess. I seen that damned boat pull away, but the brush was so thick I didn't take in what was going on until I heard you yelling. By the time I got moving, it was gone."

"We're real close to him, though," Longarm pointed out. "It ought not to be too hard to pick up his trail from wherever he gets off the river."

A cackle of laughter rose behind them. Longarm, Travers, and Dove turned in unison to face the house. On the veranda stood a bent old man whose mouth, gaping with laughter, showed two or three snaggled yellow front teeth in an expanse of pink gums. He was totally bald, but badly in need of a shave. He wore a dirt-streaked, tattered shirt and butternut jeans, and was barefoot. The woman standing next to him was not quite so old, and had a more complete allotment of teeth. She was laughing as hard as the old man, but hers was silent laughter.

Next to the woman was another woman, much younger than either of her companions. Her features were irregular, but animated; in different surroundings, wearing something other than the sleazy, faded sateen dress she had on, men might have found her attractive. Her face was twisted in a sneering smirk. Unlike the older woman and the man, she had on shoes.

"Too smart for you, wasn't he?" she called. "You didn't think you had any chance of sneaking up on Sim, did you?"

"They almost got him, Francy!" Dove retorted hotly. Next time they'll get him, and that'll be the end of your precious Sim!"

"Don't bet on it!" Francy snapped. "He'll be back, and you know what you'll get when he catches up with you!"

His voice pitched low, Longarm asked Dove, "That hospitable bunch would be the Blount family, I take it?"

"Yes. Old Sim, Ma, and Francy."

"No use asking them anything, then," he said.

"Why not?" Travers asked. He raised his voice.

"Listen, you people! I'm a Texas Ranger and this man with me's a United States Marshal. If you don't tell us where Sim Blount's gone to, we'll—"

"Do what?" Francy asked. "Put us in jail? Shoot us down? I don't know where Sim's heading, and even if I did, I wouldn't tell you!"

"Yippee! That's the way, Francy!" the old man cackled. "Don't let on y' know a thing! Your ma and me won't either! Make 'em find out theirselves!"

"Shut up, Pa!" Francy commanded. She turned back to face the three standing by the creek. "Now all of you get off our land! You've got nothing on any of us here! Pa, tell 'em what you'll do if they don't move fast enough."

"I'll take m' shotgun to you, that's what I'll do," the old gaffer said in a high-pitched voice. "I'm still good enough to dust y'all outa here with it! And I'm spry enough to chase y', too! Y'll find that out if you don't hyper fast as y' can git!"

Looking at the three, Longarm felt more pity than anger. He remembered people like this from the days of his boyhood in the hard-scrabble hills of West Virginia. He said to Blount, "You don't need to take a gun to us, old man. We'll be as glad to go as you'll be to see us leave."

Travers objected, "Ain't we even going to search the house? We might find something inside that'd give us a hint where Blount might be heading for."

"We'll search it if you want to," Longarm replied. "Me, I think it'd just be wasting time. Sim Blount's too smart to leave anything behind that'd help us."

"I hear what you two're saying!" old Sim called. "You got no right to search my house, no more'n you got a right even to be on m' land! Maggie, go get my shotgun! Looks like I got to give these men a lesson!"

"You put a damper on, old man!" Travers called back. "If we decide to take a look, the law gives us a right to. We'll make up our minds what we're going to do!"

"Let's don't push him too hard," Longarm suggested in a half-whisper. "Thing we'd better do is get out of here without fiddling around any longer and get on Blount's new trail."

"I guess you're right," Travers agreed. "But I hate to let an old bastard like that one think he's bluffed me and made me drop out of the pot."

Maggie Blount had already started toward the door leading inside the house when Longarm called, "You won't need your shotgun, old man. We're going."

Old Sim greeted Longarm's announcement with another burst of high-pitched, cackling laughter. "See, Maggie?" he gasped when he'd stopped laughing. He pointed a gnarled finger in the direction of Longarm, Travers, and Dove. "I guess I c'n still play first fiddle when I take a mind to. Francy, you be sure to tell—"

Francy spoke quickly: "Pa, I told you once to shut up! Now, you keep quiet. You got your way. They're going to leave."

While the trio on the veranda watched, grinning, Longarm, Travers, and Dove retraced their steps across the cleared ground to the winding, narrow trail. They walked along the trail in the silence that comes from frustration. Going through the swamp, they passed the still-twitching carcass of the water moccasin without comment, though to each of them the thought occurred that if it hadn't been for the snake, their errand might have been successful. Mounted, with Dove again on the rump of Travers's horse, they rode down the main trail to the river. Travers pulled rein at the water's edge and Longarm, behind him, also stopped.

"What's the matter?" he asked the ranger.

"Nothing. I just got to get used to being in daylight again."

Longarm realized for the first time that he'd been squinting ever since they'd emerged into normal sunshine from the perpetual twilight of the Big Thicket. He looked at the dancing wavelets of the Trinity, and at Tews's store on the opposite bank, and said to Dove, "I bet your pa's going to be mad when you get back home."

"Pap's been mad at me before. He's always got over it, and I guess he will this time."

"Maybe after he finds out we're lawmen, he'll feel better about you helping us," Travers suggested. "We'll stop and tell him and see if that won't ease things between you."

"Oh, you won't have to do that. I'm not going to ride back with you. I'll stay here until you've gone on after Sim, and then go home. Whatever Pap thinks I've been up to, he won't have anything to throw back to me."

"Now, wait a minute—" Travers began.

Longarm said emphatically, "You heard what Dove wants to do. Let her be. That's the least way we can thank her for trying to give us a hand." To Dove he said, "I wish we could do more than just say thanks. You sure did your best, and it wasn't your fault we ain't bringing Blount out with us."

"I hope you catch him before he can circle around and get back here again," Dove replied. "You heard what Francy said."

"We heard her, all right. Don't worry. We'll stay on his tail so close he won't get a chance to hurt you."

"We damned well *better* stay on his tail," Travers growled. "Well, if you're finished saying your good-byes, Long, let's get moving. Sooner we start, the quicker we'll catch up to Blount."

They nudged their horses into the river. When they'd splashed through the shallows a short distance, Longarm turned back to wave a goodbye to Dove, but she'd already disappeared into the thick brush that lined the bank. Travers caught the movement of his companion's body and turned in his saddle.

"Damn you, Long!" he said angrily. "You sure euchered me outa getting any of that ass! I was figuring on puttin' it to that girl tonight."

"That was before we let Blount slip out of our hands, which was mostly my fault, I guess. Like I said this morning, I kept clear of her. Hell, Travers, you know that."

"Yeah, I know. That was sour grapes talking," Travers admitted. "Just the same, that was a mighty choice piece. I hated to have to turn my back on it." Then, after a few moments, he added, "But I'll tell you something. I think I'd pass up that Dove girl if I had a choice between screwing her and Francy. You can just tell by looking at her that she knows all the movements."

"Francy?" Longarm said, more to make friendly

conversation than because he had any real interest. "Hell, man, she can't hold a candle to Dove for looks."

"I grant you that. But women with quick tempers is the best lays, and that Francy's a holy terror. Why, the way she told her step-pa to shut up when she wanted to have her say, and the way he done just what she told him to——"

"Wait a minute," Longarm interrupted. He frowned, trying to recall an elusive memory. "You just made me remember something I'd overlooked. It was what the old man started out to say just before Francy yelled at him to shut up."

"What was that?"

"I'm trying to think. Let's see. Old Sim said whatever it was just before that. Then he commenced threatening to get out his shotgun and I got concerned about keeping him from starting something we might have to finish, and that drove what Francy had said clear out of my mind."

"Well, think harder, Longarm. Because I don't remember what everybody said."

"I recall it now. It wasn't what Francy said, though; it was what old Sim started to say just before she told him to keep quiet. He said something about Francy not letting on she knew where young Sim was heading. I think it was, 'Don't let on you know anything, and me and your ma won't either.' "

"Yeah." Travers's face now wore a thoughtful frown that matched Longarm's. "I seem to remember that now. But I don't see as it means anything."

"That wasn't all of it. A little bit later, just when we were walking away from the creek, Francy cut him off fast again. And what he'd said was, 'Francy, you be sure to tell——' And right there, she busted in and told him to keep quiet."

"I don't remember that. But I was fighting down my mad right about then. I guess I could've let it go by me." Travers shook his head. "I still don't see as it means anything."

"Like hell it don't! The way I read what he said the first time, Francy knows where Sim's heading."

"What if she does? She'd never tell us nothing."

"That's not all of it. The second time, what old Sim

127

was starting to say was, 'Francy, you be sure to tell young Sim about what I done, when you see him,' or something to that effect."

"Oh, now hold on! You're putting an awful lot of meaning on what the old fellow never finished saying," Travers objected.

"I wouldn't be too sure of that," Longarm said slowly. "If you put that with what Dove told us about how Sim was putting it to Francy when they were kids, she might still be one of his bedmates, one he'd take along when he was going to hide out. Sure as shit stinks, he'd be able to trust her, when he might not feel so sure with a woman he didn't know so well."

Travers digested Longarm's suggestion slowly and thoroughly before he spoke. "You just might be right. Blount sure would want him a lady friend, if he was figuring on hiding out for a long spell, from what I've learned about his ways."

Longarm said, "It all hangs together, as far as I can see."

The ranger gestured impatiently. "All right. Say it does. What good is it to us?"

"If Francy's going to join up with Sim, she's going to leave here pretty soon. I'd bet they were getting ready to take off together when we showed up and spoiled their plans." Longarm shrugged. "All we've got to do is follow Francy, and she'll lead us to Sim."

"Suppose she don't leave for a week? Blount could be anyplace by then," Travers pointed out.

"I never said it wasn't a gamble," Longarm reminded him. "What we've got to decide on is whether the odds are on our side or his."

"A man that made his living gambling told me at one time that it don't much matter what game you're playing, when you first start out the odds is fifty-fifty whether you're going to win or lose. It's only later in the game that they'll tilt one way or the other."

Longarm grinned wryly. "We ain't exactly starting out on a new game. Unless you figure we finished one back there in the Thicket, and we're starting now from raw."

Travers didn't answer directly. Instead he asked,

"You're pretty sure you've got this thing figured right, ain't you?"

"Like your gambling friend told you, it looks to me like the odds right now are fifty-fifty."

"If we gamble wrong, Blount might get away clean."

"Not likely. It'll be easy to pick up his trail, starting from here. He's got to come ashore on one side of the river or the other. He's got to land his boat someplace where he can get a horse, or catch a train or a stage," Longarm pointed out. "Spotting his boat wouldn't be any trick. That slug I put through the stern's going to make it stick out like a sore thumb."

"That's occurred to me, too. All we'd have to do would be for you to take one side of the river and me take the other, and ask questions while we move downstream."

"You saying you feel like gambling?" Longarm asked.

"It wouldn't be my first gamble." Travers grinned, and Longarm heaved an inward sigh of relief when he sensed that the current of animosity that had been flowing between them seemed to have been at least temporarily diverted. The ranger went on, "If you got the deal cased right, and Francy leads us to Blount, it'd sure beat trying to pick up his trail by ourselves."

"It's settled then?"

"Far as I'm concerned it is. Only we better decide how long we're going to wait for her to come out of the Thicket. I'd say if she don't show up by this time tomorrow, we call it a loss, and take out after Blount again by ourselves."

"That's fair enough," Longarm agreed. He nudged the claybank into motion. "Let's get on ashore and find a place where we can watch the river without her spotting us." Then he added, "If she comes out, that is."

They found the place they were looking for in a clump of live oaks that stood on a little rocky knoll a short distance downstream from Tews's store. The knoll lifted them only fifteen or twenty feet above the general level of the rolling terrain that sloped down to the river, but that was enough to give them a clear view of the green wall of the Thicket on the opposite bank. The trees that grew on the little rise were thick enough to hide them and their horses, but not too thick to obscure their view and make watching difficult.

Longarm and Travers took turns keeping an eye on the Thicket. They had no trouble spotting the mouth of the creek that had been Blount's escape route, and it was only a little more difficult to locate the small gap in the vegetation that marked the beginning of the trail they'd taken to reach the Blount house. They had no way of knowing how Francy would travel, if she traveled at all. There could have been another boat moored on the side of the house, or there could have been a horse tethered in some nearby clearing, or out of sight in the shed they'd seen. It didn't really matter, they agreed, whether Francy rowed or rode. Either way, they were sure to see her.

Both of the lawmen were veterans of countless stakeouts. Neither of them could remember how many hours they'd spent waiting concealed at some place where a fugitive they were after might be expected to appear. They didn't make hard work of their watching, but took turns resting, sleeping, or just lying stretched out on their bedrolls relaxing, while the sun tracked down to the west through the long afternoon.

"One thing we didn't take into account, Long," Travers said as the sky behind their vantage point began to turn pink. "How in hell are we going to spot her if she takes a notion to travel at night? She could slip past us easy as hell in the dark."

"I guess we'll just have to count that as part of the gamble," Longarm replied. "I don't much think she'll pick on the nighttime, though. Hell, she won't be expecting us or anybody else to be watching for her. Far as she knows, we're long gone."

"Well, we got another hour or two to find out," Travers said, consoling both of them. "After that, it's a full moon and early moonrise. So maybe we ain't screwed ourselves with this deal, after all."

Longarm was watching and Travers was dozing when Francy came out of the Thicket. For a moment, he couldn't believe what he was seeing. He blinked his

130

eyes several times to ease them and to reassure himself that they weren't playing tricks on him.

He was more than a little certain that he recognized the horse as the freshly broken mustang that Blount had traded his dapple for at the farm a little way from Round Rock. The animal was a hammerhead mustang with the rough, patchy coat of a wild horse that hadn't yet had enough grooming to get smoothed and shiny. The rider caught his eye more than the horse did.

It was Francy on the horse, Longarm was sure, even at the distance from which he was looking at her. But she'd discarded the sleazy sateen dress she'd been wearing when he'd seen her earlier in the day, and really gotten gussied up. Now she wore a long black velvet dress, with a lace insert down the front and a high lace collar. She was riding sidesaddle, and as the horse waded deeper and deeper, nearing the center channel, she lifted her legs to rest them in front of the saddle, just as he and Travers had done when they crossed the stream on horseback. Even at a distance, Longarm could see the fancy stitching on the knee-high button-shoes Francy had on.

There was only one thing that didn't jibe with the image she presented of a genteel young lady out for a refreshing afternoon canter. In a saddle scabbard that slanted down on the off-side of the mustang, she carried a rifle. As the water came up higher on the mustang's flanks, Francy lifted out the rifle with the smooth movement of one accustomed to handling it, and rested it across her lap.

As soon as he'd made absolutely sure he was right about the identity of the woman on the mustang, Longarm called, "Travers! Come take a look! Francy's come out of the Thicket, and I'll bet anything I've got she's on her way to meet Blount. I'd say the gamble's paid off. As of right now, we're back in business!"

Chapter 12

"Hell!" Travers exclaimed. "She ain't coming straight across."

He'd jumped out of his bedroll at Longarm's call, and the two had been watching as Francy guided her horse across the river.

"Look at her!" the ranger went on. "That slant she's taking is going to put her ashore a half-mile downstream from us."

"It won't matter much," Longarm told him, "unless there's more than one road along this side of the river, or a place where she can leave her horse and catch a train or get on a stagecoach. Is there? You know the territory better'n I do."

Travers thought for a moment. "There's no road along the east bank of the river for the next ten miles, that I recall. On beyond that, there's a better road on the other side than on this one. And there's damn few places between here and Galveston Bay where she can catch a stage. The one place she could get on a train would be at Buffalo Bayou. But the railroad she'd be riding is just a little jerkwater line that don't go noplace yet."

"We've got nothing to worry about then, have we?" Longarm said. "All we've got to do is stay behind her far enough so she won't spot us, then close up a little bit when we get near any town where she might be meeting up with Blount."

"Nothing to it, the way you're talking," Travers said with a smile. "I hope it turns out that easy."

"It'll be a sight easier than trying to pick up Blount's trail," Longarm pointed out. "He can duck and dodge around and make following him tough titty. Francy

132

can't do that. Why, in the getup she's wearing, a blind man'd notice her at midnight."

"Dressed like she is, she sure don't figure to be on the road very long," Travers said.

"No," Longarm agreed. "She's heading for a town of some kind. What's your idea? Where'd she be going?"

Travers took off his hat and scratched his head vigorously. "Not too damned many places she could go. There's Anahuac, at the mouth of the river; Allen's Landing, across the bay from there on Buffalo Bayou; then there's the Allen brothers' town westward from the landing, the one they call Houston, but it's just a little place, nothing like Fort Worth or Austin or San Antonio. There's Beaumont, but that's a right far piece east, unless Blount's heading for New Orleans. I'd say the likeliest place is Galveston."

"Hmm. I ain't ever been to Galveston, but it's got the reputation of being a crooks' hangout, like New Orleans, or any other port town. Does that still hold true, or is it all talk?"

"Oh, it's true enough, all right. Has been ever since it's been there. Still is. We keep a real close eye on it."

"That's likely where Blount was aiming for, then. Bad as he's wanted now, he might've decided the only way to get out is on a ship. He'd be too cagey to risk a border crossing into Mexico, and it's one hell of a long way from here up north to the Red River."

"Damned if I don't think you've hit it, Longarm."

Longarm had noticed one thing about Travers. When things were going along well between them, and they were on good terms, he'd always call him "Longarm," but when the ranger got riled, he'd shorten it to "Long" in a tone that was anything but friendly.

Which ain't so odd, old son, Longarm thought as he stood beside Travers on the knoll, watching Francy negotiate the last few yards of the river crossing. *Neither one of us is used to a lot of partnering. We got our own ideas, and we're used to doing just about what we please without looking to anybody else for a by-your-leave. But anyhow, we've got past the time when we were sparring like a couple of banty roosters after the same hen. It won't last, though. The minute we take Sim Blount, we'll be at it worse than ever, trying to settle which one of us is going to take him in to hand over to the judge and hangman.*

Aloud, he said to Travers, "We'll know soon enough, I guess. Right now, we got something else to think about."

"Her?" Travers jerked a thumb at the woman crossing the river.

"Yep. Her. Francy's going to get a pretty good start on us, slanting downriver the way she's doing. Looks to me like we better get our gear stowed and follow along after her."

After the difficulty they'd had keeping on Blount's trail—all the stops looking for information, all the uncertainty of the times when they were sure he'd slipped away from them—following Francy amounted to a pleasant, slow ride along the river.

She made no effort to cover her tracks. Apparently she thought Longarm and Travers had gone snipe-chasing after her stepbrother when they left the Thicket, and if she gave a thought to the possibility that someone might be trailing her, her actions didn't show it.

On the first evening, she covered less than a dozen miles, and crossed the Trinity again to the east bank, where she stayed at an inn—a boardinghouse, in spite of the sign it bore—in the little hamlet of Liberty. Longarm and Travers made their camp outside the town, under a huge spreading holly tree, and were in the saloon across the town square from the inn when Francy came out the next morning, still wearing her black velvet dress, to resume her journey.

"She's got to be heading for Anahuac." There was certainty in Travers's statement. "There just ain't another place she can be going, after she turned south at the fork where we thought we'd lost her."

They'd let Francy get a half-hour's start on them when she left the inn. When they reached a fork in the road, three or four miles outside the town, they'd been forced to spend a busy two hours in hard riding to learn that Francy had taken the south fork instead of staying on the main road east. After that, though Travers swore

134

there weren't any more forks ahead, they'd been more careful. For the rest of the day, they took turns riding ahead until they caught sight of the rider in the black velvet dress on the road in front of them. Once the scout had seen her, he'd stop and wait for the other to catch up. They weren't sure such care was really necessary, because Francy still rode as though she were at the head of a Fourth of July parade, but doing it that way broke the monotony and gave them little time alone.

"How far is this Anahuac?" Longarm asked.

"From here? Maybe twenty miles more. It's just a good day's ride from Liberty, unless you're in a hurry. Which she don't appear to be."

"Nothing there that'd keep Blount hanging around the place, is there?"

"Hell, there's nothing there that'd make anybody even want to stop. Unless it's to wait for the ferry to go to Galveston. You see, Longarm, Anahuac used to be the capital, back when Texas was a nation instead of a state. It sort of died out when they moved the capital to Austin. About all it is now's a bunch of tumbledown houses and some wharves."

"That ferryboat you said something about, Travers —how long does it take to get to Galveston?"

Travers blinked and jerked his head around to face the marshal. "Damned if you don't ask more fool questions than any man I ever rode with! What in hell difference does it make?"

"I don't know yet. That's what I'm trying to find out from you," Longarm said patiently. "What kind of boat is it, steam or sail?"

"Last time I was down this way, and that'd be about three years back, they was running a little paddle-wheel steamboat. I don't imagine they've changed since then."

"You remember how much of a trip it was then, to Galveston?"

"Damn it, I'm trying to. Seems like it took a little bit longer than two hours going, and close to three hours coming back.

"Why the big difference?"

135

Exasperated, Travers almost shouted, "Now what the hell does that have to do with us?"

"Nothing, maybe. But it just might. Listen, Travers, when you've got a rat with a bolthole handy, and you're trying to set a trap for him, you look around to find out if he's got a spare hole someplace that he might use. Then you put out a trap at both of those holes. If you don't get him at one, you might get him at the other."

Aware now that Longarm wasn't just trying to satisfy an idle curiosity, the ranger took time to think back, then answered more calmly, "It's like this. Anahuac's up at the top of Trinity Bay, and Trinity Bay turns into Galveston Bay to the south of the town. Now, the ferry goes to Galveston, and then it circles back along the west shore and stops in two or three little places there, like Allen's Landing, for instance. Does that satisfy you?"

"It sure does. And it might be important to us."

"Damned if I see how."

"Stop and think about it a minute. You expect us to get on the ferryboat that Francy takes to go to Galveston?"

"Why, hell no! She'd see us for sure on that little boat."

"All right. She gets off in Galveston. Now, we can't follow her until the next ferry sails. What the hell's she going to be doing, those five hours? That's close to half a day. And we're not out in the country, in Galveston. It's a sizable town, as I understand it."

"Yeah, it's a pretty big place," Travers agreed. "Six, maybe seven thousand by now. Not quite as big as Austin or Fort Worth, but a good-sized town."

"With a hell of a lot of houses and streets and people milling around, maybe some of 'em women wearing black velvet dresses."

Slowly, Travers said, "I see what you been getting at. Damn! We got ourselves a puzzle, ain't we?"

"Maybe. But not one we can't work out. Let's think about it while we ride along here for a spell, and see if we don't come up with an answer."

After they'd ridden in silence for perhaps a quarter of an hour, Longarm said, "Maybe there's a way to

136

handle things so we don't spook Francy. I ain't so sure it'll work, because I don't know how far apart places are, or even if there's any places where we'll need for 'em to be."

"I guess I remember enough about the lay of the land down there to fill in whatever gaps you can't," Travers volunteered.

"I'm hoping you can. Let's begin with the ferryboat. You said it swung up the west shore of the bay, Galveston, Trinity, they're just the same as one, the way I understand it."

"That's right. Trinity Bay, where Anahuac is, and Galveston Bay, they're all the same stretch of water."

"All right. Now where's the place closest to Anahuac that the ferryboat stops at?"

Travers's fingers sought his chin and he began scratching while he thought. "There's two places between Allen's Landing and Anahuac where it puts in, but I'm damned if I can remember the names of 'em. One's an old Confederate shipyard at the mouth of a creek, and the other one's a little ways beyond it, on a neck of land that sticks out into the bay."

"You got any idea how far either one of 'em might be from Anahuac, by road?"

Again Travers scratched for the answer. It didn't quite surface in his mind. He shook his head. "I don't recall, Longarm. But it can't be more than ten or twelve miles."

"And it'd take the ferry a while to get to Anahuac from that last place it stops?"

"Yep. But I couldn't say how long. Half an hour, maybe."

Longarm squinted and looked up at the sky, as though the solution to their problem might be written there. "Suppose one of us was to put on speed and ride ahead, get to one of those ferryboat stops about the time Francy got to Anahuac. Now, if he got on that ferryboat, showed the captain his badge, and told him he needed a place to hide until the boat got to Galveston—I reckon that could be arranged?"

"I don't imagine that'd be any trouble at all." Travers began to grin. "So one of us will be on the ferryboat when Francy gets on it at Anahuac. And

137

he'll ride with her to Galveston, follow her, and then we'll know right to a tee where Blount's hiding!"

"If he don't come meet her at the boat, that is," Longarm amended. "Which he just might do."

The ranger slapped his thigh and said admiringly, "By God, Longarm, that's what I call a real slick scheme! I don't see how we can miss!"

"If it works," Longarm said, holding up a cautioning hand. "It's another gamble. But whichever one of us don't ride ahead and get on the ferry will be following Francy to Anahuac, and maybe there'd be some way of getting aboard without her noticing him. That'd be too big of a gamble to count on, though. I'll bet there won't be but five or six people get on there."

"Hell, Longarm, if one of us is already on the boat, it won't make much difference. Whoever follows Francy to Anahuac can just take the next ferryboat. It'll be up to the fellow that's already on board to follow her and Sim and spot their hideout."

"That's how I see it, Travers. And I think you're the one that ought to be on that boat."

"Why me? It's your idea."

"Whose idea it is don't signify. You've been to Galveston before; you'll feel more at home there. And you'd be more likely than me to know any shortcuts between here and the rivermouth that'd get you to wherever you'll need to go to catch the damn boat."

"Well—whatever you say, I'll go along with. There's only one thing about this scheme that bothers me."

"What's that?"

"How in hell can we be sure Francy's going to take the same boat I'm hiding on?"

"Well, there's only one boat makes the run, ain't that right?"

"Far as I know, it is."

"Then just get on the damn thing and stay on it till she gets on. If she don't go on to Anahuac, I'll be waiting to tell you when the boat pulls in there."

"I guess that's about the best we can do to copper our bets," Travers admitted. "All right, Longarm. That's how we'll play it."

They rode on together, not hurrying, for Travers was positive there was no destination other than

138

Anahuac for which Francy could possibly be heading. Travers was not a talkative man in any situation, Longarm had found, but the ranger was even more silent than usual as they continued south along the road in the hot sunshine of early afternoon.

Now the character of the land was undergoing still another change. The road itself revealed this; when they'd crossed the Trinity to Liberty, and started south from there, the rutted, hoof-pocked surface had still been the rich, dark brown—almost black—of the riverbottom. Now it was streaked with a lighter soil, lighter in both texture and color. The surface was no longer firm, giving back a resounding thump when a horse's hoof struck it. Now the hoof made almost no sound when it was set down in the softer earth.

They rode along a wide, rounded hump on which the road had been beaten by the hooves of horses and draft-oxen and by the wheels of farm wagons. On their right, the land sloped down to the river, wider and shallower here as it neared the point where it would flow into the salt water. On that side, the dark hue of riverbottom loam absorbed the sun's rays. To their left, the lighter soil, earth that had once been sand on the shores of the Gulf of Mexico before the gulf receded, glistened in the sun's rays, and reflected its heat.

There were cottonwoods, a few loblolly pines, and bushes growing in the riverbottom soil and for a short distance east from the road, then the big trees vanished and their places were taken by lower, wider-branched oaks, and the brush gave way to tall grass that rippled when a breeze passed.

"We ought to come to a place pretty soon where I'll find a road leading west," Travers said. He'd been getting edgier with each mile they put behind them, and Longarm could tell that the ranger was anxious to begin what could be the final part of their long, frustrating pursuit.

"You're sure there *is* a road?"

"Of course I'm sure. I went over it in the other direction when I was down here before. I just can't recall exactly where it branches off of this one."

"How far'll I be from Anahuac, when we come to that fork?"

"Eight, maybe ten miles. About an hour's easy riding."

"And you figure it'll take you how long to get where you can board the ferryboat?"

"About the same. Oh, allow another half-hour or so."

"And you said the ferry took about half an hour to sail to Anahuac from where you'd be getting on it, as I recall."

"That's as close as I can put it. Don't worry, though. I'll ask when the last ferry left there, and if the timing don't work out right, I'll just go on into Galveston and we'll meet there."

"I was coming to that. You got a ranger head-quarters there, or someplace like that, that I can find easy?"

"No. We don't put men in big towns, you know, where they've got a police force." Travers scratched at his jaw for a moment, then said, "I'd guess the best place is the Catholic church. Folks in Galveston call it the Cathedral. You can't miss it, and it ain't too far from the ferry landing."

"I'll manage to find it. There's not much way to set a time. If you get there first, you wait till I show up. If I get there first, I'll wait for you."

They rode for another quarter-hour before Travers reined in at a dusty fork that led off the road along which they'd been riding. From its appearance, the fork was seldom used. There were few ruts or wheel marks on its surface, and weeds grew down its center.

"This is the place," Travers said. "Now that I see it, I remember. It slants down to the bay, then runs along it. I know where we are now. Anahuac's about eight miles further on."

Longarm nodded. "All right. See you in Galveston, then."

They were not men who wasted time and energy on handshakes, wishes for good luck, or the other cere-monial amenities of parting. Travers poked a heel into his horse's flank and pulled the animal's head over. He moved off down the fork. Longarm fished out a

140

cheroot and lit it. He sat puffing, surrounded by a blue-gray cloud of fragrant smoke, watching Travers until the ranger vanished around the first bend in the fork. Then he poked his own horse into a walk and went on toward Anahuac.

Riding alone gave him more time to think. Longarm went over the plan they were beginning to carry out, step by step. There were holes in it, he knew. The assumptions on which they'd based their future moves were uncertain, based on what Travers remembered from a time several years in the past, and things might have changed. They were operating on a timetable that might not hold up, and on the actions of people over whom they had no control.

From the beginning, when he'd first formed the scheme, he'd considered the possibility that Blount might be sending Francy out as a decoy, to draw them off in one direction while the fugitive himself went in another. After thinking out that line of reasoning, he'd discarded it as not quite probable. He just didn't credit Blount with all that much cunning. All in all, Longarm decided, the odds were in favor of their scheme, loose and chancy as it was.

Besides that, old son, he thought as his horse covered the few remaining miles in a steady pace, *when you're the extra pig in the litter, you grab at whatever tit you can scrabble your nose up and and then you do the best you can to get whatever milk's left in it.*

Travers's memory for distance had been good, Longarm told himself as he saw ahead the final, long slant that led to the shallow brown waters of the bay. At the edge of the water, a cluster of houses stood. Even from the spot some distance away where Longarm stopped to study them, he could tell that a lot of them were falling down. There were piles of hewn stone blocks and half-disintegrated adobe bricks between many of the structures that remained standing. Off to one side, away from what was left of the town, a series of sawtoothed walls stood near the water's edge; from the looks of the ruin, Longarm judged that there must have been a fortified area there at one time. A pier jutted out into the bay. At its end a few dories and three or four small sailing craft swung and swayed on mooring ropes.

It sure ain't such a much of a place, Longarm thought as he studied it. *If Francy's there waiting for that ferryboat, it's going to be one hell of a hard job to keep her from spotting me. Best thing I can do is duck inside the first saloon I come to. That's the one place I'll know she can't get in. Or a barbershop. A hot bath and a real shave'd make me feel a lot better. If the town's got such a thing as a barbershop. It'll damn sure have a saloon or two; this place is still in Texas.*

Before riding into the town, Longarm dismounted and took his coat out of his bedroll. Francy had only seen him when he was wearing a vest over his shirt, and it was worth a gamble that she might not recognize him at a glance if he had on a coat this time. He shook the wrinkles out of the coat as best he could and slid his arms into its sleeves, then swung back into the saddle and headed for the town.

He was still on Anahuac's outskirts when he noticed the sign he'd been hoping to see: LIVERY STABLE. Longarm pulled the claybank over into the stableyard. Two or three farm wagons, a surrey, and a shay leaning forward on its shafts stood in front of a pole corral where a number of horses plodded about aimlessly. There was the generally acrid smell of all stables in the air.

A man wearing a straw sombrero with a ragged brim ambled out of the barn that stood a few paces away from the corral and asked, *"Sí, señor?* You want something?"

"Right this minute, all I want is a little information. How much you charge to board a horse?"

"Ten cents the day, *señor.* For the week, fifty cents. Is not so much if you leave him a month."

"Thanks." Longarm was inspecting the horses in the corral while he listened. He thought he spotted the patch-coated mustang that Blount had traded for at the farm outside Round Rock. He asked, "You get quite a few to board, I guess? People riding in to catch the ferry over to Galveston?"

"Not so many. But a few."

142

Longarm pointed to the mustang. "That one there looks like one that passed me on the road into town. You recall whose it is?"

"Oh, *sí, señor*. A beautiful lady, all in black. She is one like you just say, to take the ferry."

"Well, I'm planning to catch it myself, but I'll want my horse to get around on. The lady who brought that one in, she's caught a boat already, I guess?"

"Oh no, *señor*. The lady is not get here in time. She is wait in town now for the next trip. The boat, he don't get here again for a while."

"How long is a while?" Longarm asked.

"Pretty soon now, I guess." The man shrugged. *"Quién sabe?"*

"Yeah." Longarm smiled. *"Quién sabe*'s right. Well, *gracias, amigo*. I'll bring the horse back out here, or send somebody with it, after a while."

As he rode on into the town, Longarm felt five pounds lighter and ten years younger. Every piece of his risky, loosely knit scheme seemed to be falling into place. All that was needed now was for Travers to catch the ferry before it came around the bay to Anahuac.

And he'll have plenty of time, Longarm thought as the looked at the decaying buildings that lined the dusty street, searching for the saloon and barber shop. *If our luck holds out, we'll have Sim Blount in handcuffs before sunup tomorrow.*

Chapter 13

Anahuac was the next thing to deserted. Longarm surveyed the situation as the claybank meandered at its own slow walk down a street devoid of people. Many of the buildings he passed were in ruins, and most of the others had the vacant look that a building presents when its windows are shuttered or made blind by pulled-down shades. Before he'd gotten halfway to the center of town, while still a safe distance from the wharf on the waterfront at its southern edge, he wheeled the gelding and started back the way he'd come in.

Just ain't a bit of use me parading down to that wharf, he replied to the sense of caution that had stirred his retreat. *Too much risk Francy might spot me. Why, hell, I stand out like the balls on a bull, as few folks as are stirring around.*

He circled the outskirts of Anahuac until he found a place where he could watch the wharf from a safe distance, then he dismounted and sat down on the sandy ground. It seemed a long wait before the little paddlewheel ferryboat came into sight, pushing at a leisurely pace through the bay's quiet yellow water. The steamer's whistle tooted in a series of sharp blasts while it was still some distance from the dock, and the signal stirred a bit of movement. A half-dozen people appeared after a few moments, walking across the strip of cleared land between the town's last houses and the landing.

Longarm had the fast-declining sun at his back instead of in his face when he turned away from watching the approaching ferryboat to inspect the passengers going to the wharf. They made a slow parade from the town's edge, across the clear ground, and even if

Francy hadn't been the only unescorted woman among them, she'd have been easy to spot. Her long black dress would have made her stand out in any crowd, except one gathering for a funeral. He watched until the disembarking passengers had left the boat and those making the trip to Galveston had boarded. When the boat backed away from the pier and turned south toward the Gulf, Longarm heaved a sigh of relief and headed back toward Anahuac.

Now he felt free to move around as he pleased. He rambled through the decaying streets until he found a saloon with a barbershop across from it, and lingered over the only Maryland rye he'd run across since leaving Denver. He wasn't inclined to worry or hurry. Even though the free-lunch counter offered only the standard small-town fare of boiled eggs, drying summer sausage, and salted cheese, he made two trips to it between drinks. It was a relief to eat anything that hadn't come out of his saddlebags.

Refreshed, he crossed to the barbershop and lazed for a while in a tub of hot water before stretching out in the chair. Being shaved always seemed to stimulate Longarm's thoughts, and this time was no exception. The idea began to form in his mind while the barber was removing a week's growth of itching stubble from his cheeks, and it grew and matured while the man was trimming his hair and mustache. By the time the barber had macassared his hair and restored his mustache to its usual longhorn sweep, he'd decided to act on the new plan.

"Is that ferryboat that pulled out a while ago the only way a man in a hurry can get to Galveston from here?" he asked the barber while waiting for his change.

"It is unless you want to charter one of them little sailing ketches that's tied up at the pier."

"You got any idea how much they'd want? You see, I'm a stranger to boats and such. I don't mind paying a fair price, but when I'm dickering with somebody, I like to know the going rate before I say yes or no."

"Don't blame you a bit, mister." The barber thought for a moment, glancing at the Regulator clock that hung, with its lazily swinging pendulum, next to the flyspecked mirror. "Well, if you hit up some of them charter fellows down there, they'd likely stick you five or six dollars for the trip. But you go ask around for Del—he's my kid brother. Del oysters, but oystering's finished now till fall. Tell him I said to carry you to Galveston for three dollars. If he don't want to, he'll know somebody who will."

"Now, I appreciate that," Longarm said. "And I'll sure do it, right away."

Sunset was near before Longarm located Del and delivered the barber's message. The young sailor looked at Longarm, taking in his travel-stained clothes and spurred boots. "That your horse, up at the end of the pier?"

"Mine till I give him back to the army. Why?"

"Generally, a man riding a horse wants me to take him and the animal both."

"What's wrong with that?"

"Oh, nothing. Except I'll expect four bits extra for the trouble of cleaning up the hold afterward. You don't think I'll shovel horseshit for free, do you, mister? If I enjoyed doing that, I'd stay on shore."

"That's fair enough," Longarm agreed. "How soon can we start?"

"Right now. I'd say you're in a hurry to get to Galveston, or you'd've waited and taken the next ferry for thirty cents."

It took them a few minutes to persuade the claybank to walk out on the echoing boards of the wharf and to take the small step off it to the sloop's deck and into its shallow, open hold—more a cockpit than anything else. When the gelding was finally tethered in place, Del said, "I'm ready if you are."

"No use wasting time." Longarm looked at the sun, now dropping into the bay. "I guess you can find your way in the dark?"

"There's plenty of navigation lights for me to go by. I guess you don't know much about sailing, but I'll get you to Galveston just about as quick as the ferry would in broad daylight."

"Well, now, I ain't in that big of a hurry. Just get me there safe and sound, that's all I'm asking."

To Longarm, who was a dry-land man, the twenty-five mile trip in the sloop across the calm water of Galveston Bay was the equivalent of an ocean voyage.

He had a few second thoughts at the very beginning, after Del had shoved the craft away from the wharf and the vessel rocked in the gentle swell before its sail was raised. He'd felt more swaying and rocking on the backs of some of the half-broken mustangs he'd encountered, but a horse was something he understood and could control. He found himself gripping the gunwales of the little sloop while Del busied himself with the lines, getting up canvas.

His nervousness vanished as soon as the vessel found weigh and began to move briskly forward. He took note of the casual manner in which Del handled the tiller, holding it with a knee hooked over it when running before a trailing wind, and lashing it with a loop of rope when he had to go forward to adjust the jib when it was necessary to tack. And after Del pointed out the navigation lights by which he set his course, Longarm got over the feeling that they were sailing blindly into a black nowhere. Even before the lights of Galveston began to change from a general haze into individual pinpoints, he was enjoying the novel trip. When they'd wrestled the gelding ashore at the fisherman's jetty where Del usually berthed his vessel during oyster season, Longarm was genuinely sorry that the trip had been so short.

Streetlights had not yet come to Galveston, nor had street-name signs, but in the wide-open waterfront district through which he first passed, kerosene flares and reflector lanterns outside the saloons, gambling houses, and brothels made the streets noon-bright. The narrow thoroughfares were crowded with pleasure-seekers ready to guide a stranger, and Longarm had no trouble getting directions to the Cathedral. There was less light on the streets he took to the central section, but Center Street was flare-lighted for part of its length.

When he reached the great structure, with its soaring spires and high, arched windows, enough light trickled through the stained glass of the windows and the tall, open doors to give him a clear view of the church itself and the street in front of it. He walked

147

the claybank slowly around the massive stone church, looking for Travers, but there was no sign of the ranger. After circling twice, Longarm pulled the horse's reins through the ring of one of the iron hitching posts that lined the brick curbing around the Cathedral and walked over to the steps of the church. He sat down and prepared to wait.

A half-hour passed, and Travers did not appear. Longarm was getting hungry, and hunger made him impatient. He was about ready to go look for supper and a drink when he spotted the ranger coming along the sidewalk, dodging through the trickle of worshippers headed for the early-evening Mass. Travers saw Longarm at about the same time, and hurried his steps. Longarm went to the sidewalk to meet him.

"Well?" he asked Travers. "Did we pull it off?"

"Oh, I connected with the ferryboat, and got the captain to tuck me away out of sight in a cupboard. And Francy got on, and I kept an eye on her when she got off, and by God, Longarm, you was right. Sim Blount was there to meet her!"

Longarm looked narrowly at the Ranger. His well-honed instincts told him there was something wrong. He asked, "Well? You followed Blount and the girl, didn't you? You know where Blount's hideout is?"

"Not—not exactly," Travers said hesitantly. "You see, I got off the boat all right, and followed 'em along the wharf. And everything would've gone slick as fresh owl shit except for one thing."

Longarm was almost afraid to ask, but he finally did. "What thing?"

"That goddamned Sim Blount had a hack waiting for him and the girl at the end of the wharf! They hopped into it and the hackie shook his reins and they took off!"

"Well, damn it, Travers! Wasn't there another hack close by you could've hired to follow 'em in?"

"Not a one! Listen, I chased after that hack on foot. I run as fast as I could, faster'n I've ever run before in my life. I just couldn't catch up with 'em, no matter how hard I tried. I didn't give up till I was plumb blowed."

"Did you get a good look at the hackman? And the

hack? A good enough look so you'd know 'em again if you seen 'em?"

"Where the hell you think I been? I been going to every hack stand in Galveston, trying to find that one. But goddamn it, the hackie looked like every other jehu and the hack was just plain old black, like most of 'em are. There wasn't one goddamn thing about it that'd make it different from the others I seen while I was trying to find it."

Longarm fought back the temptation to lash out at Travers for his incompetence. He knew the ranger probably felt worse than he did himself over having lost Blount's trail. Raising a ruckus with Travers wouldn't do a bit of good.

"Now, that's a hell of a thing to have happen," he said consolingly. "But I've had men slip away from me, and I guess Blount's not the first one to've slid past you."

"He ain't the first, but there's been damned few! I tell you, Longarm, there wasn't one blessed thing I could do about it."

"Sure. I know that. Well, we're still ahead of the game. We know Blount's in Galveston, we know Francy's with him, and all we got to do now is find 'em."

"Easy enough to say." Travers's voice reflected his glumness. "I feel like a fool, the way it happened. But there wasn't a way at all I could've got off of that boat any sooner. And if I could've run anymore, I'd still be running after 'em."

"Hell, I know that. It wasn't rightly your fault."

"It was too. If I'd of thought I was going to lose 'em, I'd of shot the damn cab-horse and stopped 'em. Or let off a slug or two into the back of it, maybe got in a lucky shot that'd take care of Blount. By the time I seen the only way to stop 'em was to use my gun, there was so many people between me and the hack that I didn't dare to shoot."

"Maybe shooting would've been a mistake anyway, unless it was a sure shot. The way it stands now, Blount likely didn't see you chasing after him. It wasn't an open hack, was it?"

"No. It was the closed kind, just a little window in

the back. Maybe he didn't spot me, at that." Travers brightened. "If he had, he'd of told the hackman to whip up."

"Chances are, he don't know we're so close to him. We'll dig him up, don't worry. But before we start digging, I got to have some supper." Longarm started for the curb. "Come on. Let's put ourselves outside of a big steak. We'll work out what to do while we're eating." He stopped at the hitching post.

Travers stared at the claybank gelding. "How the devil did you get that horse over here with you?"

"On the little boat I hired to sail me over. Why?"

"Because I had to leave mine behind, damn it! They wouldn't let me take it on board the ferry."

"Chances are you won't need it. There's hacks we can hire."

"Yeah." Travers's voice was bitter. "Except when you need one so bad you can taste it."

Longarm freed the reins and stepped off the curb. "I'll lead the gelding, we'll walk. There ought to be a place close by where we can eat."

"I don't see how you can be hungry. I've lost my appetite, maybe for good."

They began walking. Longarm said, "Forget about your bad luck. We'll find Blount and the woman. Don't forget, we're on an island here. There's no way they can get off, except on a ship." He stopped suddenly.

Travers said bitterly, "That just occurred to you, I guess. I've had a while to think about it. What if they sail out before we catch up with 'em? There's a dozen ships goes out of this port every day, heading everywhere in the world."

"That just means we'll have to find 'em fast, before they catch on we've followed 'em here," Longarm said.

"I wish you wouldn't act so damn cheerful about this mess." Travers shook his head mournfully. "You're making me feel worse than if you got cussing mad."

"What good would that do? I'm not—" Longarm didn't finish what he'd been about to say. He pointed ahead. "There's a restaurant, over on the other side of the street. You feel like giving it a try? It might not be much good, but I'm hungry enough to risk it."

"Makes me no difference. Whatever I eat right now's going to taste like horseshit anyhow."

They ate in silence until halfway through the meal, when Longarm suddenly said, "You've handled cases in Galveston before. What's the police force here like?"

"I don't know all that much about it. You know how the rangers work. Like you do. We don't mix with local police unless things get out of hand pretty bad." Travers's eyes narrowed. "Look here, Long, if you're thinking about asking for help, forget it. Blount killed a ranger, and we handle our own cases. We don't go begging anybody to give us a hand when one of our boys has been murdered."

"I'm not thinking about help. We need information."

"You'd play hell getting any you could trust from the Galveston cops. You tagged this town back before we started for it: it's a crook's town, always has been. Hell, you got to remember, it was one of them pirate brothers, the Lafittes, that started the settlement here. It's wide open, and you know what that means."

The tall deputy marshal let out a sigh. "Yep. Crooked lawmen."

"I got the idea, when I was here before, that the local folks is sorta proud of the reputation their town's got. Anyway, it seems like nobody wants to put a lid on it."

Longarm nodded. He'd seen wide-open towns elsewhere, and what he'd seen prompted his next remark. "In a town like this one, there's always a big man down in the open district. He's the one that settles fusses the law can't be called in on, fixes bail for the district people that get in trouble. He's the man I'm looking for."

"If there's a man like that here, I don't know who it is."

"I didn't expect you would. Like you said, you rangers don't mix up in things a city police force generally handles. But there's man like that that here, and he's the one I want to find."

151

"You go bringing the locals into this, and whatever deal we had between us is off, Long."

"You mean you'll welsh on me?"

"Not unless you make me. Which is what you'd be doing."

"I don't see it that way."

"Well, I sure as hell do!"

"All right. I guess I can find him on my own."

"Now wait a minute! If we're going to keep working together, we'll go all the way or not at all."

"You're in damn poor shape to say that, Travers." Longarm's voice was steel-cold. "You're the one who let Blount slip away, not me." It was a dirty punch, and he knew it, but he had to bring Travers into line. When the ranger sat sullenly silent, Longarm said, "All right. I'll make a deal with you. No local police, but I'll go down to the district myself to find the man I want."

"How?"

"I don't know how, yet. I'll find him, though."

"All it sounds to me like what you've got in mind is fishing around, wasting time."

"You're entitled to your opinion." Longarm's patience was wearing thin. "Maybe you were right a minute ago, when you said you wanted to call off the deal we've got."

"It's a hell of a poor deal, if it don't work both ways. You expect me to bull ahead whichever way you want to go. Well, I'm damned if I'm going to let you be the one to call all the shots!"

"If you'll think back a ways, Travers, you'll remember that whatever I've wanted to do's turned out to be right. If I'd let you call the shots back in Round Rock, we'd be way the hell up on the Red River now, waiting for Blount to show up, and he'd be laughing up his sleeve at us here in Galveston. Then, after I figured out which way he was going to run, and we caught up with him, you let him give you the slip. Or did you?"

"Just what the hell do you mean by that?"

"You take it any way you want. You're out to get Blount for the rangers, so he can stand trial in Texas. I want to take him back to Denver for a federal trial.

It seems damned funny to me that you'd let him get out of your sight when he and Francy joined up at the ferry dock."

"You calling me a liar, Long?"

"Like I just said, take it any way you want."

"I don't have to stand for that from any man, U.S. marshal or not." Travers stood up and tossed his crumpled napkin on the table. "We've got no more deal, Long. You go after Blount on your own. I'll go after him my way."

"That suits me fine!" Longarm was almost as angry as the ranger.

"And me too! I've stood about all your fancy jawbone I can!"

"And I got no use for a man that sneaks around behind my back and tries to take advantage of me in a deal he wasn't smart enough to set up!"

"If you mean I'm lying to you about losing Blount, Long, you're wrong. Right this minute, I don't know where they are, any more'n you do. And that's a fact!"

"All right, Travers. Maybe I was too quick to accuse you of lying. But it don't change anything, does it?"

"No. I'd say we've both got our bellies full of each other."

Longarm nodded. "That's about the way of it. At least we know where we stand."

"You remember one thing, though. You might be smarter than me; maybe you'll even find Blount before I do. You'll never get him out of Texas, though. If you take him first, I'll see that every damned ranger on the force turns out to keep you from getting him to the border!"

Travers turned and stamped out of the cafe. Longarm sat without moving and watched him disappear through the door.

Chapter 14

When Travers was out of sight, Longarm pushed away what was left of his steak. He hadn't exactly lost his appetite, but thinking had suddenly become more important to him than eating. He caught the waiter's eye and motioned him to the table.

"Yes, sir? What can I get you?"

"A bottle of Maryland rye. I know you got some over there at your bar; I had a sip before we sat down to eat."

"Yes, sir. Right away."

For the better part of an hour, Longarm sat sipping the sturdy whiskey and letting his thoughts flow. The restaurant emptied as the night grew later, until he looked around and realized that he was the only one left, besides the waiter and the cashier. They were both eyeing him, and signs of impatience were beginning to show on their faces. Longarm signaled to the waiter.

"I guess it's getting on for closing time, and I hate to hold you folks up, but I'm a U.S. marshal on a case, and I've got to ask you for some help." Longarm took out his wallet and showed the man his badge. The waiter was visibly impressed.

"We'll do what we can, Marshal. Just tell me what you need."

"First off, I'll be obliged if you'll close up. Then, if you got a newspaper and a pair of scissors and some paste, I'll appreciate getting the use of your table for a few minutes. Oh yes, if you got some folding money in the till, I'll swap you gold for it."

"Of course, Marshal." If Longarm's requests seemed strange to him, the waiter managed to keep a straight face. "I'll get them for you. How much currency will you need?"

"I got about a hundred dollars in double eagles. That'd be five twenties, if you got that many."

Within minutes, everything Longarm had asked for was on the table. He folded the newspaper the length of the sheet and, using one of the twenty-dollar bills as a pattern, cut the newspaper into four stacks of rectangles the exact size of the bill. Then he cut thin strips from the newspaper's margins that were left over, and, after putting a bill on the top and bottom of each stack, wrapped the strips around the stacks to make packets of equal thickness. At a glance, it looked as though they were twenty-dollar bills bundled by a bank into packets of a thousand dollars each. He tucked two of the packets into each of the side pockets of his coat, swallowed a final drink, and stood up. The waiter came over at once.

"Will that be all, Marshal?"

"Just one more thing, then I'll leave you and you can go home. Tell me where I'll find a livery stable close by, one I can trust."

After a moment's thought, the waiter said, "You'll be on Center Street when you go out. Go across the street, and turn to the right at the next corner. In the middle of the block, there's a livery stable I'm sure you can depend on."

"Thanks. I guess the man that owns this place is back in the kitchen. While you're figuring up my bill, I'd like to step back there and thank him for a good supper and all the extra service you gave me."

"There is no bill. Marshal. I own the restaurant. I couldn't keep from overhearing you say you're going after the big man who protects local crooks. He collects a tribute from businesses such as mine, you see. He calls it insurance, I call it blackmail. Go after him, Marshal. I'm on your side."

As livery stables went, the one recommended by the restaurant proprietor looked all right to Longarm. He told the liveryman, when he handed over the gelding's reins, "Feed him and water him, and let him stand with a loose girth, but don't unsaddle him. I might need him in a hurry." He indicated the Winchester in its saddle

155

scabbard. "Is that rifle going to be safe here?" He took out his wallet and showed the liveryman his badge. He didn't want to have the man report him as an outlaw who might be planning to run after committing a crime in the neighborhood.

"Your gear'll be safe here, Marshal. You don't need to worry."

Longarm nodded. He was about to put the wallet back in his pocket when a thought occurred to him. He took out the few bills left in it, unpinned the badge and fastened it inside the waistband of his trousers, then dropped the wallet into one of his saddlebags.

As he left the livery stable and headed for the waterfront, Longarm wasted no energy by hashing over in his mind the break he and Travers had made. He'd already decided, before going into the restaurant, that with the tension between them increased by the ranger's failure to keep on Blount's trail, if there was to be a break it ought to take place before they caught up with Blount as a team. Travers's threats had underlined to Longarm the wisdom of their parting. He wasn't making the mistake of underestimating Travers, but at the same time, he was willing to gamble that the ranger couldn't win the race they were now running to be first to nab their common quarry.

Lighting a cheroot, Longarm left a cloud of fragrant smoke behind him in the warm, moist night air. He thought, *Sure, it's a gamble, old son. But hell, everything is anyhow. And maybe I ain't got much to gamble with but that cardsharp's bankroll and a lot of gall. But after all these years spent catching crooks, I found out one thing about 'em for sure. Crooks feel safest when they're in places where there's others on the wrong side of the law. And since I'm looking for a crook on the run, that's the kind of place I got to go to pick up his trail.*

If he'd thought the waterfront district was crowded and rowdy when he'd passed through it earlier, Longarm discovered that he'd underestimated. Now, toward midnight, the streets were packed even more thickly. The kerosene flares and reflector lanterns in front of the saloons and gambling halls and the bright red lights that marked the whorehouses shone even more garishly,

156

and at some of the joints, barkers had been stationed outside to steer prospects to the games, girls, and liquor behind the doors.

Close to the spot he judged to be the district's center, Longarm stopped. He stood and let the pleasure-seekers jostle him while he studied the signs, trying to decide which of the saloons or gambling joints looked the most promising as a starting point. The places had an appearance of sameness about them, which certainly wasn't true of the men who crowded the streets.

There were sailors wearing billed cloth caps and tasseled, knit stocking caps; dockworkers and roustabouts in sweat-stained dungarees; cowhands wearing tight-legged pants over high-heeled boots and with Stetsons on their heads; farmers in overalls and straw hats; city-dwellers from all levels of society, from pale, ageless men clad in shabby, shiny serge coats to florid-faced men dressed in obviously expensive tailored suits. Some of them walked with a purpose, heading for places they visited regularly; others were obviously trying to decide which of the joints would give them the most action for the amount of money they could afford to spend.

And a lot of 'em's going to be real damn sick tomorrow, he reflected. *They're going to learn you got to pay a price when you go out to see the elephant and listen to the owl.*

He decided, after a few minutes' study, that he wasn't going to be able to hit the place he wanted to find with his first shot. With a shrug, he went into the nearest gambling house.

In spite of the crowds on the street, there were few players inside. A table of euchre was fully filled in a corner just inside the door, and a monte table on the other side was getting a little play. The roulette layout that dominated the center of the room had a handful of bettors, and at the back, a dice table was holding the attention of three or four men with its over-under-seven layout. There were only five poker players at the round table nearest the bar, and after he'd given the other games a quick glance, Longarm walked over to the poker table and watched until the hand being played was finished.

"You got room for one more?" he asked the dealer.

In reply, the man waved to one of the empty chairs. "Sit in, my friend. Table stakes, and no shy bets. Jackpots. House takes even hands. If that's the kind of game you're looking for, you've found it."

"Just let me get something to wet my whistle with, and I'll join in with you." Longarm turned to the bar.

"No need to go over there," the dealer said. "You'll have a drink served by the house as soon as you sit down. After that, you pay for what you want, of course."

"Well, that's right nice." Longarm settled into one of the vacant chairs. The barman came over to the table, and stood waiting until Longarm said, "Maryland rye. Just like it comes out of the bottle."

He fished through his pockets when the house man rattled chips suggestively. He let the dealer glimpse his Mississippi bankroll briefly while he dug deep into his right-hand pocket and produced the three twenty-dollar gold pieces he'd had left after leaving the restaurant. "These'll be enough to get me started," he said, tossing the double eagles across to the dealer. "I'll save the folding money till I need it."

Longarm had counted on winning one or two of the first hands played, and the dealer didn't disappoint him. He took the second hand with a low straight, and the fourth with three queens. Both pots were small, though, and Longarm decided it was time to make his play.

"This damn game's too slow," he told the dealer. "Cash me in. I come in here looking for a faro layout, where a man can get some quick action for his money. Only you ain't got one, so I guess I'll go find someplace that has."

"Now, I hate to see you go away feeling unsatisfied, friend," the dealer said. "Especially since you're a stranger in town."

"How'd you know that?"

"If you'd been to Galveston before, you'd know where to find the kind of game you're looking for," the man replied. Then he added, "Now I'll tell you something for your own good, friend. A man carrying the size roll you are wants to get in a game he's sure is

158

straight. If you don't mind me doing you a favor, I'll tell you where you can find it."

"Well, I'd take that right kindly," Longarm said.

Dropping his voice, the dealer said, "Turn right when you go outside. Middle of the next block, you'll see a black door without any sign on it, just a number, 33. Tell the doorman that Roger sent you. He'll fix you up."

Longarm took his time leaving and walking to the next block. He was certain that the dealer had sent a runner ahead to alert whoever ran the place known as "33," and he wanted to be sure the runner got there ahead of him. Apparently his delay did what he'd intended it to, for when he mentioned the name "Roger" to the burly individual who opened the door marked 33, there was no delay whatever in swinging it wide for him to enter. He stepped into a small, bare room.

"If you're carrying a gun, sir, I'll have to ask you to check it with me," the doorman said.

He was polite but firm, and his eyes were fixed on the bulge of Longarm's Colt made under his coat. Longarm saw that he didn't have much choice.

"Might as well give you my whole rig, then." He unbuckled his gunbelt and handed it over. "You give out a check or something?"

"No, sir. I'll remember it's yours, though, when you get ready to leave. Now I'll just introduce you to Miss Elsie, and leave you to get acquainted. She'll see that you're taken care of properly."

Miss Elsie turned out to be a henna-rinsed woman of uncertain age and obviously corseted architecture. Her hair approached the hue of ketchup; her skin was the color of a white china plate; her eyes were the green of peas fresh from the garden; her lips were like strawberries at their ripest during the hour or so when they reach their peak, before they begin to grow soft. The rouge on her cheeks matched that on her lips, and the lining-pencil used to darken her eyebrows, as well as the mascara on her lashes, would have been kinder if it had been a shade lighter. Her face was round, though not as round as the breasts that had been squeezed into a corset an inch or so too small to contain them; they bulged lavishly outward, overflowing the bodice of her green satin dress that squeezed inward at the waist, then flared over high, broad hips and swept, in shimmering cascades of sequins, to the floor. She could have been any age beyond thirty. For all that, Longarm found her interesting in an overpowering sort of way.

"Now, you just call me Elsie," she said. "And instead of you giving me the kind of false name most men use when they come in here to have a good time away from the wife and kiddies, I'll just call you honey."

"If you'd feel more at home doing that, Elsie, why it suits me." Privately, Longarm thought Elsie probably had a bad memory for names, and called all men by the same nickname to avoid possible embarrassment.

"Now you tell me what you want, and I'll see that you get it," Elsie went on. "If you'd like to go in and try your luck at one of the games, that's what we'll do. And if you'd rather go into one of the little private parlors and sit down and have a drink or two before you play, we can do that. Or if there's something else you'd rather do first, we can go up to my room."

"I like all them things, Elsie," Longarm said. "But I got a real urge to double the money I picked up when I split a partnership a little while ago, so why don't we go look at the tables?"

"Then you come right along with me, honey." Elsie slid her hand into the crook of Longarm's elbow and guided him through the doorway into a quietly luxurious chamber, deeply carpeted, papered with pale blue flocked wallpaper, and lighted by globed gas lamps over the eight or ten gaming tables that were spaced around it, and by crystal gas sconces dotted along the walls.

In contrast to the first gambling house Longarm had visited, this one was well occupied, and almost without exception, the players looked as though they could afford to lose whatever sum the house took them for. Aside from the rattle of the balls in the two roulette tables that were spinning simultaneously at separate tables, and an occasional voice raised in calling a raffle at the chuck-luck table, the room was very quiet.

"What was it you were telling me about closing a big deal?" Elsie asked as they walked slowly around the room.

"Oh, I done all right." Longarm took Elsie's hand and slipped it into his coat pocket, letting her feel the two Mississippi bankroll packets it contained. "Them's twenties. Bank run out of big bills, so I had to take some chickenfeed. There's more in the pocket on the other side."

"Oh my, you really did make a killing, honey!" Elsie said.

"And I aim to double my money, if you got the right kind of faro game going."

"You'll find it's one you'll like," she assured him.

They reached the faro table and stopped. Longarm said. "I don't play until after I watch for a minute or two. If I don't get a good feeling, I move on."

"I sure hope you don't feel like moving on from here," Elsie told him, squeezing his arm. "I like big, strong men like you. They make me feel all hot inside."

"You're just telling me that," Longarm replied. "Now, you just stand by me quiet for a minute, while I study out how the cards are running. I never buck the tiger in faro till I've done that."

Ten or twelve players were crowded up to the table, which had the traditional layout of the spade suit painted on its green felt surface. The slowest of them in placing his bet was a tall white-haired man wearing the gold-braided blue coat of a sea captain. He dropped his markers to play the ten three ways to win and the five to lose. The dealer glanced around the table and called, "No more bets, gents!"

One of his hands had been resting on the shuffle board on which the draw box stood. He raised the hand and waved it, then let it stay on the draw box for a split-second while he took another look at the layout. Then he slid the exposed card off the top of the draw box and dropped it in hoc, revealing the newly exposed card in the draw box with the same motion. The card was a five. There was only one marker on the five painted on the layout.

"Sorry, but you're whipsawed, captain," the dealer said, sweeping up all the markers except the one belonging to the player who'd bet the five to win. He dropped two markers on the winning card, and the player who'd bet it picked up his winnings.

Still addressing the big loser, the dealer went on, "Your luck's changed in the last hour, captain. That's too bad. I'll tell you what. It's time to call the turn, and I'll give you back some of the money you've dropped."

"I'll take you up on that," the captain said. "Right now, four-to-one odds look good to me." He studied the case-keeper's frame for a moment. "You've got the nine, ten, and jack left in the box. I'll take them to come up in reverse order." He dropped a marker on each of the cards on the layout, starting with the Jack.

Longarm had spotted the game as rigged the moment he saw the extra-thick shuffle board; the dealer's momentary hesitation while he'd had his hand on the draw box had confirmed the crooked play. He'd seen those extra-thick shuffling boards before; inside was an ingenious spring mechanism that could slide out into the dealer's hand any one of six cards he chose from a selection inside the board's hollow interior. The dealer, choosing a card that on the layout had the lowest bet or no bets at all, palmed the card from the shuffle board and slipped it dexterously into the draw box to be exposed on the next turn.

While the dealer was asking the other players which of them wanted to call the turn differently from the captain's choice, Longarm said to Elsie, "I'll wait till after the shuffle before I start bucking the tiger. There's only three cards left in this draw. Why don't you go get us something to drink while we're waiting? You get whatever you like best for yourself, and make mine Maryland rye."

"Why, sure, honey," Elsie smiled. She held out a hand, and Longarm fished out a gold eagle to put in it. "Now don't you go running off," she said coyly as she turned to go. "I'll be back in just a minute."

At the table, the players had finished betting. The dealer had been resting his hand on the shuffle board, as before, while he'd waited. He brought the hand up in the short wave indicating that betting was closed, and again hesitated with the hand on the draw box while he looked over the layout. Then he exposed the next card in the draw box. It was a ten.

"Hard luck, captain!" he said. "You should've waited for this turn to bet the ten."

"Yes. Too bad I didn't." The captain turned to leave the layout and the dealer asked, "Not giving up, are you? Your luck's bound to change after the shuffle."

"Oh, I'll be back," the captain told him. "I'm just not interested in split odds on those last two cards."

Longarm had been trying to decide just how he was going to create the kind of disturbance he had in mind, one that would get the attention of the owner of the gambling joint. His plan, when he'd set out to find the boss of the waterfront district, had been to create a ruckus that would attract the attention of the man he sought. A disgruntled loser might be the key, and he had one handy in the person of the sea captain. As the captain turned away from the faro table, Longarm slid a cigar from his vest pocket and made quick work of biting off the end. When the captain started past him, he put a hand on the man's blue-sleeved arm.

"Excuse me, captain. Can I trouble you for a light?"

"Why, of course." The captain took a metal match case from his pocket and began fumbling with the lid.

While the captain was working at removing the match case's waterproof top, Longarm said in a low voice, "You're in a crooked game. I don't mean to butt into your affair, but there just ain't a way in the world for you to win at that table."

"Who are you? Why are you telling me this?" the seafarer asked.

"That don't matter. I'm just doing you a favor. You make up your own mind whether you want to call these crooks or not."

Distracted, the captain had forgotten Longarm's request for a match. Longarm saw that the faro dealer was watching them. In a voice loud enough to carry to the table, he said, "Too bad you can't get at your matches, but thanks just the same."

He walked away, leaving the captain staring after him, then went to one of the players at the faro table and repeated his request for a light. As soon as he had the cheroot glowing, he stepped back.

Elsie returned with the drinks. Longarm downed his while she was still sipping at the frothy whiskey sour she'd gotten for herself. He kept an eye on the faro table. The dealer had turned another card and was waiting for bets to be placed on the last draw. Longarm told Elsie, "If I'm going to get in that game after the shuffle, I better find me a bathroom right now."

"Of course, honey. It's that door over in the corner at the back of the room. You go ahead, I'll wait right here."

Just as Longarm reached for the knob, the door of the bathroom opened and the captain came out. He said, "If it's not asking too much, tell me how you know that faro game's rigged."

Longarm looked around, making sure there was no one within earshot. In as few words as possible, he explained how the cheating had been done. "It gives the house two times the odds it'd get in an honest game," he concluded. "When you got whipsawed a while ago, the dealer done that on purpose. If it was me, I'd brace the boss of this place and get my money back."

"No, I won't do that," the captain said slowly. "But if you hadn't warned me, I'd be back to that table to lose some more. I'm grateful to you. My name's Summers, by the way. My ship's the *Falcon*. If you're down that way, step aboard. I feel that I owe you something, Mr.—"

"My name don't matter," Longarm said quickly. "Now, if you'll excuse me, I got urgent business in that toilet."

In the privacy of the bathroom, Longarm frowned thoughtfully as he stood in front of the urinal. He wasn't going to get the argument started that he'd hoped for; now he had to find another way to smoke out the man he was trying to find. Looking at his image in the mirror as he buttoned his fly, he said to himself, *Well, old son, I guess whoever said it first got it right. You want to get a job done, the only way to go about it is to do it yourself.*

Chapter 15

Elsie was showing signs of impatience when Longarm got back. "If you're going to play on this draw, you'd better hurry up and buy your markers," she said. "He's already shuffled and put the deck in the box."

"Well, you stay close by and bring me luck," Longarm told her. He stepped up to the table, pulling two of the packets of his Mississippi bankroll from his pocket. He slapped them on the edge of the layout. When the dealer looked at him, Longarm asked challengingly, "What's your limit on this table, mister?"

"Fifty on one-card bets, twenty on combinations," the man replied. "You ready to buy in?"

"Not yet, I ain't. I don't play piking games. You take that limit off, and I'll buck your tiger till hell freezes over."

"Sorry, I can't raise the limit. The boss is the only one who can do that."

"You get him out here, then. Maybe he'll accommodate me when he sees I've got what I need to back my play." Longarm waved the packets of paper in front of the dealer's face. "And this is just part of it." He saw the man's eyes flicker toward Elsie and turned in time to catch the tiny nod with which she replied.

"I'll see what I can do," the dealer said. He jerked his head at the casekeeper. "See if he wants to accommodate the gent." The casekeeper left, and the dealer told the other players, "It'll be a minute or two before we start the next draw. If you'll tell the lady your pleasure, the house will buy you a drink while you're waiting." As the players were drifting away to give Elsie their orders, the dealer said to Longarm, "I imagine the boss will be glad to accommodate you. I know I sure would, if it was up to me."

165

"I'll just bet you would," Longarm said with a smile. The smile didn't reach his eyes. "But maybe your boss won't say yes so quick, when I tell him I want a new draw box and shuffle board before I buy in."

"If you've got something on your mind, come out with it. Don't beat around the bush," the dealer snapped.

"I figure you know what I mean. I been watching you deal."

Frowning, the dealer called, "Elsie! I need to talk to you before you take those orders to the barkeep!"

Elsie went to the dealer and he whispered to her. She started off in the direction the casekeeper had taken, looking over her shoulder at Longarm as she walked. Her face was anything but serene. Longarm said nothing and looked above the dealer's head at a spot somewhere between the faro table and the back wall.

Elsie and the casekeeper came back to the table together. The casekeeper went to the dealer and said something in a low voice. Elsie kept her face turned, avoiding Longarm's eyes. The casekeeper finished his conversation with the dealer and came over to Longarm.

"You mind stepping over to the office with me, mister? The boss wants to talk to you a minute," he said.

"You lead the way. I'll be right behind you."

The office into which the casekeeper ushered him was gray. Walls, ceiling, carpet, curtains, all were in shades that ranged from pearl to thundercloud gray. The desk and chairs continued the color motif. So did the man sitting behind the desk. His suit was flawlessly tailored of dark gray cheviot; his shirt was the palest possible ash; his cravat was a smoke gray that was almost black. The man's skin was as gray as his suit. Only his eyes and hair contrasted with the unremitting gray of the man's office and clothing, to startling effect. Both were midnight black, and the eyes had the obsidian opacity that is usually seen only in the lidless eyes of a snake.

On the desk in front of the gray-black man lay Longarm's gunbelt, with his .44 Colt, which he'd surrendered to the doorman, lying beside the holster. He was tempted to scoop up the Colt, but his good sense told him he'd be making a fool's move if he did so.

Ignoring Longarm, the man asked the casekeeper, "Did you make sure he's clean?"

"No, sir. I didn't think it'd look right to the customers if I did it where they could watch."

"You're right. Do it now. Then you can go."

Quickly, with practiced fingers, the casekeeper patted Longarm's beltline and armpits, turned back his cuff to be sure he didn't have a sleeve-gun, then ran his hands down his legs to feel for a knee-holster or a boottop knife sheath. Longarm kept his face expressionless and submitted to the search.

"He's clean," the casekeeper said. The gray man nodded and waved a hand. The casekeeper left.

"You can sit down," the gray man told Longarm. When Longarm reached for the nearest chair to move it opposite the desk, he added sharply, "I said sit down, I didn't say move the chair."

Without replying, Longarm sat down.

The man leaned forward, placing his forearms on the desktop and his fingertips together. "Now. Tell me why you came here," he said. "You're no mechanic, even if you are sharp enough to spot my dealer's move." When Longarm still said nothing, the man picked up the Colt. "Your gun gives you away. Only a professional files off the front sight this way. Who sent you?"

"Nobody sent me. I walked in under my own steam."

"Stop sparring with me. What's your name?"

"You wouldn't know it," Longarm replied.

"Try me out; I might surprise you. I know a lot of names of men I've never seen." When Longarm said nothing, he went on, "Very well. Tell me my name."

"I'd like to be able to. If I'd known it, I wouldn't've had to act like a fool outside, there."

Slowly, the gray man nodded. "I see. Not a bad idea. You might never have gotten in to see me if you hadn't."

"That's how I figured it. Sorry if I gave your people a bad time, but you just said why I had to do it."

"Are you trying to tell me you came in here without knowing who to ask for? Or whether you were even in the right place?"

"That's about the size of it."

"You took a long chance."

"Not so long. I knew you had a place down here in the district. Hell, when I heard about you, I didn't think I'd ever need to look you up. I don't even recall who it was told me about you, or where. Might've been one of the Casey boys up in the Nation. Might've been Tod Hunter over in Arkansas, or Sim Blount, or Lem Giles."

"You're damned free with everybody's name except your own."

"If you've got to call me something, Jones is as good as anything else, until I'm sure about a few things."

"Tell me what they are."

"I've heard you're good at finding a man a hole he can duck in and pull closed after him, or getting him out of the country."

"I thought that might be what brought you here, after I saw your gun. I'm surprised you handed it over at the door."

"I was close enough by then to figure I wasn't taking too much of a risk."

"Where is it you're wanted?"

"Now, you know better than to ask me that," Longarm countered.

The man leaned back in his chair and shrugged.

"I can't help you unless I know the whole story."

Longarm shook his head. "Not now. Not until we set a price. Maybe not the whole story then."

For a moment, the gray man seemed about to ask something else. Then he smiled, a quick twitch of his thin gash of a mouth. He picked up the Colt. "How good are you with this?"

"That's a fool question. If I say I'm good, you'll wonder if I'm bragging. If I say I ain't, you'll know I'm lying. Best I can tell you is I know which end to hold it by and where to point it when I got to use it. And where the lead's going to hit when I pull the trigger. That satisfy you?"

"Better than if you'd bragged or acted bashful. I'm

inclined to believe your outlandish story." He laid the Colt back on the desk. "You were naming names a minute ago. You know the men they belong to, I suppose?"

"If I didn't know 'em, I wouldn't name 'em."

"So any of them would know your name? Your face too? And vouch for you? I don't deal blindly, you understand."

"I'll face any of them I named," Longarm said. "There's one or two I'd like to see, and there's one or two I never got along with too good. I can't think of none who'd be around here, though." He frowned. "Hold on. Ed Casey might be. Or Sim Blount. I've heard 'em both mention Galveston."

"If I could produce either of them, would you face them?"

"Try me." Longarm knew the gray man couldn't produce Casey. He'd delivered Casey to Denver just a few days before leaving for Texas. And he'd meant it when he'd said he'd be glad to see Blount.

"Where are you staying?"

"Right here, until you find me a place that's safer."

"I haven't said I'd do that. Or that I can. And safe places for a man like you cost money, I don't have to tell you that."

"Name a figure. It don't have to be cheap. I'd imagine the girl, or one of your men, already told you I can afford to pay."

"You've got about four thousand in bank-banded currency in your coat pockets."

Longarm smiled thinly. "Your folks don't miss a bet. Ain't that enough loose change for a man to carry?"

"It's a start." The gray man sat thinking for a few moments, then he said, "I'm going to take a chance on you." He raised his voice slightly. "You can come in now, Zilker."

A panel in the wall behind the desk slid open and the man who'd been on duty at the door when Longarm arrived stepped into the room, holstering his pistol. He pressed a toe hard on the carpet in front of the opening and the panel closed noiselessly. Longarm kept his face impassive.

169

"Take this man over to the Clark Street house," the gray man instructed Zilker. "He says Blount will vouch for him. Sim will tell you his name when he sees him. If Sim says he's all right, bring him back here, and we'll put him up at Angelina's, if he's willing to pay for his keep."

"What if Sim don't come through for him?"

"Then bring back the money he's got in his pockets."

Longarm knew what had been left unsaid. He decided it was time for him to improve his chances. "Sim's going to come through. And I feel right lonesome without that Colt. If somebody who knows me happens to spot me and throws down on me, I'll feel downright naked."

"You don't have to worry. Zilker will handle anybody who gives you trouble."

"I never looked to another man to nursemaid me. If somebody gets in my way, I'd sooner handle things myself."

"There's not much chance you'll run into anyone at this time of night," the gray man pointed out. He hesitated, looked at the Colt, and picked it up. "Still, I can understand how you feel." He handed the revolver to Zilker. "Unload it and let him carry it. If Sim passes him, give him the cartridges." While Longarm strapped on his gunbelt, Zilker unloaded the Colt's cylinder and dropped the shells from it into his hamlike hand, then put them in his pocket and handed the empty revolver to Longarm.

Longarm looked at the gun for a moment, nodded at the gray man, and said, "Well, I got half a gun here. I guess you're due half of a thank you." He holstered the Colt and turned to Zilker. "I'm ready whenever you are."

Zilker motioned for Longarm to walk ahead of him. They went through the main gambling room and out onto the street. Longarm noticed, as they passed through the entry, that Zilker's place as guardian of the door had been taken by another man about his equal in bulk and features. He wondered how many plug-uglies the gray man had working for him.

Outside, the crowds had diminished somewhat, but there were still enough men wandering around to fill the narrow street. The lights still flared, and the touts in front of the doorways still buttonholed those passing by and tried to persuade them to sample the diversions within.

"We'll take a hack," Zilker said as they left the bustle of the district and turned into a quieter thoroughfare. The only light here was provided by the elongated yellow rectangles that showed at the tops and bottoms of saloon batwing doors. A hack or two stood in front of most of the saloons, while the horses that drew the boxy carriages stood patiently, getting a bit of rest while the hackies refreshed themselves inside.

Zilker pushed open the batwings of the first saloon they came to and called, "Hackie!" When the driver came out, wiping his lips, Zilker told him, "Drop us at the corner of Clark and 18th." He let Longarm get into the cab, then followed him, sitting on the seat behind the driver; the two men faced one another in the high-topped enclosed carriage.

After the hack had rattled over the woodblock paving for several minutes, Longarm asked Zilker, "How far away is this place we're going to?"

"We'll be there soon enough," Zilker answered curtly. "What difference does it make? You're not going anywhere else."

"Just curious." When they'd ridden a short distance farther, he asked, "What's your boss's name, anyhow? I never did catch it."

"If he'd wanted you to know, he'd of told you."

From then on, Longarm gave up trying to pry any information out of his guard. There were a lot of things he'd hoped to learn on the way to Blount's hideout, but it was pretty apparent that he'd get no help from the close-mouthed Zilker.

Woodblock pavement gave way to gravel. The hack's wheels crunched and grated for a while as they rolled over the pebbles, then the grating suddenly stopped and they were rolling silently on an unpaved street. Shortly after they'd left the pavement, the hackie pulled up his horse. He flipped open the slide that separated the driver's seat from the passenger compartment and said, "Here's your corner. You want me to come back for you or wait? If I wait, I'll have

171

to charge you an extra two bits, but if you're going back to town tonight, it's going to be a long walk before you'll pick up a hack."

"You better wait," Zilker said, handing the driver a dollar bill. "That'll pay for the trip and your time and the ride back to town." To Longarm he said, "I'll get out first. Then you'll walk in front of me, straight up Clark Street. I'll tell you which house to go into."

Even before he'd maneuvered the gray man into bringing him face-to-face with Blount, Longarm had realized the risks he'd be taking and had chosen to accept them. He was luckier than he might have been, he thought as he got out of the hack and set off in the direction Zilker had ordered him to take. The gray man could have had Blount brought to the gambling hall to identify Longarm. It hadn't been a likely possibility, but it could have happened that way. As it worked out, he was in a reasonably good situation. At least he'd have only Zilker and Blount—and perhaps Francy—to handle. He'd faced a lot bigger odds before.

Here, the isolation of the neighborhood was on his side. As he got out of the hack, he could see that the street was sparsely settled. The houses were few and spaced widely apart; vacant lots stood between many of them. None of the dwellings were lighted. The moon hadn't yet risen. There were no sidewalks, and the big deputy marshal, walking a step or so ahead of Zilker, had to feel his way along the narrow dirt trail that pedestrians had beaten through the coarse sawgrass that grew from the houses down to the unpaved street.

As soon as he'd seen how few houses there were, Longarm knew that until Zilker had led him to the very door of the hideout, he'd be unable to take any kind of action. Without Zilker, he'd have no way of knowing which of the houses was being used by Blount—and presumably, by Francy as well—until they were at their destination. He'd need good timing and more than a sprinkling of luck, he thought, to immobilize Zilker and take Blount.

"All right," Zilker said after they'd passed the first four houses and several lots on which no houses stood.

"It's the next place. Go up on the porch, but don't knock. Let me do that."

He's got some kind of signal, then, Longarm thought. *That ain't good. Cuts me shorter on time than I'd figured.*

Zilker rapped on the door three times, paused, rapped twice, paused again, then rapped once. Longarm was ready when the big plug-ugly let his arm fall to his side. He snaked his watch chain through his hand and lifted his derringer from the vest pocket where it had stayed hidden through the two searches he'd undergone earlier. Zilker had stepped in front of Longarm to knock, and now the lawman pressed the cold muzzle of the derringer to the man's neck, just behind his jawbone.

"Stand real still, Zilker. Don't even bat an eye, and don't say a word, or you won't live long enough to say another one."

"You're bluffing. I've got the shells out of your gun."

"I've got another gun, Zilker. Stand still and keep quiet." Longarm dropped his voice in mid-sentence because he'd heard footsteps shuffling toward the door.

Zilker heard them too, and made the mistake of acting on his belief that Longarm was trying to bluff him with an unloaded gun. He grabbed for the pistol that he wore high on his right side. Longarm had no choice. He triggered the derringer.

Pressed hard against Zilker's neck as the little pistol was, its report was no louder than a cough. Zilker slumped, dead. Longarm pushed his crumpling body hard against the wall and shuffled his feet on the porch floor to press against the corpse with his own body, holding the limp form almost erect.

Longarm released his grip on the derringer and let it dangle from his watch chain. He reached under Zilker's coat from behind and yanked out the dead man's gun. He wasn't about to find himself face-to-face with Simaeus Blount armed with a derringer that now had a live load in only one of its twin barrels.

He got his hand on the gun just in time. The door swung open in a burst of yellow lamplight. A sleepy-eyed Blount, wearing a nightshirt, and holding a lamp

173

in one hand and a revolver in the other, peered out into the blackness of the porch.

Longarm was standing now where he was half-hidden behind Zilker's body. The corpse was slipping slowly to the floor in spite of all the pressure he was putting on it with his own body.

Blount was squinting into the dark, the light from the lamp making him half-blind. He saw Zilker's lolling head.

"What's the matter with you, Zilker?" he asked. "Are you drunk?"

Longarm chose that instant as the time to move. He stepped back and let Zilker's corpse continue to crumple downward. Blount's eyes instinctively followed the falling body.

That was what Longarm had counted on. He took no chances. Stepping forward, he swung the revolver he'd taken from Zilker in a roundhouse blow that caught Blount squarely on the side of the head. The outlaw grunted and fell like a steer poleaxed by a slaughterhouse executioner. His gun dropped to the floor, and so did the lamp he'd been holding in his other hand.

With the musical tinkle of breaking glass, the lamp's chimney shattered when it hit the floor. Kerosene gushed out from the ventholes around its collar. The wick hadn't been extinguished by the lamp's fall, and the gushing kerosene was ignited; it flared up in puffy clouds of black smoke and tongues of orange-yellow flame.

Longarm had extinguished an occasional out-of-hand campfire by trampling the flames with his booted feet, but he found himself dancing an idiot's jig when he tried to give the kerosene fire the same treatment. It refused to die. As quickly as he'd smothered one patch of blazing carpet with a bootsole and moved to another, the last one reignited.

He wasn't giving his attention to anything but putting out the fire until a woman's voice called, "Sim! What're you doing?"

Francy appeared in the doorway across the room from the entry. She wore a filmy, flowing nightgown that revealed far more than it hid, and suggested as much as it showed. She stopped in the doorway, unable to take in the scene that greeted her eyes. She failed to recognize Longarm at first. She'd seen him only once before, and then for just a few minutes, in the Big Thicket. At that time he'd been without the long Prince Albert coat that now flapped around his knees as he tried to put out the blazing rug.

She started toward Blount, who was still unconscious on the floor. Halfway there, she recognized Longarm. With an angry shriek, she changed course and headed for him.

"Damn you! You've killed Sim and now you're trying to burn me alive!"

Francy ran toward Longarm, her fingers curled into claws, going for his eyes.

Chapter 16

Longarm had stamped out almost all the burning patches of the carpet when Francy came in. When she headed for Blount, he returned to putting out the fire. The room had little light, only the glow that trickled through the partly opened door leading to the back of the house. He didn't see Francy when she changed course and headed for him.

A half-dozen steps away, Francy leaped. Longarm was bending over. She sailed through the air, her night-gown billowing, and landed on his back. An arm went around his neck and she wrapped her legs around his waist. Then, with her free hand, Francy began clawing at Longarm's eyes.

"You son of a bitch!" she screamed. "You've killed Sim, and you're out to do me in next! But I'll tear your eyes out first, your murdering blueback bastard!"

Longarm's quick reactions saved his vision. He grabbed Francy's clawed, threatening hand before it quite reached his face, and yanked it to one side. He let the gun in his other hand fall to the floor and wrenched away the arm she'd wrapped around his neck. Then he whirled, and the sudden speed of his turn shot her body back and down.

Francy hadn't quite managed to get her ankles locked around Longarm's waist. As he kept spinning, she lost her hold, flew across the room, and landed on a patch of carpet that was still smoldering. With a yell of pain, she rolled off the hot spot and began beating at the flimsy material of her nightgown, which was beginning to char and smoke.

Longarm scooped up the gun he'd dropped. Blount was stirring, and Francy was back on her feet, ready to attack again, if he could judge by the glare in her green cat-eyes, slitted now in anger.

"Keep your distance," Longarm warned her. "You being a woman don't get you any special treatment. I'd as soon shoot you as I would him." He jerked his head toward Blount, who was now trying to sit up.

"Oh, I'll just bet you would!" Francy sneered. "Don't worry. I've got a lot of living to do yet. I'll stay where I am."

"That's being smart," Longarm told her. He still kept an eye on her while he stepped over to Blount, grabbed him by an arm, and dragged him clear of the door. Even this late, there was a chance that somebody might walk by and see what was going on. He thought about dragging Zilker's body inside, but decided the risk that anybody would notice the dark shape on the dark porch wasn't great.

Blount was conscious now, swaying on his feet. Longarm got his first really clear look at the outlaw, and didn't like what he saw. Blount was broad everywhere: face, shoulders, belly, and hips. He'd been a brawler, his face showed that. His nose had been smashed, his jaw was lumpy, his brows beetled. His neck was as big around as his bulging jaws were wide. His mouth struck a discordant note; it was small and pursed, with thin, downturned lips. He wore a night-shirt, and from its short sleeves, his arms showed hairy and muscled. So did his legs. He wasn't a man who Longarm thought he'd want to be seen with unless Blount was wearing handcuffs and Longarm was leading him to jail.

Blount raised a hand and felt his head, then rubbed his face. For the first time, he realized what had happened. "Shit!" he grated. "Guess I didn't give you enough credit, Long. How in hell did you find me here? I was pretty damn sure Kester wouldn't sell me out."

"Who's Kester?" Longarm asked, before he realized Blount must be referring to the gray man.

"Don't play me for a fool," Blount snapped. "I heard that code knock he said anybody he sent here would use." He frowned. "And that was Zilker you was standing in back of, when I opened the door. Don't try to tell me Kester didn't tell you where I was. Hell, he even sent his own man along, so I'd be sure to open up."

"I won't tell you anything, Blount," Longarm replied. "If you think you know how I found you, go on and think it. Right now we got other fish to fry. You two start getting into your clothes. We're all going on a little trip."

"You can't take me in!" Francy protested. "I'm not wanted for breaking any law!"

"You're consorting with a known criminal," Longarm told her. "I can arrest you for that and for helping him get away from me, up in the Thicket. Either way, I can stand you up in front of a judge. If he wants to let you off, that'll be up to him."

"Nobody's going to put me in jail on a flimsy charge like that!" she sniffed.

"Maybe, maybe not. That don't change a thing, as far as right now's concerned," Longarm told her. "Come on; we'll get on back to wherever your clothes are. And don't give me any trouble, or I'll take you in just the way you're dressed now."

Blount studied the revolver in Longarm's hand and decided he didn't want to argue with it. He started toward the lighted door. Longarm snapped, "You stay right close to him, Francy. I don't want you two more'n a foot apart."

Francy glared, but obeyed. Longarm followed them into the adjoining room. It was a bedroom, scantily furnished with a double bed, a dresser, and a chair. Clothing lay on the chair and on the floor, and there were a half-dozen bottles, empty as well as unopened, on the dresser. Longarm didn't need to guess very hard to figure out that the pair had been dividing their time between the bed and the bottles.

Get your clothes on now, and make it fast!" Longarm commanded. "I ain't feeling very patient right now."

"You don't mean you're going to stand there and watch while I dress!" Francy said indignantly.

"I wouldn't turn my back on you," Longarm said flatly. "And it's likely I won't be the first man that's seen you in the altogether. Go on and dress, before I decide to march you off in your nightgown."

Francy gave him an ugly look, and made a point of turning her back on him and slipping her shift on over her head, then letting her nightgown fall to the floor. Longarm paid no more attention to her than he did to Blount, who had a distracted look on his face while he pulled on his clothes.

He's working something out, some scheme to get away, Longarm told himself. *And now that I got him, I sure don't want to have to run him to earth again. Damn Travers! I could sure use him now. I didn't figure on having to handle both of 'em at once!*

Neither Blount nor Francy hurried in their dressing. They seemed to be hoping that if they took as long a time as possible, some miracle might take place, and they'd find themselves free. Longarm waited as though he had all night.

Which ain't so far off the mark, he thought. *I still got no more idea than a jackassrabbit where I'm going to take these two. There's times when being stuck on an island can be a downright damn nuisance! Right now, I need me a boat of some kind! Even a rowboat would beat taking 'em to the police. If that Kester fellow didn't find out where they were, Travers might. I'd sure give a pretty piece for my own private navy right now!*

Thinking of ships suddenly reminded him of Captain Summers. He had no idea when the *Falcon* was supposed to sail, but Summers had volunteered to help him, and the captain had seemed grateful enough to be sincere in his offer.

Unless he's like a lot of folks, all blow and no go, Longarm thought. *Sure would work me out of a fix, though, if Summers'd take us to the closest real land. I wouldn't care much where he'd set us ashore, as long as it was away from Galveston. Well, hell, all he can do is say no. I'll just, by God, have to give it a try!*

By the time his two prisoners were dressed, Longarm's plan was fully formed. When they finally faced him, fully clothed, he said, "Now you two lay down there, across the bed. On your faces. Seeing as there's two of you, and I'm by myself without my handcuffs handy, I'll have to tie you up."

Longarm worked as fast as he could; he knew that by now he and Zilker should have finished their errand and returned to the gambling joint. Kester, if that was the gray man's name, was going to start wondering where they were, and if Longarm gauged the underworld boss correctly, he'd send a couple of his plug-uglies out to the house to see what was holding them up. He couldn't afford to waste a bit of time.

He had a bit of trouble tearing a bedsheet into strips without laying down his gun or relaxing his vigilance, but he finally managed to get the job done by grasping the hem of the sheet between his teeth and ripping strips off with his free hand. Then, being careful never to let himself get into a position where he'd be vulnerable to a sudden surprise move by his prisoners, he tied them Shoshone-style.

He lashed Blount's right wrist to Francy's left wrist first. Then he tied her left ankle to Blount's right ankle. He completed the job by tying Blount's left wrist to his left ankle with a twisted strip of sheeting that forced Blount to keep his arm straight down at his left side. Finally he tied Francy's right arm in similar fashion. When he'd finished, neither one of them could bring a hand across to reach either wrist or ankle knots without lying down and contorting their bodies. They could move only by cooperating with one another, yet they'd be able to walk slowly if they were careful.

He helped them to stand up, and watched as the pair tried a few experimental steps around the room. Longarm was satisfied that they'd be unable to escape. Given some time alone and without any interruption, time for them to get used to moving together, they might manage, but Longarm had no intention of giving them that much time. As for running from him once they were outside the house, he'd learned how much a runner depends on his arms for balance, and how difficult it was for two people of different sizes, bound together by their ankles, to keep their steps in unison even at a slow walk.

"All right, that'll do," he told Blount and Francy

when he was satisfied at last. "I'll clean up what few little chores are left to do here, then we'll be ready to go."

"Go where?" Blount demanded. "You got us, but how the hell you think you can keep us? You're a fool, Long. Kester's got his fingers into every pie in Galveston. He gives orders to the police, and they jump. You might as well cut us free now as take us to jail. We'd be out before you'd turned your back."

"Oh, I already figured that was the way of things in this town," Longarm told Blount cheerfully. "Anyhow, I don't cotton to turning over any prisoners of mine to anybody but my chief, in Denver. He's the one who told me to bring you back to him alive, or else you'd be dead by now."

"Denver!" Francy laughed, a few staccato, unladylike snorts. "That's a thousand miles from here! You've got to sleep sometime, Long, and Sim will have us loose before we're halfway there!"

"I'd expect him to try whatever tricks he knows," Longarm replied calmly. "We'll just have to see if his tricks are better'n mine, won't we? Now, I've had about enough jawboning from you two. I'll do my chores, and we'll head out."

His first chore was to reload his Colt, using the shells he always carried loose in his coat pockets. He reloaded the discharged barrel of the derringer at the same time, and replaced the ugly little snub-nosed weapon in his vest pocket. He picked up the revolvers he'd taken from Zilker and Blount and dropped one in each coat pocket. Finally, leaving Blount and Francy to follow at their own slower pace, he opened the front door and dragged Zilker's body inside the house. He took the front door key down from its nail on the wall inside, next to the door, and after Blount and Francy came out to the porch, hobbling and stumbling as they got used to their new style of walking, he locked the front door and tossed the key into the sawgrass that grew thickly in the yard. He saw no need to make it easy for Kester's men when they came to investigate.

After several unsuccessful tries, when their legs didn't move right together, the bound pair managed to get down the steps leading from the porch. Francy had apparently brought no dress besides the black velvet outfit she'd worn away from the Big Thicket, and its long skirt kept tangling them up. She finally got hold of the dress with her right hand and gathered it up to free her feet. Longarm saw right then that he needn't worry too much about the pair outdistancing him if it came to a foot race. He got the feeling, from their swearing struggles, that they'd had some idea of that kind and were finding out that whatever scheme they'd hatched wasn't going to work.

Longarm herded the hobbled couple in front of him along the narrow path until, after several stops to disentangle them from the sawgrass, the little procession moved out into the road. The hack was standing where he'd left it, with the driver curled up on the front seat asleep. Longarm poked the man awake. The hackie's eyes goggled when he saw the strange couple in their bindings, but with the aplomb of cabbies from time's beginning, he recovered at once and accepted it as just one of the unusual situations encountered in the day's work.

"Where you want to go now, mister?" he asked Longarm between yawns.

"There's a livery stable just off the main street. I forget its name. It's close to the big church. Think you can find it?"

"Sure. O'Malley's. Off Center Street, a little ways from the Cathedral. That's where you want to go?"

"That's the first place. After we pick up my horse there, I'll give you the rest of it." Longarm turned to his prisoners. "All right, into the hack with you."

Getting the pair inside took some doing, but they finally maneuvered up the strap-step and into the carriage. Longarm seated Blount and Francy, who were silent now, and glowering angrily, in the back seat. He sat on the seat facing them. The hackie geed his horse and the carriage rolled off.

At the livery stable, Longarm got the claybank and tied its reins to the back axle of the hack. He said to the driver, "You think you can find a ship that's tied up to one of those piers along the waterfront?"

"Mister, you give me its name, I'll take you to it. There ain't anyplace in this town I can't take you to."

"It's the *Falcon*. That's all I know about it."

"You're as good as on board," the hackman assured him.

True to his word, the carriage rumbled hollowly over the planks of a wharf within a few minutes after they'd pulled away from the livery stable. Longarm looked out of the small window in the hack's door, and saw the masts and rigging of ships sliding past. His nerves had tightened when they entered the district, but the passage through it had been without incident.

By now, the gray of dawn was showing. There were only a handful of men on the street. The barkers had called it quits, although the kerosene flares and red lights still shone as brightly as ever. Those still abroad were either too engrossed in their search for pleasure, or too exhausted after having found it, to pay any attention to a solitary hack, even one that was trailed by a saddled claybank gelding.

Longarm heard the rumble of the hack's wheels on the boards of the wharf fade away as the driver reined in. The slide in the end of the carriage opened and the driver's face appeared in the opening.

"There's the ship you're looking for. The *Falcon*."

Longarm leaned forward and looked out. The vessel looked imposing enough; it had three tall masts that swayed gently against the brightening sky. He told the hackie, "Wait for me just a minute. And sort of keep an eye on these two, will you? I don't think they can break loose, but I don't aim to risk it."

"Now wait a minute!" the man protested. "I ain't about to get mixed up in something that might get me into trouble!"

"You'll get in more trouble if you don't watch 'em," Longarm replied. "Look here." He reached for his wallet before remembering he'd left it in his saddlebags and that his badge was pinned inside his trouser waistband. He got the badge free while the driver squinted curiously at Blount and Francy, who were squirming in the back seat. Showing the badge to the driver, Longarm said, "I'm a U.S. marshal, and these two are my prisoners. I'm getting ready to take 'em on that ship. Now do like I told you to, and keep an eye on 'em for me. I won't be gone but a minute."

"Well . . ." the hackman drawled out the word while he made up his mind, but Longarm's badge had tilted the scales. "I guess it's all right. But don't be gone too long. I'm new at this."

From the wharf, the *Falcon* looked deserted, but before Longarm could step from the gangplank to the deck, the sailor on anchor watch appeared out of the wheelhouse. "You looking for somebody, matey? Because if you are, you'd better come back later, when the hands are piped to."

"I'm looking for Captain Summers, and my business won't wait until later." Again the lawman showed his badge. "My name's Long. Me and the captain got acquainted earlier tonight. Just tell him the fellow that saved his wallet's on board asking for him."

"I sure hope he'll be glad to see you," the sailor said. "Captain didn't come back aboard until late. If I roust him out of his bunk now, and you ain't who you say you are, it'll be my ass he'll take it out on."

"Go on and call him," Longarm said. "It'll be tougher on you if he finds out I was here and you didn't let him know."

Summers appeared in a few minutes, pulling on a peajacket over his nightshirt. He recognized Longarm at once. "Why, you're the man—damn it, I don't think you ever told me your name."

"I didn't for a reason, Captain. It's Long, Custis Long. I'm a deputy U.S. marshal out of Denver. Back in that gambling joint, I didn't want anybody to catch on to who I was."

"I see. Well, Marshal, what brings you to the *Falcon*?"

"I suppose you do. What you said about me calling on you for help, or if I needed something—I sure hope you meant it."

"I did. What's your problem? Money? If it is, I've still got some left, thanks to you."

"Maybe what I need right now ain't as easy as money." Using as few words as possible, Longarm sketched his problem. He concluded, "So you see, I got two things going against me. If the Texas Rangers find out I've got those two, they're going to want to take them away from me. I don't think they'd care much more about the woman than I do, but they want Blount to stand trial in Texas. If that fellow Kester catches up with me, he'll do his best to take them away from me, on account of he was supposed to be keeping them where the law wouldn't find them. Either way, I got to get those two off this damn island, or I'm between a rock and a hard place."

Summers said nothing until he'd thought over Long-arm's explanation, then he nodded. "I can see your situation, Marshal. I want to help you every way I can, but I've got to put the interests of the ship's owners first. I'm not due to sail until tomorrow. I've still got freight to unload."

"Captain, it don't matter to me if we go today or tomorrow or the next day, as long as Travers or Kester don't catch up to us."

"I can understand why you'd be worried about the rangers," Summers said. "They're a hard group of men, and they've got the power in Texas to do just about what they want to. But this man Kester's a criminal. Do you really think he'd dare bother you?"

"You ain't met him and talked to him. I got him tagged as a real tough man. He won't let anything stop him from what he sets out to do."

"But why? You didn't hurt him."

"I did, the way he'd look at it. When a crook gets to be a sort of boss, the way Kester is, he can't afford slipups, and he can't let anybody make a fool of him."

"And you caused him to slip up, and made him look stupid."

"I done more than that. I had to shoot one of his main men. I don't reckon he's found out about that yet, but he's bound to, pretty quick."

"I see. That changes things, doesn't it?"

"You're damned right it does. It ain't just that I took Blount and his woman out of a hidey-hole he guaranteed them would be safe; that'd be bad enough. But with his flunky dead, it's up to Kester to get me now. If he don't, he'll start to slide downhill. And he's smart enough to know it, and tough enough to do something about it. The Indians call it saving face."

185

After thinking this over for a moment, Summers nodded thoughtfully. "Yes, I guess I can see that. Responsibility goes with authority. Well, setting you ashore on the mainland won't be any trouble. I've got to put in at Allen's Landing and Morgan's Point to take on cargo. Fortunately, we aren't carrying any passengers out of Galveston, so I can accommodate you and your prisoners on board until we sail. Would that help you?"

"You just don't know how much." Longarm took Summers's hand and shook it heartily. "I'll go get my prisoners."

"Oh—just a minute, Marshal," Summers said. "I guess that horse behind the hack is yours?"

"In a manner of speaking. It's an army remount."

"I don't see how I can take it along too. We're not fitted to carry animals."

Longarm thought about this for a moment, then said, "You mentioned those places you were going to take on a load. Is there a railroad line running into either one of them?"

"There is to Allen's Point."

"I figured there'd have to be some way of getting goods to the dock," Longarm nodded. "Well, then, don't worry about the horse, Captain. I'll get word to the army where he is, and let them figure out how to get him back where he belongs."

Blount and Francy were getting restless when Longarm got back to the carriage. She complained, "You sure don't show much regard for us, damn it! Being tied the way we are is real miserable."

"Too bad," Longarm said curtly. "Well, you'll get to stretch your legs a little bit now. Come on, both of you."

"Where to?" Blount asked.

"You'll find out soon enough." Longarm left them to work out as best they could a way of getting out of the hack while he gave the hackman an extra dollar for his help and instructed him to take the gelding back to the livery stable to board until the army picked it up. He went back, stopping for a moment to watch Blount and Francy contorting their way through the hack's narrow door, and took his saddle off the claybank. They were ready to move by the time he'd done that, and Longarm marched them up the gangplank to the deck of the *Falcon*.

"Soon as the captain shows me where he's going to put us, I'll get the lashings off you and put cuffs on you," he told Blount and Francy. "And I wouldn't advise you to try getting away. There's a Texas Ranger prowling around Galveston on your trail. If he gets hold of you, you'll get worse treatment than staying handcuffed in a ship's cabin."

Summers came back on deck. "I've got cabins for you on the main deck." He turned to Longarm, "You didn't say whether or not you wanted to keep them where you can watch them, so I've told the purser to put you in separate cabins."

"I'd just as soon keep the two of them apart," Longarm said. "Keep 'em from plotting together. And I sure don't enjoy being in their company any more than I have to be."

As on all ships, the *Falcon*'s cabins were equipped with a variety of ringbolts and stanchions to which furniture and luggage could be lashed to keep them from shifting when the ship rolled in heavy seas. Longarm handcuffed Blount to a ringbolt beside the bunk, which put him in a position where he could sit or lie down with no more discomfort than an outstretched arm. Before leaving the outlaw, he searched him to be sure he had no lockpicks or other tools that could be used on the cuffs.

With his spare pair of handcuffs, he secured Francy to the stanchion that ran between the floor and ceiling of the cabin and held the bunk in place. He didn't bother to search her; the black velvet dress had no pockets, and they'd left the hideout in such a hurry that she hadn't brought along a handbag. He did take her hairpins, much to her displeasure.

"How do you expect me to look nice, with my hair strung down my back?" she complained.

"There's nobody on board going to see you," he replied. "And you might as well get used to traveling rough. From here to Denver ain't exactly going to be a trip on a parlor car."

"You'll never get Sim to Denver," she taunted.

"He'll get loose and go free, and maybe fix you so you can't follow him in the bargain."

With his prisoners safe, Longarm went to his own cabin and stretched out on the bunk. He'd been on his feet for almost forty-eight hours without any real rest, but until now, things had been happening so fast that he hadn't had time to feel tired. He told himself sleepily that he'd just lay there for a minute or so, then he'd go up and see if the captain would pour that drink he'd invited him to have the night before. In the midst of taking a cheroot out of his vest pocket, he fell asleep.

Longarm didn't know how long he'd been sleeping when an urgent knocking woke him seconds before the door of his cabin opened and a sailor said, "Marshal, Captain Summers sends his compliments and asks if you'd step to the upper deck for a minute. There's a gang of toughs gathering on the wharf, and the captain says it looks to him like they're getting ready to attack the ship!"

Chapter 17

Longarm almost knocked the sailor down as he rushed past him in the narrow passageway, hurrying to get to the deck. When he reached the top of the narrow stairway and emerged into the open, he was surprised to see that dusk was settling down. He hadn't realized until then that he'd slept that long.

Captain Summers was standing beside the ship's rail, his eyes fixed on the wharf. "I didn't like to bother you, Marshal," he told the lawman. "Perhaps I'm worrying needlessly, but those men have been drifting along the wharf for the past hour."

Longarm looked at the little knot of about a dozen roughly dressed men who stood on the far side of the wharf, a short distance from the *Falcon*'s berth. He didn't recognize any of them, but that didn't signify. They obviously weren't sailors or dockworkers who would have had any reason for being there. Most of them looked like street toughs, the kind of men Kester could mobilize on short notice with very little effort.

"They damn sure ain't Rangers," Longarm told Summers. "So they're bound to be Kester's crew."

"You mean he'd have the gall to attack the *Falcon*?"

"I mean he'd have the gall to do damn near anything. From what I've learned, he pays enough graft to the police so he can get away with murder."

"That's a rough-looking bunch over there," Summers commented. "I didn't pay any attention to them at first. Then I thought of what you'd told me about Kester and his need to hold his stature. Then I began to worry."

"Well, I'm sure sorry it's happening, if it does," Longarm told the captain. "I didn't figure Kester would catch up to me as fast as he must've."

"How did he, I wonder?"

The marshal sighed and shook his head.

"It'd be easy for a man like Kester to find out almost anything that goes on in Galveston. The hackie who took me and Kester's man out to where those two downstairs were holed up could've told him, or somebody at the livery stable where my horse is. Or it might just have been somebody who saw us parading out of the hack and onto the ship, here at the wharf."

"This may sound like a foolish question to you, Marshal but what are we going to do if those men *do* attack the *Falcon*?"

"That depends." Longarm looked at the toughs again. "You still ain't ready to sail off?"

"Not until the tide peaks. That's another three hours, almost four. It'll start to turn in an hour, but it won't be full high for two more. But we're high in the water now. We can ride over the sandbars in three hours."

"Looks like we'll just have to fight 'em off then," Longarm said calmly as he pulled a cheroot from his pocket and stuck it between his front teeth.

"Fight? With what?" Summers asked, his eyes wide.

"You mean you got no guns on this ship?" Longarm asked incredulously.

"Oh, we have a few. Three or four rifles and a couple of shotguns. The mates and I have pistols. We're merchant mariners, Marshal, not the navy."

"I'll bet you got a bunch of old navy hands in your crew, though. North or South, it don't matter. I'll deputize all or part of 'em; that'll make things legal."

After a moment's thought, Summers said, "I'd guess more than half my crew's seen navy service. Not just North and South during the War, but British or French or Portuguese."

"Then we got nothing to worry about."

"I'm afraid we have. I'll be held accountable by my owners if the *Falcon* should get damaged."

"Well now, I don't think Kester's going to bring up any cannon, Captain."

"I was thinking about torches," Summers said, echoing the greatest fear of any seafarer, fire on board ship.

"They'll have to get near enough to throw 'em,"

Longarm reminded him. "I got my Winchester and my Colt—" he suddenly remembered the two pistols he'd taken from Zilker and Blount; when he'd taken out the handcuffs, he'd dropped the guns into his saddlebags because they were dragging at his coat— "and two spare pistols I'll be glad for your men to use. I'll guarantee none of those yahoos will get near enough to toss a torch on board."

While Longarm and Summers talked, the light had grown dimmer. Dusk was changing to nightfall. In the growing gloom they could see that more men had joined the waiting group; there were at least twenty on the wharf now.

"What do you think they're waiting for?" the captain asked.

"Somebody to tell them what to do." Longarm was relieved that Summers didn't seem to be nervous. He went on, "We might as well be getting ready. Even if we ain't sure yet whether or not they've come down here to give us trouble, it ain't smart to wait until we find out. You get your men and guns together, Captain. I'll swear them in as deputies, just as soon as I check up on my prisoners."

Blount was asleep; apparently the night had been as much of a strain on him as it had been on Longarm. Francy was wide awake. She glared at Longarm when he opened the door and looked in.

"What do you want now? Can't a lady have any privacy? Next time, knock before you open my door!" she snapped.

Maybe I'd knock if I was getting ready to go into a real lady's room," Longarm shot back. "Right now, I'm just checking up on a prisoner."

"If I'm a prisoner, I'm entitled to be fed," Francy said. "You haven't offered us a bite to eat, and I'm starving."

"Supper'll be along after while," Longarm replied. "You look healthy enough to me. Missing a meal won't hurt you."

He went to his own cabin, ransacked his saddlebags for ammunition, and picked up the two pistols as well as his Winchester. Back on deck, he found the men

191

Summers had promised him assembled in a little knot, but there was no sign of the captain.

A tall, rawboned man of about fifty volunteered, "The captain had business below. Said to tell you to go ahead."

"You men know what you're here for?" he asked.

All of them nodded. Longarm looked at them. They were a strangely assorted group. All were bearded, and their beards were trimmed short. They weren't dressed alike, but there was a family similarity in what they wore. Whether their breeches were made of sail canvas, denim, linsey, or lightweight cotton, they'd been chopped off at the knees. Most had on pullovers, jersey or cotton knit. Some were bareheaded, and some had on stocking caps or billed cloth caps. One sported a cockaded tam. They ranged in age from late youth to one or two who'd never see middle-age again.

He looked at their weapons. There was one good Winchester among the three rifles. The other rifles were Colts, which Longarm had never liked because the side-blast from the cylinders when the guns were fired obscured a man's vision at critical moments. There were two shotguns, both double-barreled. Four had pistols stuck in their belts, and two had no weapons at all. Longarm handed these two his extra pistols.

"How many of you men were in a navy?" he asked. Without exception, they all nodded. His second question was, "All of you know how to shoot then?"

When there was another universal bobbing of heads, Longarm felt better.

"You don't need to do any fancy shooting, now," he told them. "We ain't setting out to kill anybody. Don't shoot first, but don't wait to shoot back. You're just protecting yourself. Now stay in back of the bannister around the deck, here."

"We call it the gunnel, Marshal," one of the men said.

"Call it what you like, just stay low in back of it. Leave me to do the lookout's job. When I yell 'shoot,' you pop up and aim fast and shoot, then pop down again. You got that?"

"Hell, we've fought afore," a rawboned man said.

"We'll look out for ourselves. The *Falcon*'s our ship, we don't want her harmed."

"Sure, you don't," Longarm agreed. "But I don't want you men hurt, either." He singled out the men with the shotguns. "Now, you two, I want you at the ends of the line. Don't waste shells trying to shoot across the wharf; wait till a bunch gets up close."

They nodded. In the little group of sailors, there were a few whispers.

"You got anything you want to ask me?" Longarm asked.

"What's the law going to say about all this?" one of them piped up.

"Hell, you men *are* the law. Captain Summers is going to put your names down on a list, and I'm going to write out that I swore you all in as my deputies. That makes you officers of the law, helping me to protect life and property. What you are, is a federal posse." Longarm pointed to the rawboned man who'd spoken earlier. "What's your name?"

"Tim Babcock."

"New Englander, ain't you?"

"Vermont by way of Maine."

"I've heard tell that New England men understand a rifle," Longarm said, still sizing Babcock up.

"I kept game on my family's table from the time I was eight."

"You still in practice?"

"Ayup. Not as good as when I hunted every day."

Longarm made up his mind. He pointed upward, at the mainmast that rose from the center of the *Falcon*'s deck. "If I was to ask you to climb up there and sharpshoot, would it bother you?"

Babcock shook his head. "Wouldn't bother me. Too whippy way up there to do good shooting, though."

"I don't mean clear to the top. That first platform."

"You mean the maintop."

"Damn it, I just said not the top, the platform."

"Platform's called the maintop. That where you want me?"

"Whatever it's called, that's where I want you. Most of those fellows on the wharf are going to have pistols. If you see any of them carrying a rifle or sneaking up on the ship, pick 'em off. Remember what I said about not killing."

"Can't guarantee I won't kill somebody, if the ship rolls."

"If you do, it ain't your fault. Just don't *try* to."

Nodding curtly, the rawboned man turned away and started climbing the shrouds to the maintop.

Longarm stationed his handful of defending sailors along the *Falcon*'s rail, behind the ship's stout oak gunwales. Just as he was getting them positioned, Summers appeared.

"You're ready, I see," the captain observed. "I had to get everything stowed away below, so we can cast off and make weigh the minute the tide turns." He jerked his head in the direction of the wharf. "Have they made any moves yet?"

"No. They're still waiting for something. Maybe more men, maybe for whoever's going to take charge of things to get here," Longarm answered. "I been keeping an eye on 'em while I got your men set out. We're ready, any time they start something."

At the point where the *Falcon* was moored, the wharf was perhaps fifty or sixty feet wide. Darkness was almost complete by now; only a line of after-sunset gray showed in the west. In the dimness, the mob across from the ship could be seen now only as a dark blob, changing in shape as the waiting men moved around. There were no other ships moored near the *Falcon*; the closest was a good two hundred yards down the wharf. Lights showed on board the neighboring ship, and on a vessel moored at an even greater distance in the opposite direction. The captain had apparently ordered that no lights be shown on the *Falcon*, for the darkness around it was almost complete.

Suddenly a match flickered and flamed from the knot of men across the wharf. It was followed by another, and the glare of two kerosene reflector lanterns bathed the midships section of the *Falcon* in a blaze of light.

Longarm didn't hesitate. He shouldered his Winchester, sighted into the center of one of the reflectors,

194

and pulled the trigger, and with a metallic clang, the reflector went dark.

At almost the same time, a shot echoed Longarm's from the maintop and the second lantern was darkened. Babcock had reacted almost as quickly as had Longarm.

From the clot of men on the wharf a streak of muzzle-blast showed, then the light crack of a pistol shot preceded by a fraction of a second the thud of a lead slug into the ship's side. There was an angry shout from across the wharf. Seconds ticked away, but no more lights showed and there were no more shots. Voices could be heard from the attackers, but the distance was too great to discern anything but a murmur. The noise lasted for several moments, then stopped.

"Wonder what they're up to over there," one of the men at the ship's rail muttered.

"Getting ready for a rush at us, I'd say," another replied.

"Wish they'd do it and get it over with," the first man murmured.

"Well, don't give 'em a target by talking," Longarm cautioned. The speakers fell quiet. Longarm strained both his ears and his eyes, trying to make out what the men on the wharf were doing. Except for a vague sound or two, indicating that some kind of movement was going on, there was no clue as to their activities.

Then, from the obscurity, a voice called, "Long! Marshal Long!"

"I'm here," Longarm replied, after thinking for a moment. He was pretty sure the voice was Kester's, but he couldn't figure out how the underworld boss had discovered his identity.

"I'm willing to give you a chance to deal," the man called.

"No deals, Kester," Longarm shouted back. "Save your wind."

"You've found out my name, have you?"

"That was easy," Longarm called back. You found out mine, didn't you?"

"I found out more than that. They call you Longarm and you've got a reputation for being a hard character.

195

If you don't give me Blount and his woman, I'm going to find out whether you can live up to it."

"Any time you're ready," Longarm replied. "If you found out my name and what folks say about me, you found out I don't deal with crooks." When he stopped talking, Longarm heard again the scraping sounds that had been faintly audible before. Now they were closer and louder. Instead of swearing at himself for falling for Kester's trick, Longarm whispered loudly enough for the sailors on either side of him to hear, "Pass the word to the shotgun men. They're trying to sneak up. Count five and shoot down at the wharf, ten or twelve feet from the ship!"

Longarm counted the seconds. As he reached seven, the shotguns blasted almost as one weapon. In the orange glare of the muzzle-flashes he saw Kester's men. They were about where he'd judged they'd be, a dozen feet from the *Falcon*'s sides, stretching in a thin line along the wharf.

On the heels of the twin blasts, shots began popping from the opposite side of the wharf again. The explosions were mingled with yelps of pain from those who'd been trying to creep up on the ship. The cries were drowned by a scattering of rifle blasts as the *Falcon*'s defenders returned the fire.

"Hold up! Quit shooting!" the marshal called to his men.

As the rifle shots ended, they heard the thudding of running footsteps on the wharf's echoing boards. The attackers were retreating, but the pistol fire kept up. Then an unintelligible shout sounded from across the pier, and the pistol shots straggled into silence.

"How did you know that was Kester calling to you?" Summers asked Longarm, keeping his voice low.

"Couldn't have been anybody else. He's the only one interested enough in those two downstairs to try to get 'em. Unless it's the rangers, and as far as I know, there's only one ranger in Galveston right now."

"I'm surprised Kester had the impudence to attack us so openly," the captain said. His frown was invisible, but it was reflected in the tone of his voice. "Isn't he afraid of the police at all?"

"Hell, from what I hear, it's the other way around,"

Longarm replied. "Kester must just about *own* the damned police force."

"What will they do next, I wonder?" Summers asked.

"Hard to say. But they'll do something, you can bet on that. And if I judge Kester right, he won't waste any more breath on palavering. He'll just send his men boring in."

As though to validate Longarm's prediction, pinpoints of light from a dozen matches dotted the blackness across from the *Falcon*. The pinpoints vanished in smoky orange flames that flared up along the ranks of Kester's plug-uglies.

"They're going to try to set the ship on fire!" Summers gasped. He hurried away from the rail, and Longarm heard his voice a few seconds later, muffled, shouting a command.

There was no time to wonder about the captain, though. From the opposite side of the wharf, men were running forward, whirling their torches. The light of the firebrands bathed the wharf and the ship in a devil's glare of crimson as the torch bearers rushed toward the *Falcon*.

Longarm didn't need to shout a command. The trio of riflemen and the half-dozen men with pistols started firing as soon as the advance began. One of the torch carriers fell, but a man ran from the group clustered on the wharf's far side, picked up the brand, and carried it ahead.

"Shotguns!" Longarm shouted.

He'd drawn his Colt and had dropped one of the nearest thugs when the two shotguns cut loose. As before, their scattering pellets sent the raiders into a quick retreat. Three or four of them had dropped their torches, and these lay, still burning, on the boards of the pier. So far, none of the torches had set the boards ablaze, Longarm noted quickly. He did what instinct led him to do, and let off a pair of quick shots from the Colt at the nearest torch. It was made of burlap wrapped around a length of broomstick, and it fell apart under the impact of the heavy lead slugs. All that was left of the torch were a scattered few flickering scraps of burlap, and their dying flames were not strong enough to set the damp boards ablaze.

Swiveling, Longarm used his last slug on another of the torches. It jumped and started to fall apart, but was still blazing brightly enough to be dangerous. Longarm holstered the Colt in one lightning-quick move and grabbed for his Winchester, which was lying on the deck at his feet. With the Winchester, Longarm could reach the most distant torches, and he turned his attention to them. Along the rail, the other riflemen were following his example. Within minutes, all of the torches had been reduced to a few shreds of glowing cloth.

Conquering the menace of the fires had both distracted the attention of the riflemen and emptied their guns. Kester had evidently foreseen that his crew would have to make more than one attempt to set fire to the *Falcon*. Even before the sailors had put out the fallen torches, a second wave of arsonists were advancing, their blazing brands lighting the night again. This time they encountered only sporadic fire from the vessel; all the ship's defenders except two of the pistolmen were reloading.

Running faster than the men who'd tried before, the second line got close enough to the *Falcon*'s side to swing their torches and release them in blazing arcs that sailed through the black sky. One or two of the torches fell short, hit the ship's side, and dropped between ship and wharf to sizzle out harmlessly in the salt water. Enough landed on the deck, though, to pose a real and immediate threat. Here and there, the tar-filled cracks between the planking began to flare up.

Longarm was about to order his men to stamp out the flames, overlooking the fact that none of them wore shoes, when Captain Summers emerged from the forecastle hatch, followed by a party of crew members carrying huge buckets filled with water.

"All right, men!" Summers commanded, "You know what to do!"

Each of the sailors ran to a burning torch and sloshed it with water from the buckets. The fires fizzled and died.

"Below now!" Summers told the men. "Fill those

buckets again, and stand ready! The bastards might try again!"

"They sure as hell *will* try again," Longarm assured Summers as the captain came to join him at the rail. "And I got a hunch as to what it might be."

"If they try again, we'll be ready. The men are standing by below. After our talk earlier, I thought we'd better be prepared for them."

"My hunch is that Kester knows we can beat his torches now. It ain't likely he'll try that trick again." Longarm's voice grew progressively more sober as he continued, "What I'm thinking now is that he'll have one more good shot at us. A big one, next time. I figure all he's got left is to try to blow up your ship, Captain."

Summers was skeptical. "He'd have to use a bomb of some kind. How would he get the guncotton? For that matter, how would he know how to make it?"

"Don't overlook the kind of people Kester can call on," Longarm cautioned. "Safecrackers is one kind. They know better than most men how to blow something up. And Kester's a boss crook."

"You sound like you really think he'd try it!"

"If that's the way I sound, it's because that's what I think," Longarm said. "A minute ago, I asked myself what I'd do if I was in Kester's place. Blow up the ship was the answer I got."

"He'd have to set off a bomb right at the waterline for it to have the most effect," the captain said thoughtfully.

"He could send somebody in a boat over from the other side of the wharf," Longarm pointed out. "If a boat came in under the boards, we wouldn't be able to see it from the deck."

"There's a little offshore wind right now." Summers spoke as though he was thinking aloud. "A jib and a stays'l might pull our bow around and get us a little way from the wharf."

"A little way's all we'd need," Longarm assured him.

Summers wasted no time. He strode to the forecastle hatch and called, "Masthands and deckhands on deck! Shake a leg, now!"

Sailors ran onto the deck and were met by a barrage of quick-barked orders. Some ran to the mooring lines and began cutting them with large-bladed knives, while others swarmed out onto the bowsprit and up the foremast. Within minutes, the *Falcon* was freed from the pier and a pair of triangular sails above the bow were set and filling in the light offshore breeze. Slowly the prow of the vessel began to swing away from the wharf. The movement brought the sails out of the lee of the land, and the ship began to move faster. A gap of black water, blacker than the night, showed between the wharf and her stern.

Looking back at the slight, frothy wake the ship was beginning to create, Longarm saw the triangular bow of a rowboat emerge from beneath the wharf. He called to Summers, "Got to go faster, Captain! They're coming after us!"

"Break out the foreskys'l!" Summers commanded without hesitating, and men clambered up the rigging to set the sail at the top of the foremast. The *Falcon* picked up speed.

For a moment, the gap between the ship and the pursuing rowboat stayed the same, then the *Falcon* started outdistancing the smaller craft. The men in the rowboat picked up the stroke of their oars and the gap closed a bit. For a moment the rowboat gained, then a gust of wind gave the *Falcon* an extra spurt of speed.

Longarm was beginning to turn to call his congratulations to the captain when a soft crunching noise sounded from beneath the vessel. The *Falcon* shuddered and stopped.

"What's wrong, Captain?" Longarm called. "We were gaining on 'em. This ain't no time to stop!"

"I know that!" Summers snapped. "We can't help ourselves! We've run aground on a sandbar!"

Chapter 18

When he heard the captain's words, Longarm called to
the sailors who'd formed his posse, "All you men
who've been shooting, grab your guns and come back
here!"

He looked to see who was responding. No one was.
The posse members were sailors first, deputies second.
They were all aloft. Longarm looked over the *Falcon*'s
stern. The rowboat was closing the gap quickly now.
He reached for his Winchester and triggered off a
series of shots as fast as he could work the lever. At
the third shot, a huge burst of flame flowered on the
rowboat and a massive explosion boomed. The water
of the bay heaved and rippled, and the *Falcon* rocked
in spite of being aground. When the smoke of the blast
cleared and the rippled surface of the bay began to
grow calm, Longarm looked back. There was nothing
except dark water where the rowboat had been.

Suddenly the stern of the *Falcon* was crowded with
sailors hurrying to see what had happened. Captain
Summers pushed through, to stand beside Longarm.
He asked, "What happened, Marshal? That was the
damnedest explosion I've heard in a long time."

"One of my shots must've hit the bomb Kester's
men were fixing to put on your ship," Longarm said.
"Lucky shot. I wasn't aiming, it was too damn dark to
see."

"Lucky or aimed, that shot saved my ship. I'm in-
debted to you again, Marshal Long."

"I'd say it's the other way around. Your ship
wouldn't've been in any danger if you hadn't let me
bring my prisoners on it. It's me that owes you."

"Do you think Kester will try again?"

Longarm shook his head. "I misdoubt he will. No

201

way for us to know how many men he's lost in trying to get those two back. And it ain't likely he brought more than one bomb. That's about the only way he could get at us now."

"No. But I'll appreciate it if you'll keep watch, just the same," Summers said. "It won't be for very long. The tide's raising. It'll lift us off this sandbar in another couple of hours, and we'll be on our way."

"I guess I messed up your schedule, didn't I?" Longarm asked.

"Not too badly. We'll just dock at Allen's Landing earlier than I'd planned. That won't hurt your feelings, I suppose."

"A long ways from it. All I hope is that I can catch some kind of train there that'll get me and those two prisoners out of this part of Texas damn fast."

"Now, damn you, Long! That's a forty-dollar pair of boots you're ruining!" Simaeus Blount protested.

They were still aboard the *Falcon*, though the ship had put in at Allen's Landing on Buffalo Bayou before dawn. Longarm had been busy since they'd landed, arranging to go on to Denver. He wanted to get his prisoners off the vessel; there was always a chance that Kester's pride had been stung so badly by last night's defeat that he'd muster a fresh squad of flunkies and pursue them. There was also a possibility that news of last night's battle on the wharf had gotten to Travers and, if that was the case, the ranger would be on their trail too.

Blount was sitting on his bunk, one wrist still shackled to the ringbolt in the cabin wall. Francy was shackled by one ankle to the chair in which she was sitting, across the small cabin from the bunk. Longarm's wrist-and-ankle double shackle had been so effective before that he'd decided to use it again, but he didn't trust strips of bedsheet, or even rope, to hold a man like Blount and a hellcat like Francy for very long. There was still a thousand miles of Texas between his prisoners and Denver.

Longarm hadn't had any trouble closing the handcuff loop around Francy's ankle, but Blount's booted ankle had been too big. He'd decided that snapping the loop through the tough, tanned leather of the outlaw's boots just above the ankle would serve his purpose. After all, the pair would still be wearing the second set of handcuffs, Blount's right wrist shackled to Francy's left.

Longarm kept on cutting away at the boot leather. He didn't bother to look up when he answered Blount. He said, in a voice that held no hint of sympathy, "You won't be needing boots where you're going. You can get along with prison shoes until they walk you out to meet the hangman."

"That day's not in sight yet," Blount boasted.

"He's right," Francy chimed in. "It's a long trip to Denver. Nobody holds Sim very long when he's got his mind set on getting away."

Longarm had no intention of getting into any kind of argument with his prisoners. He finished his trimming and stood up, then went over to Francy and unlocked the handcuff that was fastened to the chair.

"All right. Let's get you and Blount together now, and we'll be moving out," he told her.

"I hope you've got something to travel in that's more comfortable than this cramped-up ship," she said saucily.

"You'll be surprised," he told her. "We're going in style, in our own private railroad car."

Blount let out a loud guffaw. "Any time you go first class, it's going to be snowing in hell, Long. I never seen a lawman yet that was anything but cheap."

Longarm held his tongue. He slipped the opened handcuff loop through the holes he'd made in Blount's boot and pushed the ends closed. The lock clicked. He moved to the ringbolt and unlocked the loop that passed through it, leaving the other loop on Blount's right wrist.

Blount struck like a snake. He jerked his hand back, tearing the handcuff loop from Longarm's grasp. In the same motion, he brought his arm around, swinging the steel loop like a flail, aiming it at Longarm's head. Longarm jerked his head aside in time to keep the cuff from striking his head, but it caught him a stinging blow on his left shoulder. Before Blount could strike again, the marshal's Colt was prodding Blount's belly.

"Go ahead," Longarm told him. "Move that right hand one damn inch and you'll find out what it feels like to be belly-shot with a .44. I've seen men hit in the belly take a week to die."

Blount did not move his hand. He said, "You knew damn well I was going to try that. I'll keep on trying, too. You better believe me when I tell you I ain't going with you peaceful."

By this time, Longarm had gotten a firm grasp on the handcuff with his left hand. Keeping his gun shoved hard into Blount's midsection, he closed the cuff over Francy's left wrist. She moved as though she were going to give him trouble too, but when she saw Longarm's set, angry face, she apparently thought better of it.

Longarm stepped away from the bunk. "You can have it hard or easy," he told Blount. "You got off light this time—"

"So did you," the outlaw broke in. "I aimed to brain you."

Longarm ignored the comment and went on, "If you want it hard, I'll see that you get one meal a day, bread and water, and more water than bread. By the time we get to Denver, you'll be too weak to stand up, let alone give me trouble. Or you can act decent and I'll feed you decent. Make up your mind."

"When I do, I'll let you know," Blount said curtly.

"You do that. Now, both of you, get up and move. We got a train to catch."

After their first few stumbling, uncertain steps, Blount and Francy remembered the moves they'd learned the night before when similarly shackled. They preceded Longarm up the gangway to the top deck and into the gray of dawn. The *Falcon* was moored at a low, narrow pier that jutted out into water green with moss and stagnant-smelling. Buffalo Bayou served the little town of Houston as a garbage dump and sewer, and the weak tidal current that crept up Trinity Bay's west shore was never strong enough to flush out the slough that ran to the bayou.

Captain Summers was standing at the head of the gangplank. He said, "Well, good luck to you, Marshal. At least we've had a few exciting minutes together, this short trip."

"Enough to last you a while, I hope. Thanks for your help, Captain. Remember, if you get up to Denver—"

"I still think that's too far inland for me," Summers said with a smile. "But I'll remember your invitation."

Longarm picked up his bedroll, which had been lying across his saddle near the gangplank, and slung it over his shoulder, then grasped his saddle by its horn. "All right, down the steps," he told Blount and Francy. "And if you think this gear I'm packing is going to slow me down if you try anything, you're dead wrong."

He directed the pair across the pier to a plank walkway that led them to the ground, then they walked slowly in the shifting, sandy soil to the little building he'd pointed out. As they neared it, Blount said, "You know, Francy, maybe he wasn't stretching the truth. He might have hired a private car for us, after all. That's sure a railroad station, if the sign reads the way I make it out."

Across the front of the building, which was painted in the standard railroad colors of light brown on yellow, a long sign read *Houston & Texas Central R.R.* From somewhere beyond the station, a thread of smoke rose from a locomotive. A string of boxcars stood on the siding next to the building.

Blount and Francy were walking a step or two in advance of Longarm. They stumbled now and then as their feet failed to move in unison, or as one of them stepped on one of the rocks strewn on the sandy soil around the tracks. They stopped, uncertain, when they got close to the boxcar at the rear of the string.

"Head for the station," Longarm told them. "I said we'd have a private car, and I wasn't lying. Just march right up on the platform, and we'll get aboard."

Blount threw a frowning look over his shoulder at Longarm but made no protest. He and Francy clumped up the three plank steps to the platform, and walked a few steps along it, looking at the cars beside which they were walking. All of them were boxcars, with their doors closed and sealed. There were no passenger cars on the track. The engine's tender could now be

205

seen at the head of the string of boxcars, almost even with the end of the station.

"There's our private car." Longarm pointed to the first boxcar in the string, just behind the tender. Its door was only partly closed.

Blount snorted, "I knew all along it was some kind of sell."

"It's a private car," Longarm said. "I didn't say what kind it'd be, and I sure didn't tell you it'd be the kind the nabobs use, with velvet chairs and servants to jump when you snap your fingers."

They reached the end of the platform. A short ramp had been placed between the car door and the side of the platform to span what would have been an impossibly long step over the space between platform and car. Longarm closed the gap between himself and his prisoners and gently urged them into the car.

Even though they'd grown accustomed to the gray predawn half-light through which they'd walked from the pier to the station, it was much darker inside the car. Several minutes passed before their eyes adjusted to the deeper darkness. For a few seconds, all three sets of eyes swept the car's interior. In one corner, slats had been nailed together to make a shoulder-high enclosure, a small stall. In a corner at the rear, a round cylinder, like a truncated garbage pail, rose from the bare board floor. Several bales of hay had been placed along the wall opposite the door. Otherwise the interior was bare, an uninviting vista of splintered planks sheathing sides, floor, and ceiling. The smell that pervaded the air was terrible.

"It's a goddamned immigrant car!" Blount said.

Longarm was putting his gear on the floor. He told Blount, "No, it's a step up from that. It's a railroad family car."

Railroads, expanding faster than the supply of available skilled labor permitted, were constantly transferring employees from one station to another. Those transferred were, for the most part, family men; to make their move easier, the railroads maintained cars in which the employees and their household goods—including the cow, which, in so many rural communities, was considered part of the family—were moved free of charge to their new town.

"Do you mean we've got to ride in this stinking thing all the way to Denver?" Francy demanded.

"No. Just part of the way," Longarm answered. Then he added, "I don't see what you two got to complain about. It don't smell as bad in here as it does in those swamps in the Big Thicket."

"What about eating?" Blount asked. "I don't see anything in here, and this damn jerkwater train don't have a dining car attached to it."

"We'll manage," Longarm said curtly. "Now, you two go sit down on one of them haybales while I shift the others around. We're going to be in this car a while, and we might as well make things as comfortable as we can, considering what we got to work with."

Like the ship's cabin, the family car had ringbolts set into its planked walls at intervals, to allow furniture to be lashed in place so it wouldn't shift when the train moved. Longarm pushed two of the bales under one of the bolts, then went a few steps down the wall and shoved two more under another, a safe distance from the first.

"Just because I was taught ladies first, I'll give you the choice of which place you want, Francy," he said.

Francy looked at the bales and sniffed. "I'd as soon ride in that stall with all the cow turds as on that."

"If that's what you want, I'll be glad to accommodate you," Longarm snapped. The constant complaining of the pair was setting his nerves on edge. "I'll shove two of those bales inside and shackle your leg to one of the slats." He took the handcuff key out of his vest pocket and started toward her.

Francy backed down fast. "You know I was just funning, Marshal Long. I'll take the bales over by the door there. At least I'll get a breath of fresh air now and then."

Longarm gave Blount no chance to repeat the attack he'd tried to bring off on the *Falcon*. Before removing the cuffs that connected the two prisoners, he shackled Blount's right wrist to the ringbolt above the haybales where the outlaw would spend the trip. Only after Blount was secured did the marshal take the cuffs from his boot. Then he led Francy across the car to the bales she'd selected, and transferred the cuffs from her ankle to her wrist. While he was snapping the loop through the ringbolt on the wall, the engine gave a series of toots, and couplings clanked as the train began to move.

Blount said, "Damn it, now we're on the way, and you still didn't do anything about getting us something to eat. I'm so hungry my belly thinks my throat's been cut."

Longarm looked up from shoving the remaining two haybales together to make his own bunk. "The train stops to pick up cars about ten miles up the line," he told Blount. "The station agent back at the landing says there's a store there, right by the track. You ain't the only one who feels like your bellybutton's rubbing against your backbone. I'll get us some grub while the engine's shunting up the string."

"You mind telling us where we're going?" Francy asked. "I don't suppose it makes much difference whether I like it or not, but I'm just curious to know."

"Now, you know the answer just as well as I do," Longarm replied. "We're on our way to Denver."

"Oh, I've got sense enough to understand that," she said, a bite in her tone. "I mean, where's this train going to stop?"

"If it'll make you feel better to know, we'll pull into Austin about sundown. I'd rather have headed north, but with your friend Kester still on the prod, the first train away from Galveston looked pretty good to me, and this one was it."

Francy subsided then. Longarm settled back on his own haybales and leaned against the boxcar's wall. He dozed fitfully for a few minutes while the train moved at a snail's pace over the level coastal plain. He'd get some real sleep, he told himself, after they hit the main line. Two nights awake in a row, and busy nights at that, were enough to make a man's tail drag just a little bit.

A series of short blasts sounded from the locomotive's whistle, and the train began to slow down. Longarm stood up, and Blount and Francy looked at him curiously. The whistle signaled again, and Longarm walked to the car door. Sliding it open a few inches, he peered out.

"We're pulling into the junction point, I guess," he told his prisoners. "It'll take 'em a while to make up the train, so as soon as we stop, I'll go rustle us up something to eat. I won't be all that far away, remember, and I'll be keeping an eye on the car while I'm outside. It wouldn't be smart for you to try anything, Blount. I know you're just waiting for a chance to, but I don't figure to give you one."

There was a grinding of steel on steel as the engineer began bringing the train to a stop. Longarm went to his gear, which he'd dropped in the first convenient corner when they'd gotten in the car, and picked up his Winchester.

"It ain't that I'm worried about you breaking free of those cuffs in the little time I'll be gone," he said to Blount. "But if I leave this where you can see it, you might be tempted to try. Now, you be smart and keep quiet, you hear? Yelling won't help you a bit. I'll close the door tight, and with all the ruckus they'll be raising outside, switching and stuff, nobody's going to hear you."

Longarm swung to the ground, slid the boxcar door closed, and headed for the store. It stood a hundred yards or so away, alongside a dirt road that ran parallel to the tracks. He looked back when the engine began puffing, then saw that it was heading for a water tower farther up the track, and relaxed. On a siding beyond the string of boxcars that the engine had left standing, he saw a passenger coach and combination mail and freight car waiting to be added to the train. He knew that shunting them off the siding to the main line and then getting them coupled to the boxcars would take a little while, but there wasn't any hurry. He took his time walking across the cleared ground and the road to the store.

It wasn't much of a store, he thought, looking around for food that was suitable for a pickup meal in a rattling boxcar. He settled for a stick of summer sausage, some cheese, a few crackers, and some dill pickles from the crock that stood in front of the counter. As an afterthought, he added a sack of sugar cookies. The place didn't carry whiskey, but, on second thought, Longarm figured it was a good thing. Good as a swallow of Maryland rye might taste right now, he'd better wait until he got to Austin to relax. Meanwhile, the water in his canteen would have to serve.

He'd just carried his purchases outside when he saw a man on horseback tearing up the road toward the store. Even at this distance, Longarm recognized Travers. Quickly he stepped back inside and watched through the screen door as the ranger galloped past. His first thought was that the railroad station agent at the landing had been impressed enough by Travers's badge to break the promise he'd made to keep Longarm's travel arrangements secret. Then, when Travers ignored the boxcar where Blount and Francy were, Longarm's worry eased.

It sharpened again immediately when Travers rode over to the coaches waiting on the siding and began talking to the brakeman who stood by the siding switch. The worry deepened more when the ranger tossed his horse's reins to the brakeman and swung aboard the passenger coach. From the coach, Travers could see Longarm crossing from the store to the boxcar, and that would be a dead giveaway.

Then Longarm saw his one chance. The engineer was backing from the water tower into the siding. He'd back the passenger and combination coach onto the main line and pull back through the siding to get in front of the boxcars, then back the string to couple the boxcars and the two coaches together. For a few moments, while the passenger coach moved behind the boxcars, its windows would be blinded on the side of the store and the cleared ground he had to cross.

At the moment when the passenger car rolled behind the boxcars, Longarm started running. He got to the family car with seconds to spare and slid the door open He shoved his rifle across the floor, put the sack of groceries by it, pulled himself into the car, and closed the door.

Francy and Blount watched him curiously. "In a hell of a hurry, wasn't you?" Blount asked.

"Didn't want to miss the train."

Just as Longarm spoke, the engine backed into the boxcars with a metallic clanking of couplings. Longarm stifled his sigh of relief; he knew that for the rest of the trip he'd feel like he was riding in front of fused dynamite.

Well, old son, he thought, *there ain't one thing you can do about it, so just start getting used to it.*

With a squeaking of journal boxes, a rasping of steel wheel-flanges, and a creaking of its board sides, the car began to move. Longarm picked up the sack of groceries. He said to Blount and Francy, "I guess we're all overdue for a meal. Now that we're on our way, we might as well eat."

Chapter 19

At every station where the train stopped on the day-long trip to Austin—at Cypress, Brenham, Mill Creek, Carmine, and, finally, the last station stop at McDade—Longarm peered out of the slitted door to see what Travers might be up to.

Each time, the ranger got off the passenger coach and made a beeline for the station agent's glassed-in office. At every stop, Travers hung over the agent while the agent worked the telegraph key. And at all the stops, after he'd left the station and headed back to the coach, Travers stomped along the platform like he was killing spiders.

After the second or third stop, Longarm began to smell the acrid fumes of the fuse leading to the dynamite. Knowing that Blount and Francy were watching him almost as closely as he was watching them, he couldn't allow his nose to crinkle up at the smell; he had to show the same straight face he'd always displayed. At the same time, he wondered whether Travers's repeated visits to the railroad's telegraphers were a sign that he'd found out who was traveling in the family car just behind the engine and was getting together a reception committee of rangers to surround the car in the Austin yards, or whether Travers still hadn't succeeded in tracing them since they'd left Galveston.

It's got to be one or the other, Longarm thought. *If Kester could find out we were on that ship, Travers could too. Unless he figured we'd taken the ferryboat. And then he wouldn't know whether we'd got off where we did, or someplace else, like Anahuac. But he took the train. Why'd he be on it, if he's still not sure where we are? He's bound to be fixing it so there'll be a bunch*

212

of rangers waiting in the Austin yards. And I purely don't relish the idea of a shoot-out with him and his crew, not there nor anyplace else. Besides which, Billy Vail used to be a ranger, and he's still got friends among 'em. Best thing I can do, as far as the Rangers are concerned, is cottontail around and stay clear of them between such holes as I can find.

Longarm's uncertainty continued until the train finished its leisurely ramble at the H&TC depot in Austin. There, the engineer braked to a stop at the depot only long enough for the passenger and combination coaches to be uncoupled, then pulled on into the yards with the boxcar string. Longarm kept his eyes glued to the slitted door during the few minutes it took for the train to roll the short distance and be brought to a halt. The yards were small, and the acetylene lights that stood on tall poles dotted around the area brightened it well. There was no sign of a party of rangers waiting to greet them, and no place in the narrow strip of ground the yards covered for such a group to be concealed.

During the trip, Longarm had hidden from Blount and Francy the anxiety he'd felt about the possibility of arriving in Austin to face a showdown with the rangers. Now he concealed his relief that the kind of reception he'd half-anticipated hadn't materialized. If they'd noticed him getting edgy, neither of them had said anything. He'd shackled the pair together soon after the train left McDade, not being sure he'd have time to do so later. He'd even worked an open loop of the handcuffs through a ringbolt before closing it over Francy's wrist, to keep them from being taken out of the car, if it came to that.

He told them, "I'm going to leave you two here for a few minutes. We've still got some traveling to do, and I need to find out the best way to go."

"I need to go, too," Francy said. "So if you're going to be away long, take off these handcuffs and let me use the pot."

Longarm hated to spare the time, but he freed Francy and waited while she used the toilet in the corner. The bowl was an old one, apparently salvaged from a retired passenger coach. The stream of cold air

213

that whistled up through its broken trap hadn't bothered Longarm and Blount, but it had inhibited Francy. She'd been able to use the toilet satisfactorily only while the train was standing still. She made a point of ignoring Longarm, who didn't intend to turn his back on her or Blount unless they were either handcuffed or tied. Francy stood up, flounced her long velvet skirt, and went back to the haybales.

While Longarm was replacing the handcuffs, Blount said, "I hope you don't expect us to eat the kind of fodder you've fed us all day, now that we're in a town where we can get a decent supper."

"We'll see about that, after I come back," the marshal snapped. "If we can make connections with a train going to Denver tonight, you'll be lucky to get anything at all to eat."

His hope of getting a quick connection on a train heading for Denver was ended quickly. "To bad," the station agent told him. "You missed the night train that'd get you there the shortest way. If you're in a real hurry, you can get out in the morning, but you'll have a couple of changes to make."

"Whereabouts?" Longarm asked.

"Well, the I-GN's got a train out at nine-thirty that connects at Taylor with a Katy train to Fort Worth. You get on the Fort Worth & Denver City there, and it'll get you into Denver at nine-thirty tomorrow night. Or you can lay over here, go out at noon, and get to Denver at ten o'clock tomorrow night. Only one change too, if you go that way."

Longarm considered the alternatives. Every change meant the risk of a ranger spotting his prisoners, or of Blount and Francy trying to make an escape. But the longer he stayed in Austin, where rangers were coming and going all the time, and where the force had its headquarters, the worse it could be.

"I guess I'm stuck here for the night then," Longarm said. As though he'd just remembered it, he asked the man, "Wasn't that Will Travers, the ranger, that I brushed past coming up to the station?"

"Sure was. You know Will, do you?"

"We've met." Longarm put a cheroot in his mouth

214

and lighted it to keep from having to say how just then.

Looking around conspiratorially, the agent dropped his voice to a hoarse whisper and confided, "Will's been burning our telegraph wires up all day today. Seems like he's hot on the trail of a fellow who killed a ranger a while back, only some damned U.S. marshal from outside of Texas has got this man, and he's trying to take him up north somewhere before Will and the boys catch up to him. I tell you, mister, there's going to be rangers waiting at every railroad station in Texas tonight and tomorrow, and I'm betting they'll get whoever it is they're after. You know what the rangers say, they always get their man!"

"Well, that's right interesting." Longarm looked around the deserted depot. "Is Will going to be setting up watch at your depot here? If he is, I'd like to say hello to him."

"No, our last train's in for the night; that's the one Will was on. He's gone over to the I-GN depot, with the ranger who was watching here, to check the one that's due in about an hour. But they'll be back tomorrow."

"I see. You know, I'm glad I'm on the right side of the law. I'd hate to think those rangers were out looking for me."

"I would too!" the agent said fervently.

"You been real helpful," Longarm told the agent. "Tell me one more thing. Where's the nearest restaurant that serves decent food? I'm sure hungry."

"I can't help you much there," the agent replied. "You'll have to hoof it to town to get real good food. The closest place is a good half-mile from here." As an afterthought, the man added, "You might look around outside, though. There's a hot tamale man hangs around here, his tamales are pretty good."

"Thanks. I'll look out for him."

Walking toward the door, Longarm weighed his hunger against a mile walk. He looked around the station platform and saw no one. He was just about to start walking when a voice at his elbow said, "You like nice hot tamale, *señor*?"

"I'll say I would!" Longarm grinned, now that his

problem was solved. "How much you get for them tamales?"

"Two for five *centavos,* please. Very good, very hot." The vendor had a lard can hanging by a broad leather strap around his shoulders. He lifted the lid and the spicy aroma of the tamales, kept hot by a thick cloth lining inside the can, reached Longarm's nose.

"You got something I can carry 'em in?" he asked he vendor. "Paper sack, maybe?"

"How many you going to buy?"

"Oh, about two dozen. No, better make it three dozen."

"Ay, *señor?*" The vendor scratched his head. "I think I don't got so many left. And I don't got a sack, too."

"Tell you what. You look and see how many tamales you do have, and I'll buy all of 'em, and give you a dime for your lard can to boot."

After a moment of thought the man shook his head. "I don' know. If I sell my can, I got to buy a new strap to make another one."

"You keep the strap," Longarm offered, "And I'll boost it to a quarter for the can."

For a moment, Longarm thought his second bid was going to be turned down, but the vendor's face broke into a smile and he said, "Ver' good, *señor.* My can and all the tamales, she is yours."

Longarm arrived at the boxcar just as a switching locomotive covered the squeaks that the door made when he slid it open. He'd put the lard can down to have both hands free for the door, and was bending over to pick up the can when he heard Francy's voice.

"Come on, Sim. Get all of it in me. You're not doing me any more good than I'd get from using my finger."

"Damn it, Francy," Blount said. "If you'd just get your leg up out of my way, I could cram it all in."

"My leg's up as high as it'll go. Can't you swing around any further?"

"Not with our legs cuffed together the way they are. Here. Bend your leg this way, now."

"Ahh. That's more like it. Go on. You know I like it deep."

Longarm debated breaking up what was obviously

216

going on in the car, but he decided it might improve the temper of his prisoners, so he sat down on the lard can to wait.

Francy said, "Why'd you move away? You pulled most of it out. All I've got in me now's the head."

"I couldn't twist my back around any more. Let's try it with me turned this way."

"It might be better, at that. Here. Now let me get hold of it, and—ah, there it is. Now go on in deeper."

"I'm doing the best I can. This damn handcuff on my arm keeps pulling me back."

"To hell with your arm. My leg's getting numb. Let's get back the way we were. I think it was better."

Longarm tried to picture in his mind the scene inside the car. He'd never tried it wearing handcuffs, but he imagined it would be as uncomfortable as Francy and Blount made it sound. Still, he felt a little pulsing in his crotch.

Francy said urgently, "Damn it, Sim, hurry up and get it in me! I'm so hot after all your fumbling around that I'm about to explode!"

"I'm hurrying."

"Well, it's about time. Now go on, deeper."

"There. How's that?" Blount asked.

"Better. Oh, yeah, that's a lot better. Keep it up!"

"I can't keep it up much longer; my leg's about to get twisted off. But I'm going to—I'm—how about it, Francy? Now?"

"No! Not for a while!"

"No. Right—now—now, Francy! Hang on!"

"*You* hang on! I'm not ready yet . . . oh no, Sim! Not so quick! Not—oh, damn! You did, didn't you?"

"Well, I couldn't hold back any longer, this position we're in. I couldn't help it."

"And I know you. It'll be two hours before you can get it up again. Oh, damn it! Long's going to be back pretty soon, and then we'll be across the car from each other."

"I did the best I could, Francy."

"Oh, go to hell. Let me get my dress . . ."

"Ouch! You caught my balls!"

Longarm thought he'd better let them know he was back before they started quarreling. He stood up and lifted the lard can into the car. He said, as though he hadn't heard anything, "Here's supper, such as it is." In the darkness of the car, he could just make out their forms. Francy seemed to have gotten her dress rearranged. Blount was standing, bending rather, and looked as though he was fumbling with his fly.

Francy said, "I hope you got something hot."

"I did. Hot tamales."

"Hot tamales and what?" Blount asked.

"More hot tamales. And you better eat 'em and enjoy 'em, because we're going to do some moving around a little bit later on, and we won't have time to eat again until breakfast."

Longarm's tone warned the prisoners that he wasn't in a mood to listen to any complaints. He set the can in front of them and pulled the lid off. Silently they reached in, took out a tamale apiece, and began removing the cornhusk wrapping.

Longarm did the same. He ate standing up, pacing now and again, trying to come up with a way to elude the rangers who would be watching all the railroad stations—not only in Austin, he guessed, but throughout the state, wherever rangers were stationed.

And that'd sure as hell be every town where we'd have to change trains, he thought. *There'd be no way the rangers could miss spotting us, either. One man and me, we might make it. But three of us, and one a woman, they'd have to be blind not to see. And I never heard of any blind rangers. Damn that Blount, anyhow! Why'd he have to pick out a mail coach to try and stick up? He'd ought to've had sense enough to know that nobody messes with the U.S. Mail . . .* His thinking changed direction suddenly. *Nobody messes with the U.S. Mail. Now, that'd take in the rangers too, wouldn't it? If there was a way to get the three of us in a mail coach, we'd go right past them ranger lookouts slicker'n the fat off a possum's belly.*

Longarm finished peeling the tamale he'd just taken from the lard can, and dropped the shuck to the floor. He made two bites of the spicy cornmeal-covered meat, wiped his hands on his bandanna, and picked up his Winchester.

"I'll be going out for a little while. Be back as soon

218

as I get back," he said abruptly. Francy and Blount were so surprised that they didn't have time to reply or ask questions.

Walking toward the mail car that had been uncoupled beside the depot when the train arrived, Longarm hoped the clerk hadn't finished his work yet. Usually there were enough useless forms to be filled out to keep a clerk in the car for an hour or two after the train got to its destination, though. He thought briefly of Blount and Francy, wondered if they'd try again, decided that they would, and that he didn't give a damn. He had more important things on his mind.

Luckily, the clerk was still working. Longarm tapped on the door of the combination coach. The bag-slide set into it opened a crack, and a man said, "You can't come in here, don't you know that? It's against postal regulations for me to open the door as long as there's mail in this car."

"I don't want in," Longarm told the clerk, "All I want from you is the name of the postmaster in this town, and where he lives."

"Um. Well, I don't guess it's a secret. His name's Mr. Benjamin Forbes, and he lives at 565 Seventh Street, that's just off Lavaca Avenue."

"Just in case I miss him, who's the chief postal inspector?"

"That'd be Ed Parsons. You'll likely find him at the Iron Front at this hour of the night."

"That'd be a saloon, downtown?"

"Yep. Just ask anybody you run into on the street. They'll tell you where it is."

"Thanks, friend. Go back to work now, but don't work too late."

Remembering the saloon the station agent had mentioned, Longarm headed for it on the chance that there might be a hackman who'd stopped in for a drink. There were two, swapping stories about odd customers. He listened to their talk while he downed a quick shot of Maryland rye, a pleasure he'd denied himself for too long now, then hired the one that had talked the most sensibly.

"First we'll stop at the Iron Front," he told the man.

"Ah, you're a drinker after me own heart," the hackie said, slapping the reins on his horse's back.

True to the clerk's prediction, Parsons was in the saloon. Longarm gave him his name, but no title, until the postal inspector had gone with him to a quiet corner of the rambling, busy saloon, where they could talk with at least a chance of privacy. Then Longarm showed his badge.

"A U.S. marshal? What's up? Some of our clerks in trouble?"

"No, but I am. Or could be. You recall that mail coach robbery up by Texarkana, a while back? The one that got one of our men killed trying to protect your mail?"

"Sure. I didn't work the case, but I know about it. Why?"

"Because I've got the killer, taking him up to Denver."

"Well, that's good news," Parsons said. "But I don't see that it concerns me or the postal service."

"Sure it does. Our man getting killed likely saved your man's life. I figure you owe the marshal's office for that, Mr. Parsons."

"I'll be damned!" Parsons grinned. "That's pretty strange reasoning." He thought about it for a moment, then added, "But I'd say it makes sense, in a left-handed way. Go on."

"It just happens that the same fellow who killed our man shot a Texas Ranger too. Now I've got him, and they want him. They know I've got him, and they're putting a watch out on all the railroad stations between here and the Texas line to keep me from taking him out of the state."

Parsons nodded. "I can see the rangers doing that, but I still don't understand why you're telling me all this."

"Because I want you to help me get my man across Texas."

"Now how in hell can I do that, Long?"

"You can lend me a mail coach for a day or two. And set it up so it'll be switched to the trains that'll get me where I'm going."

"Lend—you—a—mail—coach?" Parsons spaced his words out as he tried to understand Longarm's request.

"Sure. That's the one kind of railroad car the rangers won't mess with. If they knock on the door, I can tell them just what your railway clerks do; it's against regulations to open the door. Anyhow, they ain't going to look for me and my prisoners in a mail coach. At least, I'm betting they won't."

"Well, I'll be damned!" Parsons chuckled. "You've got more nerve—no, by God, it's not just nerve! It's outright gall! But you've got more than any man I've ever seen." He chuckled again. "That calls for a drink. What'll you have?"

"I never refuse a swallow of Maryland rye."

Parsons snapped his fingers to get the attention of one of the white-aproned waiters, and ordered. When they had their drinks in hand, he said. "I'm not sure I've got the authority to do what you want me to, Long."

"Now don't let's beat around the bushes, Mr. Parsons."

Longarm kept his voice level and pleasant. "We're in the same line of business, I'd say, except you're a specialist. You only go after crooks who monkey with the mail, and I go after *any* of 'em. And I know a man with a job like the one you hold can do just about what he damn well pleases. And likely nobody'd ever call him on much of what he done."

After considering this for a moment, Parsons nodded. "I suppose I'd have to agree you're right. Tell me one thing. If I do this and somebody *does* call me, will your chief get the attorney general to square me with the postmaster general?"

"That I can guarantee you. The marshal who got shot was a real special friend of Billy Vail. Billy's my chief. He'll do just about anything to get his hands on this killer I'm trying to deliver."

"I see. Now, assuming I do loan you a mail coach, where'd you be going, and when?"

"Out of Austin on the I-GN at nine-thirty in the morning," Longarm said. "Switch to the Katy at Taylor, then to the Fort Worth & Denver City in Fort Worth. Those are the regular trains; I suspicion you know their schedule better than I do. I reckon I could travel in a regular coach after I get over the Texas line, where the rangers run out of jurisdiction."

"That'd be at Texline, up in the Panhandle," Parsons said. "Well, it'd be easier if the coach stays in the state. Less trouble for me to get it hauled back, too."

"Texline," Longarm frowned. "I remember going through it a time or two. Seems like the Texas-New Mexico line cuts right through the town."

"It does. And the depot's on the Texas side by about twenty feet or so."

"I guess I could make it that far on my own," Longarm said. "But look here, Mr. Parsons, you got a direct telegraph line to Washington out of your office, like the one we got in ours up at Denver?"

"Yes. Why?"

"Maybe you'd use it to send a message that they'd relay to Billy. I can't use the regular telegraph or the railroad wires for fear the rangers will be watching 'em."

"If I know the rangers, they're watching them right now. There won't be any difficulty in getting your message relayed. What do you want to tell your chief?"

"When I'll be getting to Texline. Billy used to be a Texas Ranger. If I run into a bunch of rangers there, anything's likely to happen. If he's on hand, everything'd go off peaceful."

"I see your point. All right, Marshal Long. I'll send your wire tonight so your chief will get it in the morning. I'll have to go to my office anyhow, to arrange for that coach you're going to borrow. It'll pick up you and your prisoners at the Houston & Texas Central yards at three in the morning. That satisfactory?"

"Couldn't be better, Mr. Parsons. And this next round of drinks is on me!"

Chapter 20

Longarm couldn't tell whether Blount and Francy had tried again, or whether Francy's taunting remark about the outlaw's need to wait two hours before he was ready for seconds had kept them from trying. If they'd tried, he decided, they hadn't been any more successful than before, for both of them were in a foul mood when he got back to the family car.

Or, he thought belatedly, *maybe it's just that those hot tamales give 'em a sour stomach.*

On the other hand, Longarm felt very good. He told his prisoners, "You better get what shut-eye you can, because we'll be moving to a different car a little bit later on."

"I hope it's better than this one," Blount snapped.

"And doesn't stink the way this one does," Francy seconded.

"Don't blame me if it don't suit you. I ain't any better off than you are," Longarm pointed out. "Now, both of you settle down and sleep. I ain't of a mind to listen to you any longer."

Longarm felt that he'd barely closed his eyes when the chuffing of the yard donkey that was delivering the mail coach woke him up. He cracked open the boxcar door and looked out. The coach was being uncoupled on the next siding. He waited until the donkey puffed away, taking its crew with it, and went over to take a quick look at the coach.

It was the standard car of its type, a third longer than regular passenger coaches, made to United States Post Office specifications. Except for narrow vertical glass strips in the top of its main side door, the car was windowless, but had a line of barred vents just under the roof. It was lighted by acetylene ceiling

223

lamps. The sliding side door had a catch and double lock, and the pass-through chute, set in it for taking on mailbags, had its own lock.

Inside, the car had been painted a uniform post office gray. Most of one side was devoted to a sorting desk with pigeonholes above it and tubular steel frames designed to hold mailbags open and upright. On the side opposite the sorting desk, steel-framed bunks, which dropped like shelves from wall hinges, were on each side of the sliding main door. A steel water cooler was on a shelf on this side.

In one corner, partitions of steel mesh came out from the end and sides of the car to form a sort of cage; the mesh had openings about an inch square, and the enclosure had its own door and lock. The other end of the car was divided down its long axis by a passageway that separated two enclosures, walled off by solid partitions. Each enclosure had its own locking door. The passageway led to the vestibule, and at one end of the passage there was a cubicle with a Pullman toilet and washbasin in it. Both vestibule doors were solid, and had peepholes with sliding closures set in their top panels.

It was a typical Austin night, warm and muggy. The acetylene lamps not only gave off light, but heat. Longarm realized he was sweating by the time he'd finished inspecting the coach; he took off his coat and hung it on a wall hook beside the sorting table. He was well satisfied with what he'd seen; he'd noticed that every detail of the car was designed to perform two functions: one was to provide reasonably comfortable accommodations for the mail clerks who worked in it on long runs, and the other was to make the car theft-proof, to deny entry from outside. Which, he reminded himself, made it impossible to get out of, as well. He'd found a set of keys hanging on wall hooks, each hook identifying the door the key fitted. He could put Blount in the mesh cage, where he'd be unable to start trouble.

Longarm didn't know when the yard donkey was scheduled to come back and haul the mail coach over to the I-GN yards, but he had a hunch it would be back within the next half-hour. His watch said it was two-fifteen, and Parsons had mentioned three o'clock as a good time to switch the car. He cut his inspection short and went back to the family car.

Blount and Francy were awake. Blount complained, "Damn it, you tell us to get some sleep, then you get up and prowl around and keep us awake. Why the hell can't you make up your mind?"

"Oh, I don't have any trouble doing that, Blount. Right now, I've made up my mind it's time to switch cars," Longarm said.

"Oh God, here we go again!" Francy moaned. "My arms and legs are both sore from those damn handcuffs you make us put on wherever we go somewhere."

"This is one time I'll let you off from wearing 'em," Longarm told her. "It's not but a step away, over to the siding. And I'll move you over there as soon as I pack my gear across, then I'll come back for you, Blount."

Blount didn't bother to answer. Longarm picked up his saddle, rifle, and bedroll, and carried them across to the mail coach, then went back for Francy. When they were inside the coach, he said, "Now I'm going to handcuff you to the frame of one of these bunks for right now. Later on, after we get moving, maybe I'll see my way to letting you out of the cuffs, if you swear you won't start trouble."

"Don't do me any favors, Marshal," she said curtly. "I'm not asking you for any."

Longarm snapped the cuff on Francy's wrist and then pulled down the bunk farthest from the meshed enclosure. She sat down, arranging her wrinkled velvet skirt as though she were in a friend's parlor. He closed the open loop of the handcuffs around the bunk frame.

Francy had been looking around the car. She said, "Well, it's a lot cleaner than what we've just left. Smells better too."

"It'll do," Longarm said shortly. He was tired of both her and Blount. As far as he was concerned, the quicker he could turn them over to Billy Vail, the better he'd like it.

Back in the family car, he said to Blount, "All right. Your turn now." He unlocked the handcuff from the ringbolt and reached for the left wrist to snap it on.

225

The outlaw extended both arms, one loop of the handcuffs still on his right wrist, as though to accept the inevitable. Before the marshal could get the cuff closed on the left wrist, Blount yanked the cuffs away with a sudden jerk of his right arm. At the same time, he clawed with his free hand for Longarm's watch chain, with the derringer attached to it.

Longarm's fingers were numbed by the force with which the steel handcuff band had struck them when Blount yanked free. He caught the outlaw's left wrist just as Blount got his hand on the derringer, and forced the gun's short muzzle away from his chest. Blount triggered the derringer and its ugly, dull splat echoed in the bare car as the slug plowed harmlessly into a wall.

Blount swung his cuffed right wrist, just as he'd done on the *Falcon* when he had tried to break free, trying to use the handcuff loop as a club. Longarm parried the swing with one hand and grabbed for the dangling cuff in the same swift move. He got the handcuff chain and whipped Blount's arm downward, throwing the man off-balance, just as Blount fired the derringer's second barrel. The slug slammed into the floor, inches from Longarm's booted toe. When Blount found himself falling forward, he let go of the derringer as he tried to break his fall.

Using the leverage the handcuff gave him, Longarm kept Blount falling forward. The outlaw hit the floor, and Longarm booted him in the head. The kick stunned him and he sagged to the floor, unconscious. Longarm made sure he'd stay that way with a second kick to Blount's jaw.

Wasting no time, Longarm dragged Blount across the floor to the boxcar's open door. He left him lying in the opening, jumped to the ground, and tossed the unconscious man over his shoulder. Carrying Blount the few steps to the mail coach, Longarm thrust his shoulder up to roll the outlaw onto the floor of the mail coach.

"My God!" Francy gasped when she saw Blount's limp form. "You killed him!"

Longarm was levering himself up into the coach. "No. Just knocked him cold." He grabbed Blount's

226

wrist and dragged him to the door of the mesh-enclosed compartment. A quick step took Longarm to the row of keys hanging on the wall. He selected the one that fitted the compartment's lock, opened the door, and dragged the outlaw inside. Then he slammed the door and dropped the key into his vest pocket.

Francy finally found her voice. She said, "You mind telling me what happened over there in the other car?"

"Not a bit. Your friend tried to jump me again. I had to knock some sense into his thick head."

Blount groaned and stirred. His arms flopped as he tried to roll over. Then his eyes opened, and he raised his head. He saw the steel mesh all around him and his eyes popped wide open. He sat up and looked around.

"Damn you, Long!" he said, his voice hoarse and rasping. "You sure got a heavy hand."

"I let you off light," Longarm said unemotionally. "My chief wants you delivered alive, to stand trial for gunning down that marshal over at Texarkana." He let the words sink in before he added, "He was in a cage just like the one you're in now, remember?"

For the first time, Blount seemed to realize fully where he was, and that he was locked up. A look of panic flashed across his face for just a moment before he got control of himself. He said thickly, "You're figuring on keeping me shut up in here until you get me to Denver, I guess." It was a statement, not a question.

"You're damn right I am." Longarm spoke flatly, without emphasis. "And you'll stay in a cage or a cell until they take you out to walk up and face the hangman."

Blount's features twitched, but he said nothing.

A locomotive whistle sounded close at hand. Longarm stepped to the door, and saw the yard donkey backing up to the coach. He closed the door quickly and locked it. There was a thump and a clank, and the coach jarred as its coupling snapped into the engine's.

"Looks like we're on our way," Longarm said. He was beginning to feel almost cheerful. He dropped the unoccupied bunk and stretched out on it. "And now that I got you two fixed up so you can't bother me, I expect I'm going to enjoy the trip."

For a long trip, it was uneventful. The train to which the mail coach was attached pulled out of the I-GN depot on time. Peering through one of the narrow, glassed slits in the door, Longarm saw three men he took to be Texas Rangers standing on the depot platform scanning each passenger who boarded. There were two more rangers, wearing the same semi-uniform that Will Travers had favored, watching at Taylor when the coach was switched to the M-K&T. Neither of them seemed curious about the extra mail coach that was switched.

At Fort Worth, one of the train-watching rangers knocked on the coach door and demanded to be let inside. Longarm called back through the closed door, "I can't let nobody in, it's against postal regulations."

"Now listen to me! I'm a Texas Ranger, and I intend to take a look inside your car!"

"Mister, I don't care who you are. This car's U.S. Government property. You bring me an order signed by a postal inspector to let you in, and I will. But that's the only thing that'll get this door open!"

Other than complaining that Longarm hadn't provided food for the trip, Blount and Francy said very little as the Rock Island & Denver City train to which the coach was coupled in Fort Worth huffed up the long slope to the High Plains. Longarm told them that he was hungry too, but that didn't stop their griping.

Between Fort Worth and Amarillo, rangers checked the train at every stop, even in the smallest towns. Longarm knew this was because they were running close to the state line, with the haven of the Indian Nation only a few miles away. Beyond Amarillo, where Longarm refused another ranger's demand that he be let in for an inspection, tension in the coach began to mount. Longarm felt the air growing electrified, and he could tell by the change in the attitudes of both Blount and Francy that they were feeling it too.

I bet I know why too, he told himself as he watched Blount nervously pacing inside the mesh enclosure, and Francy constantly arranging and rearranging her long black velvet skirt. *I've left those two by themselves enough times, before we got in this car, for them to've put their heads together and concoct some kind*

228

of scheme. Except there's things they don't know about, like Billy meeting me at the state line, and us having to leave this mail coach in Texas. But they're going to try something, sure as God made little green apples. Only I don't aim to let 'em get away with whatever they've got cooked up.

All but a score of miles between them and the border had chugged away under the steady push of the engine's big pistons when Francy called to Longarm. "I need to go to the bathroom, Marshal. Do you mind?"

"Now how could I mind, if you got to go?" Longarm asked.

Blount stopped pacing long enough to say, "It's all this water we have to drink to keep our bellies feeling full. Goes right through you."

Longarm was unlocking Francy's handcuffs. She asked him, "Yeah, how much longer do we have to go without eating?"

"Not much longer. As soon as we cross the Texas line, and that's only about twenty miles from here, as I remember the country."

Francy stood up and started for the bathroom. Over her shoulder she said, "I'm sure ready. Aren't you, Sim?"

"Damn right," he agreed. Emphatically he added, "The sooner the better."

Waiting for Francy to return, Longarm went to the door and looked out at the treeless, trackless country through which they were now traveling. There was nothing but grass from where his eyes first saw earth to the long, straight horizon. He was turning away when Francy came back. She said, "You know, Marshal, this is the first time I've been this far north in Texas. I'd like to see what it's like. Can I look, too?"

"Sure. But there sure ain't much to see."

She came to the door and tried to look out through one of the slit panes, but wasn't tall enough. "Oh, damn! I'm just too short," she said. "And there's not a chair or anything for me to stand on."

Longarm's ingrained habit of being polite to women, even women prisoners, led him to offer, "Here, I'll boost you up long enough so's you can see there ain't much to look at."

He lifted Francy by the waist. So far, during the trip, they'd never been so close, and the heavy, musky scent of her body caught him by surprise. She leaned on him, her arms braced on his chest, while she gazed out at the countryside. Surprisingly soon, she said, "You're right. There isn't anything to look at. I've seen all I want to."

Longarm lowered her to the floor. He expected her to go back to the bunk, but she surprised him. She darted past him toward the cage, her arm extended. "Here! I'll keep him busy while you let yourself out, Sim!" She thrust the key she'd taken from Longarm's vest pocket through the mesh of the enclosure where Blount was confined.

Longarm grabbed for Francy, but she eluded him and ran to the far side of the car. He turned back toward the enclosure, where Blount was trying frantically to fit the key into the lock. Francy landed on Longarm's back before he'd taken two steps. She locked one arm around his neck, choking him, while covering his eyes with her free hand. Momentarily blinded, Longarm grabbed Francy's wrist and pulled away the hand that covered his eyes. She dug her fingernails into his wrist, and he had to use his other hand to pull her free. Then he twisted sharply and broke the throttling hold of her arm around his neck.

Francy stumbled and started to fall as Longarm broke her hold on him, and he grabbed her. His hand closed over a breast, firm and resilient. His other hand was pressed on her stomach, flat and smooth; under the velvet dress he felt her muscles draw tight, then relax, as she realized the futility of trying to struggle against his much greater strength. Longarm again caught her musky aroma, and the combination of woman-flesh under his hands and the blatantly sexual scent affected him strongly, although more urgent concerns prevented him from realizing it consciously.

Francy turned to look for Blount. She saw that he was still trying to put the key she'd given him into the lock. "Damn it, Sim! I gave you enough time. Why aren't you out?"

"Because that ain't the key you thought it was," Longarm told her. "Oh, I saw you studying that row

230

of keys hanging up there. And I know you saw me tuck that one away. Any damn fool ought've known what I did. I switched 'em." He walked over to the enclosure and extended a hand. "You might as well hand me that key, Blount. It won't ever fit into that lock, not if you try for a hundred years."

"To hell with it!" Blount snarled. He thrust the key through the mesh and let it fall to the floor. He beat his fists on the mesh and yelled at Francy, "Stupid bitch! You can't do anything right, can you!"

"Don't blame me!" she shouted back. Her face was flushed and sweating. "You got us in this mess! I sure didn't!"

Their argument was stopped by the train whistle. All three of them knew it signaled their arrival at Texline, the little town on the Texas-New Mexico border where the authority of the rangers ended. Longarm took Francy's arm and led her to the bunk. "Just to be safe, I'll put the cuffs on you again," he told her. When he bent down and closed the loop over her wrist he caught once again the waves of her scent emanating from her hot skin.

By now, the train was slowing down. Longarm stood at the door, watching Texline's few buildings slip past. The mail coach passed the station, went perhaps a dozen yards beyond it and stopped. Longarm remembered what the postal inspector in Austin had told him about the depot being only twenty feet inside the Texas border. He sighed with relief and opened the door of the coach. His foot sought the stirrup below the door, and he swung to the ground.

"That's him!" a man called. "He's the one they call Longarm, I've seen him before!"

Longarm whirled. Two men were running toward him; they wore the light shirts, covert trousers, and broad hats that Longarm had come to identify as the closest thing to a Texas Ranger uniform. He made no move to draw.

"Hold it, boys!" he called. "I'm in New Mexico now."

His warning didn't stop the rangers. They kept coming. A shot split the air in back of them. They turned, hands going for their pistols. The hands stopped in

231

midair. The portly figure of Billy Vail stood behind them, his revolver already drawn, his thick black eyebrows glowering under the brim of his Stetson. Slowly, the rangers raised their arms until they were extended straight out from their shoulders. Caught between Vail and Longarm, they had no other choice.

"Hell, I know you!" one of them said. "You're Billy Vail, used to be in A Company. With Jim McClintock and Bert Matthews."

"That's right," Vail agreed. "And I'm now chief U.S. marshal in this district. And you boys have just stepped over the line where your authority stops."

"Now hold on!" the second ranger protested. "That fellow just off the train's got a man we're after! A killer named Sim Blount!"

"As it happens, we're after him too," Vail replied. "And since Marshal Long's got him in custody, we'll just keep him."

"But that son of a bitch Blount shot a ranger!"

"He shot McClintock too," Vail retorted. "And I've got other reasons for wanting him. I reckon you've cooled off enough. You can let your hands down."

As they lowered their arms, one of the rangers asked Vail, "How in hell do you expect us to explain this, Billy? Captain Harvey's going to have our asses if we don't bring Blount back."

"No, he won't," Vail assured them. "I'll send him a wire and explain how it happened. I'll promise you something else. If Blount doesn't get a hanging sentence in federal court, I'll see that he's sent back to Texas, and you can take care of him."

Their heads turned toward one another as the rangers had a silent, eye-to-eye consultation. They nodded in unison, and the one who seemed to be the spokesman told Vail, "I guess that's fair. We know you'll do what you promise to."

After the rangers had walked off, a blue-capped brakeman stuck his head out cautiously from between the engine and the tender and asked, "Is there going to be any more shooting? If it's safe, I got orders to cut this first car and shut it onto that siding yonder."

"Go ahead," Longarm said, as he and Vail holstered their sixguns. "Nobody's going to shoot now."

Vail walked up to Longarm. He gazed at the mail coach and shook his head wonderingly. "I got a wire from a postal inspector in Austin that you'd be traveling in that. I didn't believe it until now." He frowned. "But why are they taking it off here?"

"I promised not to take it out of Texas," Longarm replied. The coach began to move away from them. "Hell, I got prisoners in there! Hop on, Billy. We'll talk while they're shunting."

They swung aboard. Vail saw Francy. "Who in hell is she?" he exploded. "And why has she got cuffs on?"

"That's something I'd best explain—" Longarm began.

Vail cut him off. "Save it for your report. Just tell me what she's charged with." ·

"She's not charged with anything. I brought her because when we left the ship—"

"What ship?" Vail interrupted. Then he said quickly, "No. Save that for your report too. There's no want on that woman, is there?"

"No. And I misdoubt she did anything we can hold her for. She wasn't with Blount when he pulled his Texarkana job."

"All right. Put the cuffs back on Blount. Put the woman on the next train back. Get her out of the way. I don't want any side issues cluttering up the case we've got to make against Blount."

"Now wait a minute, Billy!"

"No, you wait. Get Blount ready to go. I want to take him back to Denver with me."

"Hold on! What about me?" Longarm asked.

"I just told you. You wait." In a calmer tone, Vail explained, "You wouldn't have heard about it, but one of the passenger cars on the train had to be pulled off at Amarillo. Hotbox. They crowded the passengers from it into the other cars, but there's no more room. The station agent got them to hold me two seats, but that's all the seats there are. You would've had to come on later anyhow. I need the time on the train to question Blount."

Outside, the engine's whistle sounded as the mail coach rolled to a stop. Vail said, "Get the cuffs on Blount, right now. I can't hold up the train, it's running late as it is." He looked at Longarm and smiled. "I understand that's the Ranger's fault, holding it up for searches all along the line."

Longarm brought Blount out of the mesh cage, handcuffed. He said, "Keep an eye on him, Billy. He's slick."

"I've got leg irons in my bag. I'll keep hold of him." Vail swung out of the car and waited while Longarm helped Blount to the ground. The chief marshal said, "Remember now, tell the conductor of that train you put the woman on that she's not to get off until she's back wherever she came from!"

Longarm's last glimpse of Vail was of his chief's broad back. Vail had a firm grip on Blount's arm and was hurrying him toward the Fort Worth & Denver City mainline where the northbound train waited.

Out of habit, Longarm closed the coach door and locked it. He turned to Francy. "Well, I guess I can take the cuffs off you now."

"I guess you'd better! And in a hurry!"

Longarm removed the cuffs. Francy promptly slapped him hard across the face. He reacted by instinct and grabbed her arm. She began beating him on the chest with her free hand. Longarm tried to catch the flailing arm, but couldn't. He reached around and pulled her to him, squeezing her arm between them. The aroma of her body, musky and heated, filled his nostrils. She wriggled against him. Longarm didn't know whether it was the heat of Francy's body or the sensuous feel of her velvet dress, but he began to harden.

Her face muffled against his chest, Francy snarled, "I hate you, you son of a bitch! Damn you, let go of me!"

"Not till you say you'll stop beating at me," Longarm said. He tightened his pressure on her body.

"I will like hell!" Francy continued to struggle. She thrust her hips against his groin, trying to break his grip around her back.

He said, "You might as well stop fighting, Francy. I won't let go of you until you do."

Francy threw her head back and looked up at him. "What is it about you, anyhow? I hate you and I'm

234

mad at you, but still, I'm not all that mad." Her body shook as a shudder passed through it. "Damn it, I never can stay mad at a real man. It was that way with Sim, every time—" She shook her head sadly. "Sim's gone. And in more ways than one."

Longarm realized that Francy was no longer struggling. He slackened his grip on her, but she made no effort to pull away.

She said, the wrinkle of a puzzled frown growing between her eyebrows, "I don't understand myself sometimes."

"Sometimes we don't want to understand ourselves, Francy," Longarm suggested. He was not holding her tightly now.

"After the way you've treated me—" Francy began, then broke off and began to smile. "Oh, hell, why am I talking like this? I know what's going to happen, and so do you."

"Only if you want it to happen," he told her.

"If I've got to say it, I will! I want it to happen! I want it to happen quick!" Her hands were unbuckling his belt, then working at the buttons of his fly. Longarm pushed down the waist of his trousers. Francy held on to him with one hand while she whisked up the skirt of her long black velvet dress with the other.

He took her standing, with a sudden thrust that brought a sob from deep in Francy's throat and started her body trembling. After three deep lunges, driven into her without pausing, Francy convulsed. Her hips ground into Longarm's with a fury equal to his.

"Go on, go on!" she urged him. "Drive harder! Hurt me!"

Half in and half out of her, Longarm hesitated, startled. Francy grabbed her skirt, which was bundled between their waists. She pulled it over her head, shrugged out of the bodice of her dress, and let it fall to the floor. "My tits! Bite my tits!" she cried. Longarm bent to obey. Francy grabbed his head and pulled it to her breast. "Bite, damn it! Bite while you pound!"

Her fury transmitted itself to Longarm. He clamped his teeth hard on yielding flesh while plunging into her with quick, relentless thrusts. She began shaking, in ecstasy or pain. Longarm was surprised at his eagerness to climax. He could not wait any more than she could.

They relaxed in a quivering shudder. Francy hung limp in his arms, her body shaking with a mixture of sobs and laughter.

When he'd quit trembling, Longarm told her, "Damned if you ain't a strange woman, Francy."

"Only when I've got a man as big as you are crowding into me." She pulled away from him. "God! Even when you're soft, you're big."

"We rushed too fast. I'll hold back, next time."

"When will next time be?"

"Soon as I spread my bedroll. Might as well be comfortable."

"Will you bite and hurt me when I tell you to?"

"Any time and place you say."

"Then spread your bedroll, fast."

Longarm hurried to obey her. There was a long night before the southbound train passed through. He almost hoped the train would be late.

SPECIAL PREVIEW

Here are the opening scenes
from

LONGARM IN LINCOLN COUNTY

twelfth in the bold new
LONGARM series from Jove/HBJ

Chapter 1

For a full hour before the shot, Longarm had smelled trouble. When the shot came, he had been riding across a shallow saddleback. At once—as the rifle's crack rolled like thunder after him—he leaned well over the buckskin's neck, jabbed spurs to the animal's flanks, and galloped down the slope toward the thin trickle of a stream below him.

Now, with his horse crowded against a dark clump of juniper, and his eyes on the ridge behind him, he waited with his Winchester in his hand. The stream's cool murmur—it was only a few yards beyond the juniper—was the only sound to break the silence of the clear, brilliant day. Longarm would have liked the acrid taste of a cheroot between his lips, something to clamp his jaws down on. But things were falling in upon him too fast for that; the cheroot could easily disturb his aim. He didn't need that. Apaches seldom gave a White Eyes more than a second chance, and according to those Apaches beyond the ridge, the towering deputy marshal reckoned, he was already on borrowed time.

Longarm's gunmetal-gray shirt was heavy now with his perspiration. In this silent, withering heat, it was beginning to smell the way he felt—stale and old. He was a lean, muscular man with shoulders that tugged against the shoulder pads of his brown frock coat. His face was wind-cured and rawboned, his skin tanned to a saddle-leather brown. There was no softness in the man, not even in the gunmetal blue of his narrowed, careful eyes. His close-cropped hair was the color of fresh tobacco leaf, as was the neatly waxed longhorn mustache that flared proudly upon his upper lip. His hat was a snuff-brown Stetson, the crown telescoped in the Colorado rider fashion, positioned carefully on his head, dead center and tilted slightly forward, calvary style—a legacy from his youth, when he'd run away to ride in the War.

An Apache, dressed in buckskin shirt, breechclout, and knee-high moccasins, darted into view, his thick hair flying, rifle in hand, and flung himself across the ridge. Longarm levered and fired almost in a single motion. A plume of dirt erupted at the Apache's feet. Longarm fired again, more carefully. The Apache left his feet and flung himself behind a clump of giant saguaro cacti. Another Apache followed the first over the ridge. Longarm levered and swung his Winchester around—just as his left foot was yanked suddenly, with such violence that he was flung sideways out of his saddle.

He clung grimly to his rifle as he looked up at the reeling blue sky, then felt his back slam with breath-robbing force into the ground. He did not let himself lie still on his back. Even as he hit, he rolled over once, twice, then lurched up onto his knees. By this time, a circle of Apaches had formed around him. As they closed in, Longarm fired at the nearest of them. The shot went high. On his feet by that time, he swung the rifle like a club. The Apaches pulled back. One of them smiled—his teeth brilliant in his broad, chocolate-brown face. A knife flashed in his hand and, as the rest fell back to give him room, the Apache ducked under Longarm's second furious swing and lunged.

Longarm parried the knife with the rifle's barrel, then drove the barrel with vicious force into the Indian's midsection. A weaker man would have lost his breakfast. The Apache just bent over and went down on one knee, grasped the barrel with one hand, and flung it aside. Longarm dove at the Indian, catching him about the waist and driving him back so suddenly that he lost his footing and went down under him. Longarm sledged a few blows to the Apache's face, but they appeared to make little impression. The two men grappled for position, rolling over and over in the alkali dust, while the silent, impassive Indians kept the enclosing circle moving with them.

The Apache had long since lost his knife, but he

240

had found a rock and was using it to some effect on Longarm whenever he could work his right hand free. At last, after a particularly numbing blow to the side of his head, Longarm flung himself back and felt the Apache lift himself from him. Feigning unconsciousness, he looked up through slitted eyes and saw the Apache towering over him. Another Apache handed the brave his knife. Again the Apache smiled and raised it over his head.

Longarm had already palmed the derringer from his vest pocket. The Apache's eyes widened in surprise when he found himself staring down the twin barrels of the marshal's .44 derringer. The pistol fired with a dull splat, and the .44 slug plowed into the Apache's knife hand, which seemed to explode in a spray of blood, bone, and sinew. The knife went flying.

Sitting up, Longarm reached across his belly for his Colt, worn high in its cross-draw rig under his frock coat, but froze in the act as he heard the Winchesters around him levering almost in unison. Looking around the impassive circle, he counted at least five muzzles trained on him. Slowly he let his hand ease away from the grips of his Colt.

The shot Apache was on one knee, holding onto his shattered hand, his dark eyes blazing with fury. He turned to his tribesmen and yelled something at them. It sounded distinctly like a command to Longarm, and he had little doubt as to what the Apache had commanded them to do. Looking back at the ring of Indians, he saw the resolve harden on their round, dark faces.

A horse's pounding hooves shattered the pulsing silence. The bleeding Apache flung himself about angrily as the ring of Indians broke apart. An Apache woman rode through the break and flung herself from her pony with all the casual skill of a Plains Indian. She took one look at Longarm, then spun on the Apaches, who immediately shrank back from her angrily blazing eyes. She spoke up then, scolding them in their own tongue. What she said, Longarm had no idea, but it certainly had an effect. The rifles were suddenly lowered and the Apaches, with the single exception of the brave whom Longarm had wounded, took still another step back. The woman turned to face Longarm.

She was a dark, handsome woman with the round, rather flat face of the typical Mescalero Apache, but her hooded eyes gave her away. She was a breed. The eyes were a bright blue—almost as blue as the sky overhead. She was dressed in a buckskin skirt and jumper. On her head she wore a black bowler with a small red feather stuck in the brim.

"What are you doing on our land?" she snapped. There was no trace of an accent. Her voice was deep and musical, though, at the moment, it made no attempt to conceal her anger.

"Just riding through," Longarm replied, "on my way to Paso Robles."

"You are on Mescalaro land!"

"I know that."

"Who are you? What is your business in Paso Robles?"

"Custis Long. I'm a deputy U.S. marshal out of Denver, Colorado," Longarm replied. He bent to pick up his hat. As he slammed it against his thigh to rid it of the alkali dust, he looked at the woman. "And before I tell you my business, who might you be?"

"I am Nalin."

"Thank you, Nalin. I got the distinct impression you saved my life."

"You say you are a deputy U.S. marshal. Prove it."

Longarm reached into his breast pocket for his wallet, opened it, and showed Nalin the federal badge pinned inside it. She studied it intently for a moment, then nodded curtly. "You've come to investigate the murder of Fred Bernstein, is that right?"

"Among other things. Governor Lew Wallace is a mite upset at what's been going on in these parts, so I've come to have a look-see. Seems like I ran into a hornet's nest real quick. You people do know how to welcome a lawman, and that's a fact."

Before Nalin could reply, Longarm looked up to see a party of four mounted agency policemen clearing the ridge. They were not punishing their horses. The four Apaches were dressed in motley clothes, some with army blouses, some without. All were wearing campaign hats and were heavily armed, with bulging cartridge belts around their middles, rifles across their pommels, and sixguns in oiled, flapped army holsters. Two of them wore cavalry britches.

The Apache who had attacked Longarm took one look and slipped off through the junipers, with the rest of the Apaches following. The agency police pulled up to watch the fleeing Apaches, then started up again, two of them peeling off to follow the Indians, the rest riding on toward Longarm and Nalin.

As the two Apaches pulled up before Nalin, she spoke to them rapidly. The riders listened impassively, their cold eyes flicking in Longarm's direction only once, then nodded and rode off after the ambushers. Again, Longarm noticed, they were not punishing their horses at all. They were a most leisurely police force.

"I spoke for you," Nalin told Longarm. "You had better be who you say you are."

"And who the hell, ma'am, are you? The Mother Superior?"

She took a deep breath, then smiled. The smile was dazzling, and it completely disarmed the marshal, despite his growing impatience. "I guess I deserved that, Mr. Long. I run the agency school. I also serve as a nurse, and, more often than not, I am the only one who seems capable of interceding for my people when they run afoul of your law."

"Now just hold it a minute, Nalin. I think we better just eat this here apple one bite at a time. What was it set those people of yours onto me just now?"

"Last night an Apache woman was raped and killed by two white men, not far from here."

Longarm frowned and let that sink in. "That Apache who came after me. Was he—?"

Nalin nodded. "Yes. She was his woman. His name is Toklani. I do not believe he will forget you."

"I didn't rape his woman."

"That doesn't matter, I am afraid. It is enough that you are a White Eyes."

"Well, it matters to me."

Nalin mounted her pony in one quick jump, Indian-style, and snatched up the reins. "Follow me and I

243

will take you to my school. We can talk there, if you want."

"I want," Longarm said, reaching down and picking up his Winchester. He had already slipped his derringer back into his vest pocket. He patted it absently, then dropped the rifle into its saddle scabbard, and mounted.

Nalin led him along the streambed for better than a mile, then cut sharply through a pass. A half-mile farther along, they came to another stream and, just beyond that, a tableland, wooded somewhat more luxuriantly than the dry, bone-white land through which they had just ridden. Close in under some oversized junipers, a frame school building had been erected, with an outhouse just in back, tipping precariously on the stony ground. On the other side of the junipers, covering the tableland like a series of festering sores, were the Apache's wickiups—brush shelters fashioned of leafy branches and rotting army blankets flung over cone-shaped frameworks. A few army-type wall tents broke the monotony. The Apache settlement was not an imposing sight, nor were the Apache squaws, who were barely animated bags of bones squatting in front of the wickiups or hobbling about, tending fires. Only the children seemed truly alive and vital as they darted about in small gangs, playing their games and shrieking wildly all the while. Most of them were as dark as Nalin, and many were completely naked.

Once they caught sight of Nalin and Longarm riding across the tableland toward the junipers, they came running, their dark eyes gleaming as they encircled Longarm's horse. A few commands from Nalin dispersed them, however, and the two continued on to the schoolhouse without further incident. The white-haired squaws seemed too exhausted even to look up at them as they rode past.

They dismounted in front of the schoolhouse, and Nalin led the way into the frame building. The single classroom was neat, but stiflingly hot at the moment. The odor of chalk dust hung heavily in the air. Nalin led the way through the classroom into an apartment in back, consisting of a small kitchen and two bedrooms. A back porch containing a table and two benches also led off the kitchen, and Longarm made himself comfortable at the table while Nalin rustled up some coffee for him. He took the time to brush himself off a bit more and reload the derringer. This surprise among his armament had bailed him out of many a tough spot; it was a .44-caliber weapon with a brass ring soldered to its brass butt. A long, gold-washed chain with a clip on the end of it led from his left watch pocket where Longarm carried his Ingersoll pocket watch. He was just placing the derringer back into the vest pocket, allowing the gold chain to drape innocently across his vest front, when Nalin brought out cups and a steaming coffeepot.

As she placed the cup and pot down in front of Longarm, she smiled and put a finger to her lips, then disappeared back into the kitchen to return a moment later with a bottle of Irish whiskey. "For your coffee," she said. "I imagine you would appreciate it, after what you have been through."

Grinning gratefully, Longarm poured his coffee and added a healthy dollop of the Irish to it.

Quickly, she took the bottle off the table and went back into the kitchen. He glanced in through the open kitchen door and saw her hide the bottle well under the sink. She took pains to make sure it was hidden completely.

Out of politeness, and in consideration of his disadvantageous position, Longarm chose to overlook the illegality of the presence of liquor on an Indian reservation. He was sure the woman must be as aware of the law as he. Normally, he would have considered it ungentlemanly to drink in the presence of those who chose, or were forced, to abstain, but in view of his recent, somewhat unsettling experience, he decided to make an exception in the present case.

She turned and saw him watching her, and said, "If any of the Apache men knew I had that there, it would be gone on the instant."

"What about yourself?" Longarm asked.

"I know. I've got Indian blood. I should be just as liable to abuse the liquor, shouldn't I?"

"That's what I hear."

"It's a lie—a damned white man's lie."

Longarm grinned at her and sipped his coffee. "I just asked."

"I know. I shouldn't get angry. It's just your ignorance."

"I reckon. Tell me, Nalin—how did you get to learn so much, you being an Apache and all?" Again Longarm smiled at her, hoping she would understand that his question had no malicious intent.

The answering gleam in her eyes assured Longarm that she understood. "I was educated in Texas," she told Longarm, "in a schoolhouse run by a very remarkable woman, Mrs. Russell Olafson."

"Texas?"

"My mother was a white woman, a Texan captured by the Mescalero Apaches. My father was a famous Apache warrior who was killed by a band of Texas Rangers who tracked him and his war party, killed him, then raided our settlement. My mother was killed in the attack, but before she died, she convinced one of the rangers to take me with him. That man was Russell Olafson. He was a good man, and he kept his promise. And his wife became more than a mother to me: a teacher and a friend."

"So what are you doing back here? This is some distance from Texas and Mrs. Olafson."

"She and her husband are dead now—and I have learned there is only one kind of white man: the full-blooded variety. With the Olafsons gone, I found I really had no one that I could call a friend. The men who courted me—they wanted me because I was part Indian, a breed from whom they could expect all sorts of things." She looked away from Longarm's face and picked up her cup of coffee, holding it with fingers that trembled ever so slightly. "And so," she finished, "I came back to my people. To teach them the white man's ways, to care for them." She shook her head. "Because they are not as civilized as the white man, they accepted me almost without question. Here, at last, I have found a home."

"How old were you when Olafson took you back with him to Texas?"

"Ten years old."

Longarm nodded. "Are you paid by the federal government?"

"I am paid by no one. I was fortunate that the Olafsons left me a considerable sum. With that I have been able to build this schoolhouse and provide myself with those luxuries I had come to depend on in Texas."

"Like Irish whiskey."

She smiled. "Yes, like Irish whiskey. Now, Mr. Long, why are *you* here?"

"My friends call me Longarm," he told her.

"All right, friend Longarm. Why are you here? Is it not more than the death of that clerk, Bernstein, as you suggested earlier?"

Longarm studied the girl, wondering how much he could tell her. He still had a few questions he would like for her to answer. "Nalin, how'd you happen to come upon me when you did?"

"You mean, did I have anything to do with that ambush?"

"I have to be careful, Nalin."

"I had just dismissed the children. It was close to noon. I saw one of Toklani's brothers hurry into the camp. Soon after, the rest of the men drifted out of camp, all of them armed. I knew something was up and that it had to do with Toklani's wife. I sent word down the valley to the agency, and then left as soon as I could without attracting attention."

"It took you a while to catch up."

She smiled thinly, and for that instant Longarm saw the Indian in her, clearly and unmistakably. It blazed in her eyes. "I am sorry I did not arrive sooner, Longarm. If I had, you would not have Toklani as your enemy. But I lost their trail when they split up before the ridge. Besides, I kept well back. I did not want them to know I was following; they would not have allowed it."

Longarm nodded. "All right, Nalin. The governor, Lew Wallace, asked my office for assistance because a territorial agent he sent to Paso Robles has disappeared. Governor Wallace sent the agent in because there've been quite a few shootings in the past two months, in addition to the murder of Bernstein. Wallace wants to know what's going on. And," Longarm concluded, pausing to get her reaction, "of course there's always a chance that Billy the Kid could be behind these shootings."

"Billy the Kid?"

"You've heard of him?"

"Vaguely. But I know no such person."

"He is an adenoidal lout who's recently made a name for himself as a regulator in the Lincoln County War. He goes by a whole bunch of handles—William Bonney, Henry McArty, Billy Harrigan, Kid Antrim, to mention a few." He grinned at her. "Any of those names sound familiar?"

Nalin shook her head.

"I didn't think so. You're pretty well away from it up here. How long a ride is it to Paso Robles?"

"A good six hours. If you punished your horse, you could make it in less time. And then, of course, I don't know how good a rider you are."

"I could take some lessons from you, I reckon. But I'm in no hurry. Tell me, is there anything out of the ordinary going on in Paso Robles?"

"Out of the ordinary?"

"New faces, new activity, settlers moving in, things like that."

"There are some new people—Anglos—moving into Paso Robles, I believe. But it is still mostly a Mexican settlement. It is those white men moving through our reservation at night that bother my people," she said. "They use our land to get to the pass. And the cattle they drive before them are not their own, I am sure." She smiled slightly at this, pleased to contemplate the depravity of the White Eyes. "I would not be surprised if some of these rustlers and rapists come from Paso Robles, but this would be unusual. The Mexican ranchers and those living in the town have always been a peaceful lot." She smiled slightly. "They are too frightened of the Apache to be anything else."

Longarm nodded. Cow stealing could be behind all the shooting, he realized. It was quite possible. The pass leading through the Sacramentos came out onto the *Jornado del Muerto* trail, which, in turn, led to El Paso—a good place to unload rustled beef for a good price. But this did not entirely square with what

248

Marshal Vail had told Longarm back in Denver, which was that since General Lew Wallace had been brought in to calm things down, both sides in the Lincoln County War were keeping their asses down, which should have pretty well stopped the thieving. Unless, of course, Billy the Kid was behind it.

Longarm finished his coffee and looked across the table at Nalin. It had been a long trip from Denver. He had taken a train from Denver, getting off at Roswell in neighboring Chaves County. From there he had taken a stage up the Rio Hondo into Lincoln County. At Fort Stanton he had picked up the buckskin, preferring to ride the rest of the way on horseback. The stage had been, as usual, a numbing exercise in boredom. The only pleasure in it had been the brief acquaintance he had struck up with a Mrs. Kate Ballard, a very enterprising young widow who had confided to Longarm that she was going to open a saloon in Paso Robles. From the look of her, Longarm had judged that she was a soiled dove of some experience who had been smart enough to salt away her nefarious earnings in a sock and then hang onto it. He did not believe for one minute that she had inherited her modest fortune from her dead husband.

Longarm had found much in the woman's endowments to admire, and he was looking forward to meeting her again. Still, a six-hour ride did not strike Longarm as a very pleasant prospect, despite the likelihood of the widow Ballard's company at the end of it. As a matter of fact, he now found Nalin's company considerably more intriguing. She made excellent coffee.

But, of course, he had to be invited—and he was still, after all, in the middle of a comparatively hostile settlement. Toklani would soon be back in camp, anxious to cut out the liver of the White Eyes who had shot up his right hand and who might still be, in his eyes, the rapist who had despoiled his woman.

"Thanks for the coffee, Nalin," Longarm said, standing up. He did not try to keep the reluctance he felt out of his voice. "I reckon I better be on my way."

"You have a long ride," Nalin observed, getting to

her feet also. "Would you prefer a fresh start in the morning?"

"Now that sure does appeal to me, at that."

She smiled. "You realize the dangers if you stay here?"

"And the advantages."

Nalin frowned. "You understand, Longarm. I am just another woman. There is really nothing special about me—nothing in my Indian nature to make me any more . . . exciting than any other companion you might find on your lonely journeys."

"That's as it may be, Nalin, but why don't you let me be the judge of that."

She inclined her head slightly in his direction, as if to concede the point, and Longarm thought her already dark complexion grew a shade darker. "I do like you, Longarm," she admitted. "But again, I feel I should warn you of the danger if you remain here overnight."

"Thank you. Now I think I better see to my horse."

She smiled. "I'll go with you. When the women see me with you, they will understand that you are to be trusted. They will speak to their men."

As they stepped through the schoolhouse door, Longarm heard a commotion beyond the junipers. Apache children came running toward the schoolhouse, their eyes wide. Nalin called to one of them, obviously asking what was causing the disturbance. When the answer came, she looked at Longarm with a sympathetic smile.

"We have visitors, Longarm. The Indian agent and two of the agency police. It seems they have come to escort you from the reservation."

Longarm sighed and waited by the buckskin as three riders appeared, south of the schoolhouse. The agent was in the lead, with two of his dark-skinned keepers of the peace at his back. The agent was dressed in a dark suit, and wore a bowler hat similar to Nalin's atop his bald skull. A thin string tie was knotted at his throat. His shirt appeared filthy, even from this distance. He waved a gnarled hand in greeting as he passed through the camp on his way to the schoolhouse. When he got close enough, Longarm could see the man's bulbous, inflamed nose, the indelible mark of the inebriate. The man's cheeks were sunken, his eyes watery. He appeared to be holding himself atop his mount with some difficulty.

He reined in his horse sloppily and looked blearily down at Longarm. "You the feller shot Toklani?" he asked.

"It was self-defense. I could have aimed to kill him."

"Maybe you should've. What your business here?"

"Just passing through."

"You got a name?"

"Custis Long, deputy U.S. marshal. What's yours?"

"Caleb Longbough. I'm the agent for this here reservation. You got proof you're who you say you are?"

Longarm had started to reach for his wallet when Nalin spoke up.

"I saw his badge, Caleb. He's a lawman, all right. All the way from Denver, on his way to Paso Robles."

Caleb shifted uncomfortably in his saddle. "All right, then. I got word Toklani is still out there, fixing to even the score with you, Long. So I'm ordering you off this here reservation, and I'm giving you an escort. These two agency policemen are the best I got. They'll see to it you get out of here and safe on your way to Paso Robles."

Longarm took a deep breath. "All right, Longbough. Thank you. I'd purely appreciate the escort. But I'd like a chance to water my horse."

"You can do that on your way. There's a stream west of here. You'll pass it."

With a shrug, Longarm turned to Nalin. The smile on her face was understanding. "Reckon I'd best be riding on, after all," Longarm told her softly.

There was a mocking light in her beautiful eyes. "You can't win them all, Longarm," she replied just as softly. "But perhaps you will pass this way again."

Longarm touched the brim of his hat to her and swung into his saddle. Catching up the reins and looking back down at her, he said, "I'll make it my business to do that, Toklani or not."

"Toklani has asked me to be his woman," she said, stepping back from Longarm's horse, a direct challenge now in her eyes. "Nevertheless, I will look for your tall figure on a horse."

Longarm pulled the buckskin around and galloped ahead of his guardians out of the Mescalero encampment. Toklani wanted Nalin for his squaw! He shook his head at the thought, then put his mind to the ride ahead. Six hours to Paso Robles, Nalin had told him. Hell, with angry Apaches at his back, he should make it faster than that.

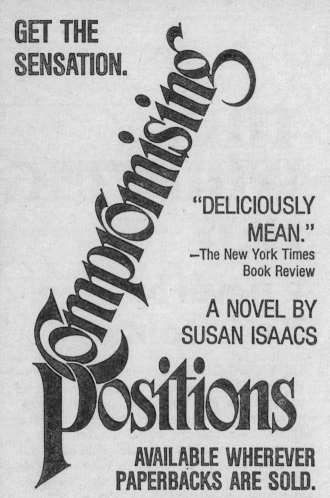

THE WHIPPING BOY

a novel by Beth Holmes

THE WHIPPING BOY is a brilliant and often terrifying portrait of 12-year-old Timmy Lowell and his parents, Evie and Dan. They were a "model" middle class family—until they realized that Timmy, their first-born, was slowly turning into a psychotic killer. His father, locked into his own terrifying world, cannot help him; can't see the evil seed growing. Only Timmy's mother, Evie, can save him...or become his next victim.